Paul Merrett

CATALYST

CATALYST

Paul Bennett

ROBERT HALE · LONDON

© Paul Bennett 2009
First published in Great Britain 2009

ISBN 978-0-7090-8803-5

Robert Hale Limited
Clerkenwell House
Clerkenwell Green
London EC1R 0HT

www.halebooks.com

2 4 6 8 10 9 7 5 3 1

Typeset in 10/13pt Dante
by Derek Doyle & Associates, Shaw Heath
Printed in the UK
by the MPG Books Group

STAGE ONE

INPUT

1

AUC Agrochemicals Division, Weedkiller Plant, Zaragoza, Spain. Twenty years ago.

Paco Ramirez did not know much about chemistry. But from what he could make out from observing the activities at the plant, it was just like cooking (not that he knew much about that either): you put some ingredients in a pot, turned up the heat and after a while you finished up with a soup or a stew or something. And, if his wife's meals were anything to go by, sometimes the result was good and sometimes it was bad. What he did know about, from the accumulated wisdom of his fifty-five years, was human behaviour – which, come to think of it, was like taking a child and cooking up a different sort of stew. And that was why Paco was muttering philosophically to himself as he worked.

If he had been English he would have been talking about the devil you know, instead of reciting some old Spanish proverb about your next donkey always being more stubborn than the last one. If he had been paying closer attention to the work in hand, he would have noticed the rupture in the fabric of the dioxin container. And if he had not had his nose broken in a fight at school, he would have smelt the gas vapourized by the heat of the sun. But that is life – history shrugs its shoulders at *ifs* and carries on its own sweet-sour way, looking only straight ahead.

Paco wiped the sweat from his brow with the back of a paint-smeared hand and climbed down the ladder propped up against the side of the twenty-metre diameter steel cylinder. He placed the long-handled brush in the tray of paint and sought out a thin sliver of shade in which to settle down for his lunch and siesta – his foreshortened siesta.

He took a sip from the neck of the brown litre bottle of Aquila beer, gave a knowing laugh and shook his head. Everyone had cheered when they had

heard the news that the man they called El Marinero was leaving. Two years
he had been the head of the factory. Two years when they had laboured
under a greater and more selfish dictator than General Franco.

'*Escoces,*' Paco hissed, simultaneously spitting on the dusty ground. The
Scotsman had mocked them, calling the whole workforce together and
declaring in the words of 'La Bamba', '*Yo no soy marinero. Soy capitan. Soy
capitan.*' And then, so there could be no misunderstanding, he had sacked ten
per cent of the workers.

Not that they had been missed. El Marinero, among other economies
made to swell profits (and increase his bonus and the chances of rapid
promotion to a bigger cog in the AUC wheel), had cut back on the mainte-
nance of the plant. That was why Paco was simply repainting the cylinder
rather than examining it and repairing those places where rust was pitting
and cracking the surface. Like heavy make-up on an old lady, he thought: it
can fool you from a distance, but doesn't bear closer inspection. Not that
there had been much of that lately either. The new man – the more stubborn
donkey – had made his own economies. With his room for manoeuvre
severely limited by the swinging axe of his predecessor, he had been reduced
to cutting the number of safety officers and, sacrilegiously, shortening the
siesta by one hour.

Paco finished the last mouthful of the crusty bread sandwich, picked a
thread of stringy ham from between his teeth and took out his cigarettes and
matches.

Why were they even bothering to store the dioxin? It had no use and no
value, just something they were stuck with when producing the weedkiller.
In the old days – the good old days – the dioxin would have been burnt. But
that cost money – too many man-hours spent on closely monitoring and
controlling the combustion. He had heard rumours that they were intending
to add it to a new product – Nemesis, it was supposed to be called. But Paco
didn't believe a word of it. Who would want a product that included highly
poisonous dioxin? No, it was just an excuse. The new man was simply stor-
ing up his problems in order to pass them, and the associated costs, on to his
successor when his time came.

Paco took a last swig of beer, placed a cigarette in his mouth and struck
the match against the side of the container.

The thin stream of escaping dioxin gas caught fire.

And set off a chain reaction.

The flame worked its way inside the half-painted cylinder. The mass of gas within ignited. A fireball erupted into the air. The steel sides shattered. Hundreds of sharp red-hot shards of shrapnel shot in all directions, peppering Paco's charred body and puncturing the thin fabric of the adjacent container.

Instantaneously, there was a second explosion.

The heat generated reached the walls of the neighbouring three dioxin containers and caused the gas to expand. As the pressure inside increased, the steel walls began to bow out. When the limit of flexion had been reached these three containers exploded in their turn. A mushroom cloud of toxic vapour rose up into the air. And hung there, like a bird of prey hovering on a thermal, waiting for the wind to carry it on a trail of death.

2

London. Present time.

The only advantage of the back staircase was that it was rarely used outside of emergencies. In every other respect it was a totally unsuitable route out of the building. A bannister that yielded as you leaned against it. An enveloping dusky darkness brought about by the absence of windows and the miserly spacing of low-wattage light bulbs. Stairs dangerously worn, their bare concrete amplifying the sound of each unsteady footstep. Walls echoing in counterpoint to the rhythm of laboured breathing. But there were no ears to hear, no eyes to witness the clandestine descent. That was the whole point.

Kit Harper managed to negotiate only two of the ten flights before his heel caught on a crumbled edge and skidded off into the gloomy void. Already unbalanced by the body he was carrying, there was nothing Harper could do to stop himself from catapulting forward. The cold, hard floor was unforgiving, his ill-cushioned bony ribcage screaming with pain. The dead weight landed on top of him, compounding his problems by knocking the wind from his chest. With the roughness of temper he pushed up and extricated himself by rolling sideways along the landing. He uttered a long and vehement curse. The sprawled heap on the floor opened one bloodshot eye and giggled.

'Come on,' Harper urged. 'Try to be some help, for chrissake.'

Harper bent down and hooked a limp arm around his shoulder, pulled Grayson into a sitting position and then rose so that both of them were standing upright. Grayson's legs wobbled, knees coming together to provide a precarious point of equilibrium. His head rolled against Harper's shoulder, mouth lolling open. Another helpless giggle brought forth a noxious stream of garlic, red wine and brandy. Harper turned his face up and to the side, half in self-defence and half in supplication to heaven, rolled his eyes and resumed the tragicomic descent.

It took a further five minutes of faltering steps and regular stops to reposition the constantly shifting burden before they reached the relative safety of the ground floor. With an awkward movement of his free arm Harper levered up on the stiff bar of the emergency exit and manoeuvred his colleague outside into the blindingly bright sunlight of the early September afternoon. Grayson closed his eyes and groaned, bringing the trace of a smile to Harper's lips: at least some stimuli were getting through to the nerve centre of the alcohol-sodden brain.

Harper whistled to the minicab waiting unhelpfully thirty yards down the street. The driver pulled alongside, climbed out slowly and, with an unsurprising lack of enthusiasm, opened the rear door and glared accusingly at Harper as the mass of floppy limbs was manhandled onto the back seat.

'Not bleeding again!' the driver moaned. 'I could refuse, Mr Harper. You know that, don't you? Well within my rights I'd be, too.'

Harper took two twenty-pound notes from his wallet and pressed them into the palm of the outstretched hand.

'All right then,' the driver responded grudgingly. 'But this is the very last time. OK? It's costing me more in cleaning bills and air freshener than I make on the journey. Straight up.'

'Just get him home, Mike,' Harper said. 'Before he passes out completely and you give yourself a hernia carrying him to his front door.'

The driver shrugged his shoulders, added a toss of his head for good measure, and finally got back into the car. Harper watched with a mixture of dread and admiration as the car was propelled with professional abandon into the stream of traffic.

He sighed deeply, knowing it was as much to do with relief at Grayson's departure as sadness for the man's condition and whatever problems had brought it about. He brushed the cobwebs and dust from the blue suit that had seen better days and stretched his aching back. He felt the pain in his side from the fall competing for sympathy with overworked muscles, turned toward the revolving doors of the front entrance to the building, and stared disbelievingly into the eyes of his boss.

'My office, Kit,' Klein said, shaking his head. 'Twenty minutes.'

Wonderful, Harper thought. Just bloody wonderful. All the cloak-and-dagger nonsense had been a complete waste of time. All the sweating and straining a total waste of energy. And what have you achieved, Kit? Pole position in Grayson's paddleless canoe, that's what.

Trust Klein, Harper thought, rubbing away subconsciously at the scar under his eye as he habitually did in times of crisis. Bloody sadist. Couldn't be 'see me now', could it? Just had to spin out the agony. A full twenty minutes to sweat over what Fate had in store.

Harper removed his hands from behind his head, swung his feet off the desk and walked across to the window of his fifth-floor office. He was a little over six feet tall, his spare frame a result of skipped meals and a high metabolic rate caused by too much nervous energy. His light-brown hair needed the luxury of a good cut: it hung a couple of centimetres over the collar of his white shirt and fell across his pale blue eyes as if to cast a veil over what lay buried beneath. He looked down at the afternoon procession of shoppers shuffling along Oxford Street. Stubbornly refused, against the internal consensus of opinion, to see them as 'punters'. It was simply another symptom of the disillusionment, the cancerous crisis of conscience that had been growing inexorably inside him over the last few years.

There was a time when Harper had regarded working in advertising as paradise with pay cheques, and his role within the agency as the pinnacle of job satisfaction. True, the 'creatives' had the most freedom and the frequent perks of attending the shoot of some commercial that 'just won't work, man,' without the golden sands and fringed palms of a Caribbean shore – albeit that the product was a bog-standard brand of lavatory cleaner. And the streetwise lads in the Production Department were the most lavishly entertained – Ascot, Aintree, Henley, Wimbledon – desperate printers and reproduction houses vying with each other for the opportunity to pour champagne down throats in order to lubricate the machinery that would sign the next contract. Account directors (or 'suits' as they were openly, and more than a little derisively, termed) received the kudos from winning a new business pitch – inadequate compensation in Harper's view for the day-to-day drudgery of covering up the mistakes of others in their team and the trials of selling the agency's sometimes dubious product to hypercritical (or perceptive, depending on what side of the fence you were on) clients. The media buyers had their daily long, drawn-out business lunches and 'seminally essential' conferences in Cannes and Monaco about how many naked angels can dance on a tabloid masthead. But it was the planner who had the real challenge.

As one of eight planners – seven and a quarter if you discounted Grayson's contribution – at Jackson, Klein and Lottersby (mercifully short-ened to JKL), Harper, when he wasn't attempting to prevent lame ducks being served up with a bitter orange sauce, spent his time solving problems of strategy and tactics: gathering evidence; making deductions; unravelling the singular mysteries of each client's business; laying bare the associated wants and needs that had to be satisfied if consumers were to be persuaded to buy some product they either couldn't afford, didn't need or both. Take a generous helping of sleuth, add an ability to empathize with people, stir together with a measure of communication skills and you have the recipe for the hybrid beast known as a planner. In that wince-inducing pretentious jargon favoured by the advertising industry – you can't glorify it by calling it a profession – Harper was an 'enabler'. He, ever contrary, preferred to see himself as a catalyst, simply providing the stimulus to the disparate ingredi-ents that go to make up the account team, sparking off a chemical reaction that would bring about an effective, and saleable, campaign.

There was still some residual enjoyment left in the job. As long as he didn't think about it too much.

And what could he do? He needed the monthly salary cheque – mortgage to pay, school fees to find, all the ongoing expenses of running a single-parent household with an old-fashioned (and, therefore, expensive) treasure of a nanny and a daughter who grew out of shoes the moment you cut off the price tag. But he couldn't change career, or the direction of his life – he wasn't qualified for anything else. Who else but an advertising agency would be indulgent enough, or just plain daft enough, to hire someone with a degree in Classics? So, he was doomed to being a solver of irrelevant puzzles, a crown prince in the kingdom of trivia.

'You can't save Grayson, you know,' Klein said matter-of-factly.

'Surely Grayson deserves a second chance,' he said.

'What do you mean *second* chance?' Klein spluttered. 'More like fifth or sixth. No, it's gone on for too long now. Reached the point of no return, I'm afraid.'

'I was given a chance once. Why not Grayson?'

'For one thing, *I* wasn't running the agency then.' Klein shook his head at the misplaced sentimental forbearance of his predecessor.

Only vehicles carry passengers, that was Klein's motto.

'And for another,' he continued, 'your situation was different. Grayson doesn't have any mitigating circumstances.'

Klein was all heart. God knows where he kept it, though. Probably locked away in his safe at home, only to be brought out at Christmas.

'And how is. . . ?' Klein consulted the file on his lap, 'Cassandra?'

Such consideration. Such spontaneity. Such ignorance! No one called his daughter Cassandra, not unless it was a reinforcement to a rebuke.

'She's fine,' Harper said.

He looked across at Klein and searched for a weakness to exploit. What he saw wasn't encouraging.

Klein was Cassius reincarnated. Lean and hungry. Cold, piercing grey eyes that showed about as much emotion as two pebbles on a beach at midnight when there's no moon. Thin lips built for sneering, but not smiling. Long aquiline nose – a tempting target only just resisted by Harper in the past – ideal for looking down. He was wearing a white shirt, plain blue tie and a charcoal suit that told you nothing and everything about the man.

'Grayson's been under a lot of stress,' Harper said lamely.

'Is that the best you can come up with? I expected something a little more imaginative from you.'

'He's worked hard on the AUC image data,' Harper said, more imaginatively.

'Let's hope so. The presentation is in three days' time. If there's so much as a single error in the figures, or the logic of the conclusions isn't impeccable, then Sir Angus will crucify us.'

Klein paused ominously, leaving the last word dangling in the air like the sword of Damocles.

'By *us*,' Harper said, 'I presume you mean the agency.'

One thin lip curled upward.

'That's what I wanted to talk to you about,' Klein said. 'I'm moving you to the AUC account. I need someone I can rely on totally and absolutely for this presentation.' Totally *and* absolutely, Harper thought: this was both serious and tautological. 'As of now, Grayson is out and you are in.'

Harper shook his head vigorously. 'You can't do that to me,' he said. 'Not AUC.'

Not only was Allied Universal Chemicals the most mind-numbingly boring account in the history of advertising, it had also earned the deserved reputation of being the agency graveyard. AUC's Chairman and Chief Executive, and Lord High Executioner, Sir Angus Cameron, was a bully of the first magnitude. Pitched up against him, Attila the Hun didn't even run a close second in the grand finals of the Tyrant of All History Contest. Within the agency, no one survived long on the AUC account: either you wilted under the pressure of the constant onslaught of Sir Angus's tongue and made a block booking with your nearest therapist, or you were unceremoniously dumped overboard because he didn't like the cut of your jib (Sir Angus was ex-Royal Marines and prone to launch into naval clichés at the slightest opportunity).

'Why can't we just ditch the bloody account?' Harper asked 'It can't be worth the aggravation or the bad feeling among the staff. How about we make a stand against Cameron? Show him that he can't push us around. That there's a limit to what money can buy.'

'Because there isn't. And because the stakes are about to be raised.' Klein's mouth puckered as he realized he had said too much. The pucker transformed itself into a tight-lipped smile of broken confidence. 'I can't say any more. Shouldn't even have told you that much. But I know I can trust you, Kit.'

'Thanks for the compliment,' he said, not taken in by the flattery. 'But it won't work. AUC isn't the right account for me. Nor I for it. Not now, or ever.'

'You're not listening, Harper,' Klein said. 'The decision has been made. As managing director, that's what I'm paid for.'

'Well, whatever you're paid, it isn't enough. Not for the price of selling the agency's soul.'

'I'll ignore that,' he said. But he wouldn't forget it, Harper knew. 'Mustn't have friction between team members.'

'I'd like to oblige,' Harper said, 'but I don't do foreign travel. In case you've forgotten, I have an agreement.'

'Not an *agreement* as such, more an *arrangement*. Unenforceable in law, I'm afraid. Anyway, I've just rescinded it.'

'You can't do that,' Harper protested.

'If you don't like it,' Klein said with a careless shrug, 'then sue me. You do have insurance to cover the legal fees, I presume?' He gave a self-satisfied sneer and settled back in the chair. Studied Harper's face to read the reaction to the threat. 'Come on, Kit, you're wasting your breath and my time.'

'Just think of the practicalities,' Harper countered, switching his attack from the concept to the execution. 'What about my other accounts? They're bound to suffer. AUC will be a drain of my time. All the background to learn. And then I'll be forever jetting back and forth to Brussels.'

'Think of all the opportunities to sample proper chocolate, mussels freshly plucked from the sea and two hundred types of beer.'

Harper snorted derisively and continued. 'AUC isn't the account for me. I'm no scientist. I know just enough about petrochemicals to know that I know nothing about petrochemicals. I wouldn't be able to handle it. I'd be totally out of my depth, waves of incomprehension pushing me down for the third time. This is commercial suicide.'

'Have you finished?' Klein said. 'Because I haven't heard anything that makes me want to change my mind. All I want from you, Harper, is one campaign. That's not much to ask, is it? As soon as that one campaign is wrapped up you can go back to burying your head in the sand. But until then, you do as I say with good grace and an overdose of commitment.'

Harper didn't bother asking 'Or what?' The consequences were crystal clear – out of the door with the imprint of Klein's crocodile loafers on his backside. He concentrated on the question *why* instead. Why him, and not one of the other planners? Any of the four women would have stood a better chance of finding a soft spot in the Cameron heart. And what about Liam, didn't he have some strange interfaculty degree – Physics and Economics or some other odd mixture? Maybe, Harper reasoned, his position was stronger than it appeared. Perhaps he had the physical as well as the moral high ground.

'I'll think about it,' he said casually.

'What!' Klein exploded. His face went red with rage, veins pulsing visibly on his forehead.

'I'll let you know tomorrow.'

Harper looked at his watch pointedly and rose to go.

'Very well, Kit,' Klein said soothingly.

Harper fought back a smile. Bingo! Capitulation. For some convoluted reason, God knows what, he thought, Klein needs *me*. None of the other planners will do.

'Just one more thing,' he said, looking down at the poorly disguised frown on Klein's face. 'I'll need a clear mind if I'm to contemplate these new responsibilities. I won't be able to focus if I'm thinking of Grayson.'

'And?'

'Why not give Grayson a stay of execution? Pay for some counselling or therapy. Put him on a month's sick leave. See how he performs after a break.'

'Agreed,' Klein said, nodding his head.

Harper walked quickly from the office and straight out of the building. He felt no joy in the victory – Pyrrhic victory, almost certainly. Klein had rolled over like a puppy dog. The stakes must be high. But what the hell was the game?

3

AUC Agrochemicals Research Facility, Den Haag, Netherlands. Six and a half years ago.

The two figures lay on their stomachs and peered intently into the half-light of the moon. Their unblinking eyes followed the slow progress of the security guard on the final stages of his hourly ritual. Damp from the grass seeped into their black clothes and their breath, escaping in slow regular bursts through the neat round holes of the balaclava helmets, hit the cold air in long misty streams. As the guard completed his tour of the compound and returned to the warmth of his office, one of the men pressed a button on his watch to start the countdown from sixty minutes; the other slid a pair of wire-cutters from the deep pocket running down the length of his thigh and began to snip at the perimeter fence.

In less than a minute they were bending back a section of wire, forming a triangular escape route, five feet high and three feet at the base. They went through the gap, each man dragging a large sack by a corner. Keeping low to the ground, they walked to the back door of the animal laboratory, letting the sacks spill their trail of fruit, grains and nuts behind them. Breathing more rapidly now, one man inserted the duplicate key into the lock. It turned smoothly, producing a sharp responsive click from the mechanism. The door swung inwards. The two men stepped quickly inside, leaving the door wide open, and surveyed the interior in the concentrated beams of their torches

It was exactly as they had been told, a long windowless room lined with mesh-fronted cages on two sides. A series of extractor fans recessed into the ceiling whirred slowly on a low-powered night setting, removing only the very worst of the smell. Even through the thick wool of the helmets, the noses of the men were stung by the sharpness of ammonia.

The animals sensed something outside their normal experience. Nearest the door, the pink eyes of white mice darted about; in the middle of the room, brown rats twitched their whiskers and emitted high-pitched squeaks of warning to each other; at the far end, rhesus monkeys retreated to the back of their cages.

Both men hesitated, the reality of the situation very different from studying the maps and planning each move. The taller of the two looked down nervously at the elasticated legs of the trousers covering the high tops of his boots as if assessing their effectiveness against intrusion. The shorter man took his time pulling a pair of thickly padded gloves over the thin leather ones he was already wearing, stretched out his hand and slid back the bolt on one of the cages containing the mice. Chastened, the taller man followed his example and together they moved quickly along the line, working top to bottom.

The theory had been that once the first animals made a bid for freedom through the door and towards the fence, then the rest would follow. Some of the mice and rats, too stupid or too sick to obey the call of their instincts, stubbornly refused to leave their cages. The two men gingerly used their torches to prod at the creatures and sweep the most reluctant outside. Soon the floor was awash with scurrying, senseless rodents and torpid barely moving bodies. Bones crunched underfoot as the men walked towards the far end of the room and the tall cages containing the pink-faced rhesus monkeys.

They swung the doors open and stood behind them, using the mesh for protection. The first of the monkeys to be released jumped down nimbly on to the tiled floor and headed for the door. Others followed in a blur of brown-grey fur. Only one remained, too weak to move, its grotesquely swollen body curled up in the fetal position at the bottom of its cage. The shorter man grabbed it by the scruff of the neck and stuffed it distastefully into the sack held open by his partner. Then both men set to work adding the broken bodies on the floor to their sacks.

Working one-handed while holding the sacks securely, the men lifted cages from the walls and laid them quietly and methodically on the floor in a pattern which would create the impression of a random act of violence.

As a final act before slipping back out into the night, the taller man took an aerosol can of paint from his jacket and sprayed the word 'Greenway' in large flowing italic letters across the bare wall. The shorter man shook his head in rebuke, grabbed the can from the other's hand and extended the uprights of the w so that it became upper case. He took one last look and smiled to himself, satisfied that it now accurately resembled the logo of the organization that would take the blame for their actions.

4

'You're late, my boy,' Saul Drummond said to Harper as he opened the door to the mansion flat on the south side of the Albert Bridge. One huge hand wrapped around his in greeting, the other slapped his forearm.

'Sorry, but it took a while to find a cab,' Harper replied, stepping into the narrow hallway. 'Hang on a minute. Why am I apologizing? I didn't even tell you I would call.'

'Klein phoned,' Saul explained. 'He knew you would come here.'

'Am I that predictable?'

'More so than Klein, it appears.'

Harper nodded his agreement. Klein was the last person he would have expected to telephone Saul. He doubted whether the pair had even exchanged Christmas cards let alone a single civil word in the three years since Saul had been the first, and only, victim of what was supposed to be a full-scale downsizing exercise. With one slash of the knife, Klein had added the role of head of planning to that of managing director and account director and, through no freak of coincidence, removed the person he saw as his greatest rival. Klein hated Drummond, always had and always would – consistent, if nothing else. His swift action in contacting Saul added to the mystery of the call to the AUC account.

Saul led Harper along the corridor to his inner sanctum. Three walls of the room were lined from floor to ceiling with wooden shelves, each shelf bowing a little in the middle as it struggled to support the weight of dauntingly thick books with equally daunting titles in a wide range of languages, some of which Harper could only guess at. The floor space was dominated by a twelve foot square Turkish rug, deep red with vibrant yellow and cream geometric designs. Near to the east-facing window was a vast partners' desk, its inlaid maroon leather top stained from years of spillages from the small bottle of Indian ink that sat off-centre to the right. On the window side of the desk stood an old high-backed chair, its leather cracked and worn, its seat hollowed by Saul's weight; on the near side was the little-used, thickly padded armchair for visitors. On the desk top were two identical cut-glass ashtrays (a little excessive, Harper thought, for a non-smoker) and a tray set with bone china teapot, two cups, sugar bowl and milk jug; they jostled for space with several piles of lined paper covered in Saul's long, flowing script.

'What are you working on?' Harper asked, as Saul poured the tea.

'Still the same book,' he replied, tapping the papers lovingly with his hand, the diamond eternity ring glinting in the light with the movement. 'This is a chapter that expounds my theory that advertising would have much increased effectiveness if it concentrated more on archetypes and less on stereotypes.'

That made sense, Harper thought, if only in Saul's unstereotypical case.

Physically, Saul 'Bulldog' Drummond was a prize bull. He was short and very stocky, that mesomorphic build where height is sacrificed to an over-generous allowance of muscle. His lined face was topped by a mop of dark hair that looked like it saw comb and brush as frequently as distant relatives. A square jaw sat upon a broad neck.

Mentally, though, Saul was a giant. But a giant dinosaur. A throwback to those days when every advertising agency had one cardigan-wearing, corduroy-trousered true intellectual on its books, his role being to enlighten and confound in equal measures, the latter to stimulate questions, the former to supply answers when all else failed. With Saul, you were lucky if you understood half of what he said – even when he boomed 'Good morning' most people found themselves wondering whether there wasn't some deeper hidden meaning they ought to be considering – but the test was to ask for clarification and not try to bluff. That was where Klein had always fallen down. The more he resorted to bluffing, the more Saul cranked the wheel of verbal obscurity, quoting in Latin or Greek, peppering sentences with words like paradigm, praxis and synecdoche until Klein's eyes glazed over or his cheeks burned red with embarrassment. That, however, was the lesser of the two reasons for Klein's hatred.

What really stuck in Klein's craw was that Saul was liked and he was not. Saul had been the *pater familias* of the agency, father figure, confessor and personal tutor to all. But Harper more than most. For some reason he had never figured out (it couldn't be anything as trivial as both of them having read Ovid and Homer in their original untranslated forms), Saul had selected

Harper as his protégé, marking him out for higher things and, as a direct consequence, Klein's undying enmity.

'I assume,' Harper said, sipping the stewed Earl Grey tea and politely trying not to wince, 'that Klein wanted to enlist your help in persuading me to join the team on AUC.'

Saul nodded his head thoughtfully.

'Therefore,' Harper said, 'I conclude that you will do your best to dissuade me.'

'No, my boy,' Saul replied. 'And don't stare at me as if I had taken on the mantle of a quisling. I happen to think that it will be for the best if you accept his offer.'

'But why?'

'Primarily because the offer is Corleonean – it is not one which you can refuse. Not if you wish to keep your job. Or indeed find another at any stage in the future. If you turn him down, Klein will surely sack you on the spot and, out of sheer spite, blacken your name within our incestuous industry. You will be forced to don the garb of a leper and no one will dare touch you.'

'You were supposed to cheer me up,' Harper said.

'And support you? Echo your reasons for refusal so that they sounded twice as convincing. Tea and sympathy, dear boy, do not always go together.'

'Now you tell me.'

'Precisely,' he said, as if Harper, his ingenuous pupil, had fallen into a masterly well-laid trap. 'Times change. And so must people.'

'But all the travel. The nights away from home.'

'You will simply have to set up a system so that you can cope,' Saul said with a dismissive wave of his hand. He took a sip of tea, pursed his lips and replaced the cup on the tray. 'And, my boy, it will do you good to get out and about more. Meet some new people. Extend your limited circle of friends.'

'What are you? My social worker or something?'

He shrugged.

'Thanks a bunch, Saul.'

Drummond looked down at the desk and pondered for a moment. Then he stretched out his arm and picked up one of the glass ashtrays. Weighed it in his hand like some expensive Frisbee. Threw it with all his force against the shelving. There was a loud crash and a shattering. Harper jolted upright in his seat and stared incredulously at Saul. But before he could open his mouth, Saul had the other ashtray in his hand and sent it spinning with identical force and trajectory to hit exactly the same spot. The ashtray bounced off this time and landed on the rug.

'What the hell did you do that for?' Harper asked, stunned.

'Just a little demonstration to show that history does not always repeat itself. That one can take from the past, but should not give in to it.'

'A touch melodramatic,' Harper said, unwilling to concede that the point had been proven. 'Not to mention lucky.'

'Well, we all deserve some luck from time to time. Trust me, my boy,' Saul said, hitting Harper with a paternal smile and then a catalogue of guilt-inducing questions. 'Haven't I always looked after you? Been your mentor and guardian angel? Didn't I teach you everything you know? Was it not I who christened you "Kit" and rescued you from the quasi-anonymity of being merely one of four Christophers within the agency? Planted your feet firmly on the first rung of the ladder by giving you a new improved brand name with a unique positioning?'

'All that and more,' Harper said quickly, before the list could be extended to the bottom.

'To everything there is a season,' Saul said in the lilting tones of an evangelist. 'You must now look to the future.'

'I thought that was exactly what I was doing.'

Saul shrugged again. Raised bushy eyebrows. 'By burying yourself in the past?'

'Give me a break, Saul.'

'I thought,' he responded with an impish smile, 'that was exactly what I was doing.'

'Did Klein,' Harper began, before the unspoken *and what I once did* hit his conscience, 'give you any reasons why it had to be me?'

'Reasons a plenty. Whether we can believe them or not is an entirely different matter. He *says* that the AUC account is a flagship for the agency – a display of its versatility and the breadth of its talent, that if one can sell petrochemical products then one can sell anything. AUC brings in business. Business which, I would suspect, is very important under the current circumstances.'

'Which are?'

'I hear rumours – and you know how our industry so loves to tittle-tattle – that the agency is going to be put up for sale. Lottersby's health is no better – liver so pickled it could end up as a Damien Hurst exhibit – and he wants to cash in his chips before he cashes in his chips, so to speak. The other two partners can't afford to buy him out, so the whole shooting match will be put up for auction. Whoever buys will have to retain the services of Jackson and Klein – ours is a people business above all, and people have a nasty habit of taking business with them when they leave – and so they will come away with job security and what I believe is termed colloquially as *a nice little earner*. The upshot is that the more business the agency has, the more profit it makes and the higher the price it will fetch.'

'Klein said something about the stakes on AUC being raised. That would fit with a dash for growth.'

'And with the concomitant dash for contraction.'

Harper shook his head as if his brain hurt.

'Explain the paradox for us mere mortals, Saul.'

'Cost-cutting, Kit. Overheads. And, in a people business, that means staff. Which is why your position is weak.'

'And yet he caved in on Grayson when he could so easily have sacked him.'

Harper explained the turn of events at the end of the meeting with Klein.

'I don't think we could ever accuse Klein of being sentimental,' Saul said, 'not when money or power is involved. It is just another means of putting pressure on you. Klein has now made *you* solely responsible for Grayson's destiny.'

'What other reasons did he give?'

'He claims that you are the best planner – what a truly parlous state the agency must be in – and that for AUC only the best will do. He also says that he needs to know where your allegiance lies – do as he says and wounds will be healed rather than rubbed with salt.'

'White man speak with forked tongue.'

'It has ever been thus.'

Harper let out a long sigh. His hand drifted to the scar on his cheek.

'Let me get this totally clear,' he said. 'If I refuse Klein, I finish up on the industry scrap heap? And if I bow to the pressure, I enter the AUC grave-yard?'

'Exactly,' Saul said. 'You seem to have the grasped the situation perfectly.'

'Which only leaves one last question.'

'Which is?'

'What do I want as the epitaph on my headstone?'

'How about *Nil carborundum illegitimi.*'

Harper smiled.

Don't let the bastards grind you down.

5

London. Four hours ago.

If he had known it would be so easy, he would have demanded more. Much more.

Dr Hans Mueller frowned. Five million pounds had seemed like a lot at the time. But now, well. . . .

'Perhaps,' he said aloud, breaking the silence of the anonymous hotel bedroom, 'a second bite of the cherry?' Mueller chuckled at the prospect of a further five million. Congratulated himself for the wisdom of only parting with one half of the valuable information. They would pay. Without question. How ironic life was. After all the years of working and searching, he had finally discovered the magic formula for success. Or should it be the equation? Information = Power.

A few weeks ago he had been grimly contemplating redundancy. Early retirement, they had euphemistically called it, from his job as head chemist at AUC.

Shock had been the first reaction. Deep anger, bitter resentment and the burning desire for vengeance had come later.

He had never been one of those painstaking scientists: intuitive discovery had been his strength – his hold over those who wielded the sword of power – and that had dried up with the years. He had become barren. Outlived his usefulness. Past success counted for nothing.

How wrong they had been. Through their petty-minded selfishness they had kicked his tired brain into producing its best idea ever. Oh, how sweetly it had transmuted the base metal of anger into the gold of revenge.

Mueller checked his watch and sighed. Five hours to go. He could have been on the plane by now if he had stayed on the home territory of Brussels, but this was a game more safely played away. And what did five hours really matter when compared to the rest of your life? Tomorrow he would be in Bangkok. Money went a long way there.

He opened the briefcase. Ran his fingers in a trembling caress over the tightly packed bundles of large-denomination notes.

There was a knock on the door.

'Room service,' said a voice. 'Your champagne, sir.'

He reached for the briefcase, closed the lid and snapped the locks shut. Turned the handle of the door and swung it open.

Cold steel tore through the flesh of his temple.

Blood poured down the jagged furrow in a warm stream. A red pool formed in his left eye.

Mueller did not see the knee that crashed into his groin. He felt an explosion of pain – such pain. Both lungs emptied. Bile rose in his throat. His plump belly contracted in an automatic, but ineffective, effort to limit the spread of the crippling spasm that coursed through his body and clawed at his brain with talon-tipped fingers.

He collapsed face down on the floor, mouth gaping fish-like as it fought to suck in air.

Nothing.

The rope was already around his neck.

His attacker was on top of him now, one knee placed in the small of his back pinning him to the floor. The short length of pure white nylon tightened, biting easily through the fleshy folds of fat and settling against the resistance of the windpipe.

Mueller raised his hands. Tried to prise them between rope and neck to ease the deadly pressure. The response made him regret the move.

The grip relaxed, providing a glimpse of a false dawn of hope. Then a gloved hand was in his hair. It jerked his head upwards, and slammed it down, breaking his nose.

The remorseless pressure was reapplied. There would be no remission this time. The outcome was inevitable.

The spirit drained from Mueller. And there was nothing to fuel the fight, no life-giving flow of oxygen to feed the muscles needed for self-defence. Mueller lost consciousness.

It was a further five minutes before the murderer relaxed his grip. Last time he had stopped prematurely. How could a man so close to death have put up such a struggle?

It would have been easier to use a gun, but much less satisfying. A gun was such a remote weapon. There was something about using your bare hands. A direct, electrifying contact with the life-force as it flowed from victim to victor.

His arms still quivering from the strain, he rolled Mueller over. Bulging eyes told all.

Satisfied, he dipped a gloved hand into the pockets of the dead man's jacket. Stood up and reached out for the briefcase. The diary he placed inside: passport, wallet and plane tickets were left for those who would search the room. He scanned the room before leaving – the rope was still round Mueller's neck. And that was exactly how it should be. The pattern was set.

6

The Information Department was a partial misnomer. Information, yes: department, no. In Harper's days as a graduate trainee (a lily-white virgin defending his honour with ineffectual naïvety until the inevitable penetration by cynicism), five people had worked here. Five intelligence-gathering magpies crouched over desks under the concentrated beams of anglepoise lamps, scouring newspapers, periodicals and reference books for salient facts or amusing titbits that might, at best, form the hook on which to hang a campaign or, at the very least, jump-start the right lobe of a copywriter's brain. Over the course of time, the electronic revolution and its uncontrollable offspring, the information superhighway, had whittled away at the annual roll-call. Now only one remained. Mab.

'Kit,' she trilled with a Southern Irish lilt and a bewitching smile. 'To what do I owe the pleasure? Do you thirst for knowledge – or just thirst?'

'Hunger might be more appropriate. But only for bite-sized chunks.'

'Would that be love-bite-sized chunks?' she said with a fluttering of her eyelashes 'You're a wicked boy, Kit.'

'And *you* are incorrigible.'

'But not, unfortunately, irresistible.'

'What I was going to say—'

'Before I so rudely interrupted.'

'—was that I already have all this to digest.'

Harper placed a twelve-inch-high stack of survey data, which he had eventually found after an exhaustive search of Grayson's landfill-site of an office, on top of Mab's desk.

'AUC,' she said, shaking her head sympathetically. 'Don't look so surprised. My job is gathering information. I also have a good ear for gossip. Good work on Grayson, by the way.'

There were times when Harper wondered if Mab wasn't so much just good at tapping the grapevine, but actually possessed some psychic power. Maybe, from her well-informed vantage point, she was simply able to predict quickly and accurately what people would do. It was another imponderable to add to the list.

For someone who sucked every conceivable source dry, she was herself still pretty much a closed book. No one even knew whether Mab was her given name, the product of her Irish ancestry or parents fixated by Shelley or Shakespeare, or if it was a contraction. (Mabel? Maybelline? Now that would make for interesting speculation. Conceived in the back of a car to the duck-walk beat of Chuck Berry?)

And no one knew her age (which, unfortunately for Harper, made the Maybelline hypothesis teasingly unprovable). His guess was somewhere a year or two either side of forty, judging purely by the as yet ill-defined laugh-lines at the corners of her twinkling green eyes and the absence of any hint of grey in her long, auburn hair, but this was otherwise hard to substantiate. Her clothes provided no clue, since her wardrobe seemed to consist solely of an unending stock of high-heeled leather boots teamed with long, flowing dresses in a variety of timeless ethnic patterns and weaves.

'Grayson,' he said, shaking his head. 'You know, he hadn't even started on preparing the presentation. I found this lot,' he stabbed at the tables accusingly with his finger, 'in an unopened box. From what I can tell at first glance, there's one volume for each of sixteen different countries!'

'All with their own individual interpretation of the word *problem*.'

Harper nodded. In his experience *pan-European* was synonymous with *nightmare*. 'And it doesn't stop there. Different samples for farmers, buyers of industrial chemicals, a rag-bag group of the media, politicians and others grandly classified as 'opinion leaders or formers', plus the good-old man and woman in the street – who, if my worst fears are realized, think of AUC as just another pill-peddling, money-grabbing drugs company. Still, at least one thing is clear – AUC isn't simply concerned about its image, it's totally obsessed by it. This is going to be one hell of a presentation.'

'How can I help?' Mab asked.

'I need some context,' he said. 'And some pointers as to how to keep my foot from drifting into my mouth. Do you have a background document on AUC?'

'I take it that you don't want the full unexpurgated version? The shining testament to the thoroughness and dedication of a professional *par excellence*?'

'How long is it?' he asked, tempted by the prospect of cladding himself in the armour of total knowledge.

'Ninety-four pages,' she said, consulting the screen where the document shone out with immodest prescience.

The temptation evaporated like dreams on a Saturday night when the lottery numbers are announced.

'Do you have a management summary?'

'You mean an Idiot's Guide?' Her eyes gave a sparkle. 'Of course I do. This is advertising, after all.'

Mab selected a few pages from within the document and instructed the computer to print them. 'I'm assuming you want hard copy, as usual.' She gestured imperiously with her hand. 'Do the honours, Kit, while we're waiting.'

Harper walked across the long room and opened a compartment in the bookcase. Reached into the concealed refrigerator. Took out a can of Coke for himself, one small, chilled, flat-bottomed glass of the type bartenders slide along countertops in Westerns and a half-full bottle of Polish vodka for Mab. He poured a measure, replaced the vodka so that it would be at the correct temperature for a refill, retraced his steps and handed her the glass. He looked longingly at it and then ripped with resignation at the tab of the can.

He had once asked her, 'Why vodka? Why not Bushmills? Guinness, even?'

'Because you never get anywhere in advertising by being predictable,' she had replied with a loud laugh.

'Still not drinking?' Mab said, taking a large appreciative gulp.

'I daren't. One drink, one sip even, would be great. Especially on a day like today. But there's no telling where it would lead. Once an alcoholic, always an alcoholic. That's what we're told.'

'We never really talked much about it, did we?'

'There's an old blues song,' he said.

'I thought there would be,' she interjected, never having appreciated his taste in music. 'By Blind Lemon Meringue or some other manic-depressive inhabitant of the Mississippi delta, I suppose?'

'Sonny Boy Williamson actually,' he replied, mustering a withering look to disguise his surprise at the closeness of her guess. 'The song goes "Don't start me talking – or I'll tell everything I know." '

'Huh!' she said.

He shrugged evasively.

She rolled her eyes, somehow managing to make the dismissive gesture seductive.

'You know,' she said, 'it's no wonder you made a lot of people very happy back then.'

Harper peered at her enquiringly.

'When you proved beyond any doubt that you couldn't walk on water,' she explained.

'Was I that much of a pain?' he said, feeling his cheeks flush with the heat of embarrassment.

'Oh, to be sure. I used to get daily requests for addresses of stockists of kryptonite.'

'Why don't you give it to me straight, Mab. You don't have to gild the lily. I can take it.'

'Don't blame me. I drew the short straw – someone in this building has to be the guardian of reality.'

'Thanks a bundle,' he said, getting up to fetch the vodka bottle.

'But someone in the building also cares,' she called after him. 'You know that, don't you, Kit? I'm here whenever you need me.'

He turned his head and nodded. Smiled his thanks this time. Then topped up her glass.

'How's Cassie?' Mab asked. 'What is she now? Three? Four?'

'Five last month.'

'Doesn't time fly.'

When you're having fun, he thought.

'She's fine,' he said instead. 'Looks more like her mother with every day.'

'That must be a mixed blessing,' she said, frowning. 'Heather was a beautiful woman, and Cassie will be blessed if she takes after her. But it must be like having a permanent reminder around the place. Makes it difficult to forget.'

'I'm not sure that I want to,' he said.

STAGE TWO

HEAT

7

Ronnie Stoker sat in his underground office – the bunker, as he liked to call it – in the AUC building and sucked mineral water through a straw so that his lips would not come into contact with the bottle or an insufficiently cleansed glass. It had been a long day – the worst of which was the flight where he had had no option but to breathe in the recirculated exhaled air of over a hundred germ-ridden passengers – and it wasn't over yet. He wouldn't be leaving the office until the phone call came through. Only when he had been assured that the honeytrap had been sprung and successfully snared its victim could he make his next move.

He leaned back in the chair and stretched out his right leg, rubbing vigorously behind the knee. The landmine had not only shattered his knee but also the career – the life – he loved so much. One moment he had been driving along the desert sands of Iraq, laughing and joking with his SAS buddies, the next, or so it seemed, he was lying racked with pain in a field hospital. The surgeons had concentrated first on teasing out of his brain the single lump of shrapnel that had robbed him of all sensation of taste and then diligently removed the fragments of metal and shards of bone from his kneecap. They had patched him up as best they could under the makeshift circumstances, but active duty was out of the window from then on. He'd endured two mind-destroying years behind a desk in military intelligence and been on the point of going stir crazy when Sir Angus – his saviour – had contacted him. At first the offer of a job as head of security at AUC had been about as appealing as jumping from out of the frying pan into the fire. But then Sir Angus had explained the details of the deal: a basic salary above his wildest dreams and 'special bonuses' for achieving the unwritten part of the job description – 'neutralize the competition, counter any opposition: and don't bother me with operational details'. New skills had needed to be acquired – industrial espionage, blackmail, administration (running two teams, one officially on the payroll, the other remunerated through the slush fund) – and soon he had felt again the old adrenaline rush.

Stoker, his mouth dry through nervous tension, took another suck through the straw and looked down at the neat line of folders on the desk.

Over the last few years he had compiled over two hundred dossiers for Sir Angus. They had reviewed four at length this morning. Spent the least time on Harper (whose role was walk on stage and walk off again). Mueller's file, however, had taken longer. Although that folder was now marked 'closed' in large black capital letters, there were still valuable lessons to be learnt. The other two dossiers had yellow stickers with the command 'Action' in Stoker's neat hand.

Both files were a worthy testament to his painstaking approach to his work. Handwritten notes. Comprehensive biographies. Timetables of movements and activities with established patterns highlighted in yellow. Grainy photographs, enlargements from fast film that needed no conspicuous flash.

He swallowed more of the cool, clean water. Lost himself in concentration for a while. Read again the details of the current operation with which he was already familiar. He was going to be especially thorough from now on.

An anxious hour passed before the call came through. If he had been a smoker, he would have got through, maybe, five or six cigarettes in that time, but he detested smoking and hated smokers. Instead, he finished the bottle of mineral water and took another from the regimental line in the refrigerator.

The mark had swallowed the bait – Stoker chuckled to himself – and now he could proceed with the other part of the plan. His hands shook with the excitement of anticipation as he rose from the desk and limped heavily from the room.

8

In another country, under different circumstances, Harper might have shouted, 'Hi, honey, I'm home.' But this was England, and there was no honey. Hadn't been for nearly five years now. Five long years now.

Cassie came running to the door to greet him in a daily ritual that, for all its total predictability, still brought a lump to his throat. He abandoned the heavy bags, bent down and spread his arms wide. She threw herself at him and he scooped her up and held her tight. Cassie was his past, present and future and he wanted to stay like this for ever, never letting her go. But five-year-olds care little for such sentimentality: she kicked her legs in the air, signalling that it was time to move on. He kissed her lightly on the cheek and lowered her gently to the floor.

He let his gaze wander over the copper-coloured hair gathered into two tight bunches tied with pink ribbon, the little snub nose that somehow always seemed to elongate and then wrinkle as a precursor to tears and the small mouth with the wide toothy smile. He stared into her chocolate-brown eyes. Into her mother's chocolate-brown eyes.

From the other end of the corridor Nanny Trent coughed politely. Harper smiled at her and nodded that it was OK for her to leave them alone and put her support-stockinged feet up for a while. It was so-called 'quality' time – a convenient guilt-reducing euphemism for those who cannot provide attention in any quantity.

Cassie took his hand and pulled him toward the kitchen. Jabbered away excitedly as she told him all about her day. As the sausages sizzled appetizingly under the grill – advertising maxim: you don't sell the sausage, you sell the sizzle – she read aloud from her book without stumbling or stuttering. She had inherited his love of reading and his photographic memory (which meant that if it was a familiar book he had to check to see whether she was actually reading).

For the next couple of hours they ate, watched some TV, Cassie played – rather than washed – in the bath and then it was story and bed. Throughout this time her favourite word was *why*. Don't ask me, he felt like saying.

After catching up with Nanny Trent's less emotional account of the events of the day and raising the subject of the trip to Brussels, Harper took a large mug of coffee and his bags through to the sitting room. He placed the coffee on the work table, set the mountain of paperwork on the floor and switched on the computer. Then he fought the nightly temptation to pour a brandy to go along with the coffee. Isn't it funny – yeah, bloody hilarious, Harper – how people react differently to adversity? He had sought solace – or was it simply anaesthesia? – in the bottle; Heather had been supported by the crutch of pills.

There had been no hint during the pregnancy of the problems to come.

No high blood pressure, no swollen ankles. Even Heather's bout of morning sickness hadn't lasted more than a few weeks. She had bloomed with the passing months, exchanging the sylphlike figure for one out of a pre-Raphaelite painting. Harper could close his eyes now and see her with perfect Technicolor clarity as she stencilled flowers on the walls of the nursery, a smear of yellow paint on her rosy cheeks; or smiled as she placed his hand on her stomach to feel the kicks; or lay in bed looking up at him, her eyes moist with tears of happiness.

Within a week of Cassie's birth, the tears had turned to ones of frustration, despair and the black dog of depression.

Harper sat down on the sofa and stared thoughtfully at the ceiling. It had been nobody's fault. Especially Cassie's. Colic, the doctor and nurses had told them, was completely inexplicable and, it seemed, incurable. They had tried every remedy on the market and, in desperation, anything ever mentioned in old wives' tales. Nothing stopped the crying. Nineteen solid hours of it, day and night, every day and every night. It wasn't long before they reached the breaking point of physical and mental exhaustion. And for Heather there was the added psychological burden of the shattering of her dreams – this wasn't how it was supposed to be. How could one love unreservedly and forge what she had been told was the important early bond when all one wanted to do was get away from the seemingly ungrateful little wretch who screamed and screamed and screamed?

Maybe, Harper thought, they had hung on too long before admitting defeat and seeking help, but most of the time they weren't thinking straight, tiredness immobilizing their brains. Pride had prevented them sending out a distress call to Heather's parents in the wilds of Scotland. When they did eventually troop along to the family doctor, he had taken one look at Heather, taut as an overwound spring, diagnosed severe postnatal depression and prescribed a course of antidepressants. After only two days on the new wonder drug, Excelsior, the improvement was indeed miraculous. Heather had relaxed and Cassie, feeding off emotions as babies do as greedily as milk, responded. Within a few weeks the colic had eased to manageable proportions and they finally became a family. Normality ruled. Heather rediscovered her maternal instincts. They both cooed over Cassie and each day became one to remember, a landmark in development rather than another simply survived.

But the time-window of happiness was to be all too brief.

Cassie was five months old when Heather noticed the lump in her breast.

And six months old when her mother died.

The cancer, showing no respect for the probabilities associated with her age (twenty-five) and her healthy lifestyle (she had never smoked), had invaded her body and spread like fire on a tinder-dry forest floor. As fast as the surgeons cut out one tumour, another appeared somewhere else.

For the first time in his life Harper had felt powerless. He prayed to every god he had ever heard of, and any nameless others who might perhaps be out there. At first it was to beg to make Heather well again. Then, as resignation set in, the plea was just to take away the pain.

Heather died – and a part of Harper died with her – on Valentine's Day. Christ, Harper thought, when Fate takes against you it never misses an opportunity to rub salt into the wound.

He broke off his reverie to stare around the room where they had often sat cuddled in each other's arms, watching the TV or listening, like now, to the prophetic sound of the blues. The screensaver on the monitor flashed at him, demanding movement, the pile of tabulations demanded attention, the brandy bottle demanded drinking. Call yourself a planner, Harper, it seemed to mock. Play with probabilities, if you wish. Predict the future, if you must. But the only certainty in this world is death and taxes.

Hell, he'd paid a lot of taxes – excise duty – in the months that followed. He'd never worked out (but maybe he didn't want to) if he had been trying to drink himself to oblivion or to death. Luckily, Saul had saved him from whichever, or both.

Having heard nothing from Harper in three weeks of what had become unsanctioned compassionate leave, Saul had made a surprise visit. Who had got the bigger surprise? Harper could vaguely recall the sound of the door being kicked in. Staring up drunkenly into Saul's angry eyes from his prone position on the floor of the sitting room, the empty bottle clutched tightly in his hand by some reflex action as he had passed out.

Saul had grabbed him roughly by the scruff of the neck, dragged him to the bathroom and held Harper's head under the cold tap. As the struggles gained in strength Saul had judged that this was the time to increase the torture – he held Harper up in front of the mirror. Forced him to recognize, and come to terms with, the manic face with the staring bloodshot eyes, sallow complexion and bristling beard. Then he unleashed the most fearful weapon of all. He pulled Harper along the corridor and into Cassie's room. Where she was lying crying with hunger in her cot, the sheets soiled where the nappy had leaked its contents. And as the final indignity, but the least of all the pain, Saul had struck him hard with a backhand sweep of his open hand. The diamond eternity ring had raked along Harper's right cheek, drawing a line of blood under the whole episode and leaving him with a scar as a permanent reminder.

Saul had told him after – long after – that he knew from the appalled look on Harper's face that he didn't have to hit him. But he couldn't stop himself. It was solely for his benefit, not Harper's.

Saul helped him through the short-term crisis, sobering him up with strong sweet coffee while he, Saul, changed Cassie and made up bottles of milk. Then, when she was sated and sleeping peacefully in Harper's arms, Saul set about the long-term. Rang Miss Trent and persuaded her out of retirement, (immediately sending out a distress call to his daily help to drop everything and come to cleanse the Augean stables that the flat had become), and started negotiations for the new working arrangement – the terms and conditions which would permit the juggling of responsibilities, keeping all the fragile eggs of baby, household and job in the air at the same time without dropping any on the floor. Strict nine-thirty to four-thirty at the office, any extra hours required to keep up with the workload to be put in at home; trade of accounts with other planners so that Harper's portfolio was entirely London-based and overnight travel unnecessary; and to compensate (and allow Saul to sell the package), salary frozen until normal service resumed.

Which, he supposed, was now. It was time, as Saul had pointed out that afternoon, to look to the future.

If this was to be the future, Harper thought, putting down the last of the volumes of survey data, then he didn't much care for it. For the last two hours he had flicked through each page, some freak synapse in his mind acting like the motor-driven shutter of a camera taking rapid mental snapshots. The pictures now developed, he found himself wondering whether AUC was one of those cultures which, if they didn't like the news, would shoot the messenger. Maybe that was Klein's game. Harper, expendable as enemies always are, was to be cast in the role of sacrificial lamb. Tethered in a Brussels boardroom until he had recounted the unpalatable cold hard facts, then ritually slaughtered.

In his time he had seen many new products slated, advertising concepts ridiculed and brand repositionings exposed cynically as exactly that, but the negative attitudes expressed against AUC represented a whole new order of rejection. The company stank. AUC didn't simply need to revamp its corporate image, it had to wipe the slate clean and start again from scratch.

The upside for the agency would be a budget to make Klein's mouth water year after profitable year (changing images takes a lot of time as well as a lot of money). The downside would be the frazzled brains of the copywriter and art director – even Stalin and Goebbels working in tandem would find it hard to rewrite this company's history and come up with a plausible alternative.

Harper sighed and fingered the scar. Realized what he was doing and picked up the agency's background document on AUC. Began reading, optimistically hoping that he would stumble across a hook, something on which to hang the new campaign.

No such luck. No serendipity. No flashes of inspiration. No leaping out of the bath and running naked down the street shouting, 'Eureka'.

One thing did catch his eye, though. And arouse his curiosity.

Admittedly his understanding of science was limited to rudiments like litmus turning red in the presence of an acid – or was it blue? – but he could see no logical explanation for AUC's recent actions. Why, he asked himself, would a company manufacturing drugs, assorted chemicals and, most pertinently, plastics of every type, shape and size, want to build up holdings in companies in the steel sector?

Like so many things in Harper's life, it just didn't make sense.

9

Belgium has a reputation, as the lager adverts might say, for being 'probably the most boring country in the world'. But all generalizations, including this one, are dangerous.

Kit Harper, steeped in the histories of Greece and Rome, liked the place. It had been Julius Caesar who had first conquered most of the country in 57 BC (or the year 696 in the Roman calendar which starts from the founding of the city – *ab urbe condita* – in 753 BC).

Subsequently the country experienced many other invasions – Spanish Inquisitors and the armies of the Habsburgs, Napoleon, the Kaiser and Hitler. And most recently, and more insidiously, the hordes of politicians, diplomats and Eurocrats with their camp followers – lawyers, businessmen and property developers. Brussels – capital of Europe, the Atlantic Alliance, Western capitalism and the AUC empire.

It is true that the city's new role as an administrative centre has done little to create an air of excitement. But the inhabitants shrug their shoulders at such criticism. 'Take it, or you leave it,' they say. 'But if you take it, you must do so on our terms.' Not a bad philosophy. Shame that it had been devalued by being adopted by the likes of Klein.

Even as the wheels of the aircraft wonderfully touched down, Harper felt the memories, happy and sad, flooding back. In the early years of his marriage, when both Heather and he had been working and the only problem they'd had with money was how to spend it, they had interspersed diving holidays in the Caribbean with many a weekend break here. Over the course of those visits he had learnt to view Brussels through the residents' eyes. Ignore, as best one could, the skyscrapers. Instead, relish the bustle of the old districts. Admire the astonishing blend of Gothic, Renaissance and baroque architecture that shouldn't work, but does. Stroll through the beautiful parks on a warm day. Sink a glass of ice cold beer at a pavement tavern. Appreciate the simple delights of what is the best example of French cuisine to be found anywhere in the world: even a fervently nationalistic Frenchman (is there, Harper wondered, any other kind?) would concede that point.

The black Mercedes taxi was travelling at 140 kilometres per hour. It zigzagged erratically from lane to lane, daring other drivers not to create gaps in the traffic along the motorway from the airport. Grudgingly, the driver slowed down to enter the tunnel that led to the heart of the city. Klein, sensing the reduction in speed, opened his eyes and let out the breath he had been holding.

'So you're clear on what you have to do tonight?' he said.

'Perfectly,' Harper said, an edge to his voice.

Klein had no sense of drama. Harper was to wine and dine someone called Charlie Mendoza, head of corporate planning, and, against his wishes, ruin the morning's presentation *and* the evening's dinner by revealing the denouement of his conclusions.

'Don't go sulky on me, Harper,' Klein said. 'Mendoza doesn't want any surprises tomorrow. It's a simple case of covering all the angles.'

'Covering what?'

'Yes, that too. But it's not for us to criticize.'

'Ours not to reason why, ours but to do as we're told and take the money?'

'Exactly, Harper. Do as you're told and take the money. It's a maxim you would do well to take to heart.'

'I prefer forewarned is forearmed. So tell me about this Charlie Mendoza. What am I up against?'

'I wouldn't want to influence your opinion. Anyway, we're here now. Just time to shower and change before dinner.' A frown appeared on Klein's face. 'You did get a new suit like I asked, didn't you?' he said.

'Yes,' Harper sighed, climbing out of the cab and retrieving his suit carrier and laptop from the boot. 'And, like you said, I'll be putting the bill on expenses. Very generous.'

'Not really,' said Klein. 'I'm going to dock it from Grayson's salary. He owes you, after all.'

Harper, his cynicism refuelled, shook his head and walked through the revolving doors of the Royal Windsor while Klein was paying the driver.

You couldn't actually say that this hotel was his favourite, but, of the many he and Heather had tried, it was the best of an indifferent bunch. The large modern hotels were completely sanitized, following a blueprint identical throughout the world. The smaller establishments with individual and idio-syncratic personalities sat directly abutting the busy streets: lacking effective double glazing, sleep was nigh on impossible except between the hours of two in the morning, when the city closed down and the beer-filled revellers finally dispersed, and six, when the noise of the giant diesel engines of the trundling street-washing trucks signalled the reopening. The Royal Windsor at least had the advantage of being conveniently located. A two-minute walk and the wonders of the Grand-Place were laid out before you. A leisurely meander through the narrow streets produced a bewildering choice of scores of equally excellent restaurants.

'You know where you're going?' Klein asked, as the two men split up to enter their rooms.

Harper nodded.

'See you at breakfast then,' Klein said.

'So what are you doing tonight?' Harper said.

'Frying a bigger fish,' said Klein, closing his door and the conversation.

Half an hour later, Harper was towelling himself dry. He took a clean white shirt from the suit carrier and checked his watch.

Nearly eight o'clock in Brussels, seven in England.

By rights, or at least by choice, he would have – should have – now been reading a bedtime story to his daughter. He picked up the phone, dialled his home number. Cassie answered on the first ring. That made him feel even more guilty.

Fifteen minutes later, dressed in the new light-grey suit, he crossed the crowded lobby and stepped outside. The evening was cool, the streets busy. Groups of businessmen with tight smiles, organized parties of tourists with video cameras and couples with interlocked hands were all heading for the Grand-Place, one of the most splendid squares in the world. The colours of the flower market were vibrant under the floodlights. The long shadows of the three hundred foot tower of the Hotel de Ville. The game of human chess being played on the giant checkerboard painted on the paving stones. The pavement cafés with their chequered tablecloths. Harper moved quickly on before he could pick out the table where he had once sat sipping a brandy and alternately gazing into Heather's eyes or up at the moon, stepped inside the covered arcade – a labyrinth of glass-fronted avenues lined with shops and eating places – and made his way to the restaurant.

The black-aproned waiter ushered him past the tables set in the middle of the room and seated him at a red velvet-lined booth in a far corner. As he sat there mentally preparing himself for the ordeal – tonight it wouldn't only be the steaks that were grilled – he couldn't help wondering why Klein had chosen this particular restaurant and, presumably, specified this particular table. Granted it was much quieter than the busy mussels and waterzooi cafés that filled the streets closest to the square, and the booth itself was ideal for a confidential conversation. But, with the subdued lighting, the rich glow of the polished wooden table, the pastel pink napkins and the almost subliminal schmaltzy music, it seemed more suited to a lover's romantic tête-à-tête than the clinical discussion of the many defects of the petrochemical industry. Maybe it was just one of those places that looked more expensive than the reality, winning the agency an undeserved brownie point from the client. He scanned the menu. Did a couple of quick calculations from Belgian francs into pounds. Said 'Jesus' under his breath. Rechecked his figures to see if he'd got the decimal point in the wrong place.

The sound of his name interrupted the (decimal) pointless exercise.

He looked up. Opened his mouth in an involuntary movement that was more shock than surprise. Made an effort to stop his jaw dropping onto the table top.

She was five foot ten, taller perhaps. Hard to judge when you're sitting down.

He jumped up.

Twenty-seven, twenty-eight, maybe. Slim – but not skinny. Well rounded where it mattered. Dressed in a pale-yellow suit, long tailored jacket and skirt with hem three inches above her shapely knees. The cut of the clothes screamed style. Straight out of the window of one of the astronomically expensive boutiques in the Galerie Louise, Harper guessed. Looked like she'd spent some time and a lot of money in a jewellers too. On her left wrist was a gold watch, its face surrounded by diamonds; on her right was a gold bracelet, the clasp two intertwined hands; around her neck a gold chain.

Her make-up was light, a touch of shadow to accentuate rather than draw attention from the eyes, a hint of colour around the full lips, a deft brushing of blusher on the high cheekbones. And to frame this beautiful face, a cascade of long copper-red hair. It seemed to catch the light and throw it back like a beacon.

Eyes of deepest brown locked onto him.

She offered her hand.

Harper wondered what to do.

Shake it?

Kiss it?

Or short-circuit proceedings by grasping it and going down on his knees and proclaiming undying love?

'Charlotte Mendoza,' she said with the hint of an accent. Canadian? East coast American? 'But you can call me Charly.'

'Kit Harper,' he said, shaking her hand. 'But then you know that already.'

She nodded. Her hair caressed her shoulders with the movement.

He stared.

'Perhaps,' she said, 'if you could let go of my hand, we might sit down.'

'Of course,' he said, feeling the blood flush his cheeks.

Pull yourself together, Harper. This is stupid. Anyway, she's almost certainly already spoken for. Some guy with the money to keep her in the style with which she seemed accustomed. He couldn't imagine she would be earning enough in corporate planning to afford such clothes – even the high-heeled ankle-strap shoes looked more catwalk than high street. And what was she doing in corporate planning anyway? Not the most glamorous of jobs – still, with looks like hers she didn't need to derive glamour from secondary sources; that would be overkill. In a little while, maybe, all would be revealed. Dream on, Harper. She probably holds all who work in advertising with utter contempt – wouldn't blame her either. And even if she doesn't, any interest she might have in you will evaporate the moment she learns you have a five-year-old daughter.

What the hell! He'd known one true love – that was more than many men managed in a lifetime. Was Heather up in heaven now, smiling down at him and shaking her head at the muddle of thoughts Charly had caused in what was supposed to be an analytical brain?

'Drink?' he said, signalling the waiter.

'Citron pressé,' she requested.

'Make that two, please,' Harper said.

She gave a little sigh. 'You don't have to, you know?'

'Don't have to what?' he asked, puzzled.

'Have the same as me. Just because I'm the client. If you want a drink, have a drink. I won't put a black mark against your name.'

'I don't drink alcohol,' he said, hoping she wouldn't probe.

'An advertising man who doesn't drink alcohol! Now I've seen everything. My education is finally complete.'

'Glad to be of service,' he said. 'Maybe we should order.'

'I'm sorry,' she said. 'I've offended you. You're not sick or something?'

'Or something,' he said, flicking through the menu.

'Come on, man of mystery. You can't leave it like that. Tell me more.'

'It's a long story. This isn't the right time or place.'

'And I'm not the right person?'

'Who knows, Charly?'

'Jeez,' she said, looking into his blue eyes. 'You're nothing like I was expecting, Harper.'

'And neither are you.'

'I'd have thought my fame would have preceded me.'

'Me too. Strange, eh? How about we wipe the slate clean and start again?'

'How about we get out of this place. It's so sweet my teeth are aching.'

They walked to the Grand-Place and found a table at a pavement café opposite Le Renard, the house of the Guild of Haberdashers. The lights of the square shone brightly against the blackness of the sky. By some unspoken and mutual agreement they sat in the shadows where it was more difficult to decipher the messages in each other's eyes. Charly was sipping pensively at a large Calvados.

'Right,' she said, 'I take it that it's not going to be good news tomorrow.'

'Let's just say that if I were Sir Angus Cameron I'd be reaching for a razor blade.'

Charly tilted her head questioningly.

'To slit my wrists,' Harper explained.

'You'd better tell me the worst.'

Harper gave it to her straight – what was the point of doing otherwise? As he explained the problem it seemed to grow before him. He didn't doubt that Allied Universal Chemicals wanted to change its image. The only question was whether it was possible. Its past record on environmental issues was frankly appalling. As far as the outside world was concerned, to AUC the only meaning of *green* was as one of three constituent colours used in magazine advertisements. In *his* judgement, he concluded, if it wasn't a lost cause then it was pretty damn close to it.

'If it's any consolation,' he said, feeling the desire to lift the frown that had taken root on her face, 'this sort of reaction isn't unusual – more extreme in this case, I admit. I've seen similar attitudes in other cases. Nobody likes big business. Most people think all business is corrupt. And the bigger the business, the more corrupt.'

'A company takes its direction, its management style, from the top,' she said, still frowning. 'Sir Angus isn't corrupt.'

'Who is to say?'

'Me,' she said, looking at him challengingly.

'Forgive me, Charly, but you can't know all that goes on behind closed doors.'

'Oh, but I do,' she snapped at him.

His heart sank. He'd touched a raw nerve and his mind fought against the logical explanation. The expensive clothes, the high position for one so young. No, don't let it be true. Don't tell me you're Sir Angus's mistress.

He turned away from her in an effort to hide his disgust – or was it simply disappointment?

'Is that it, Harper?' she said angrily. 'Sudden loss of interest, is it? I had imagined that you knew. Klein didn't brief you very well, did he?'

'Klein is a firm believer in the mushroom theory of management – keep 'em in the dark and shovel on the. . . . Anyway, what the hell! It's none of my business.'

'Sir Angus,' she began.

'I said it's none of my business,' he interrupted. 'I don't want to know.'

'I ought to slap that pretty-boy face of yours,' she said.

'It wouldn't be the first time.'

'Now why doesn't that surprise me? Maybe it's the way you jump to conclusions.'

'Look, it's a big day tomorrow. I'll call you a cab. Where do you want to go?'

'Nowhere, Harper. Not till you've heard me out.'

He gave an elongated sigh and nodded his head wearily.

'Sir Angus Cameron,' she said, 'is my grandfather.'

'Sugar!'

'Sugar?'

'Force of habit.'

'*Sorry* would have been a better choice of word, Harper.'

'Sorry, Charly. But I've just realized something. I've been stitched up.'

'You and me both, Kit. Romeo and Juliet. Ridiculous.'

He knew now why Saul hadn't dissuaded him from taking on the AUC account. Klein must have told him the plan in order to enlist his help.

'Only half ridiculous,' he said. 'Klein knew that I'd be taken with you.'

'Even with that wedding ring on your finger?'

'Because of the wedding ring on my finger.'

'Don't go all mysterious on me again.'

'It's a—'

'And if you're going to say "It's a long story" again, then please don't.'

He reached into his inside jacket pocket. Took out his wallet. Placed it on the table and paused to contemplate the wisdom of his next move.

'That,' he said, passing her a well-worn colour photograph, 'is my late wife. Notice the colour of the hair and eyes.' He waited while she studied the picture. 'Exactly the same as yours.'

'Gee, thanks,' she said, tossing the photograph back at him. 'So every time you look at me, you see her. That really makes me feel great.'

'No, it's not like that,' he protested. 'All I meant was that Klein would know that you were my type.'

'You really know how to flatter a girl.'

'I'm sorry. I'm a little out of practice.'

'Well, it can stay that way as far as I'm concerned. Don't get any ideas about me, Harper.'

'Strictly business, Mendoza,' he said. 'Which brings me to the big question. I can see Klein's motivation for this set-up – a relationship with Sir Angus Cameron's granddaughter gives him leverage, makes the account less prone to being moved. But what's in it for your grandfather?'

'That's simple,' she said. 'He wants me to leave AUC. And I am determined not to go. We've reached an impasse. He must think that if – God forbid! – I were to get involved with you, then I'd fall in with his plans and move to London.'

'And what are you supposed to do there? Perpetuate the Cameron dynasty? Settle down and have a long line of wee bairns?'

She laughed. Shook her head.

'Where do you think Klein is now?' she asked.

'With Sir Angus,' he said, knowing that the fish didn't get much bigger.

'Quite right. They're putting the finishing touches to the contract. The contract, that is, for AUC to buy the agency.'

Harper swore under his breath. 'Forgive me if I don't order champagne,' he said, 'but the idea of working for Sir Angus Cameron doesn't exactly fill me with unbridled enthusiasm.'

'Relax,' she said. 'It was never his intention to get directly involved with the agency. The acquisition simply makes commercial sense – AUC is going to be spending so much money on advertising over the next few years, my grandfather wants the profit coming back into the AUC coffers.' She gave him a sweet smile. 'No, you wouldn't be working for my grandfather, Harper. You'd be working for me. I'm supposed to be the new head of planning.'

'Sugar. Sugar. Sugar,' he said.

They stood outside an entrance to the Parc de Bruxelles across the road from Charly's apartment. The lights of the old lampposts glowed against the night sky.

'You didn't have to walk me home, you know,' Charly said.

'It was my pleasure,' Harper said, meaning it. 'Anyway, you can't be too careful.'

'Seems like London is more dangerous than Brussels nowadays,' she said.

'What do you mean?'

'Three businessmen murdered in the last week. Some sicko strangles them.' She shuddered.

'I haven't heard anything about this,' Harper said.

'The media have been told to keep a lid on it,' she explained. 'Not good for business.'

'Then how do you know?'

'One of the murdered men used to be our head chemist. Retired a couple of weeks ago. The police have been round asking questions.'

'I'm sorry,' he said. Then a thought occurred to him. 'So the atmosphere at the presentation won't be good.'

'Mueller's death won't affect it,' she said. 'He wasn't much liked.'

'Not much of an epitaph,' he said. 'Maybe all one can expect is *acta est fabula* – it's all over.'

'If you don't mind' she said, 'can we skip the homespun philosophy. It's a big day tomorrow and I need some sleep.' She paused. 'I won't ask you in, Kit. OK?'

'I understand,' he said, trying not to show his disappointment. 'See you in the morning.'

Harper stood as she entered the building and watched until a light went on and the curtains were closed. Then he gave a small sigh and turned away.

10

Kit Harper couldn't sleep. And Charly Mendoza was definitely not the reason. It was caffeine overload – too many cups of coffee too late at night. That and the presentation, of course. Drawing nearer with every minute and he still hadn't decided how to play it – Mr Nice Guy, choosing his words to sugar the pill, or the gunslinger, shooting straight and fast from the hip.

He stretched out his arm and searched around in the darkness of the unfamiliar setting. Pressed the first rocker switch he found. Flooded the room with blinding light. He blinked rapidly a few times and, when his eyes had become accustomed to the brightness, looked at his watch. Five-thirty.

He needed a walk; that was what was important. Some fresh air. In some place where he could think and, hopefully, be blessed with inspiration. Just one glimpse would do.

The park, that's where he would go. The Parc de Bruxelles.

He dressed in jeans, T-shirt, boots and leather jacket. Grabbed the plastic key card and left the room.

Acknowledging the sleepy-eyed greeting of the night porter, Harper pushed his way through the revolving doors and out into the street. The cold air sliced at him like a surgeon's scalpel. He shivered, turned up his collar and set off toward the Gare Centrale where he would then turn east.

The streets, covered by a thin blanket of mist, were still sleeping. Reluctant to face the day. Few cars. Fewer pedestrians.

Harper felt lonely. Homesick. And, above all, angry at himself.

True confessions!

Why had he told her so much? He would have been better off keeping his own counsel and remaining her man of mystery. Christ, he didn't even have the excuse of being verbose through drink. She must have been bored to tears. Certainly couldn't wait to leave him on the doorstep and escape into the safety of that wonderful old building. How lucky she was. What a wonderful view she had. Third floor front. Overlooking the park. Imagine waking up to that sight in the morning.

Still castigating himself, Harper passed through the west gate of the Parc de Bruxelles. There in front of him were the fountains, their plumes of water rising and falling in graceful arcs against the haze. His spirits lifted. A bottle is always half-full, he told himself, never half-empty. What better start to the day can you have, Harper? Selfishly enjoy the delights of this park, free of the intrusive presence of the daytime crowds.

The jogger, approaching from the left, pounded past him. He looked back and smiled knowingly at Harper, as if to say that they were fortunate men to share the secret pleasure of this hour.

The man's sweatshirt was soaked with perspiration. He was in his fifties, but lean and fit. Legs heavily muscled. Looked like he could run a marathon. Rhythmic, easy pace. Devouring the ground.

He faded quickly into the distance. Running anticlockwise around the perimeter, he disappeared behind the Theatre du Parc.

Harper, reluctant to be shamed by the older man, quickened his pace. He strode out purposefully along the central path that would bring him coincidentally to the eastern exit from the park and a view of Charly's apartment.

Twenty yards on, he heard the screams.

Long wailing cries, like a wounded animal being eaten alive. They cut sharply through the air. Shock waves of tortured pain.

Harper sprinted to the source of the sounds. The noise grew louder. It ripped at his mind. A deep chill ran down his spine.

The jogger lay on the grass, partially hidden from sight by the walls of the Theatre. A figure, sinister in black balaclava helmet and enveloping dark overcoat, stood over him, some long metal object in his hand. The weapon swept through the air. It smashed into defenceless legs.

Another scream rent the air.

The hand barely paused. It rose up again.

Closer now, Harper recognized the shape of a tyre lever.

'Stop!' he cried.

The attacker looked up.

Two pairs of eyes met across the grass.

The man hesitated.

Fight or flee? Decision time.

One last look at Harper. The weapon was thrown aside. The man turned, and with a shuffling lop-sided run, right leg dragging along the ground, headed toward the Metro station at Parc.

Harper set off in pursuit, knowing he would catch the man easily.

The man must have known that too. He spun round. Raised his right hand. Metal glinted in the rays of the morning sun. The man's arm was steady now as he took deliberate aim. A flash of light spat from the muzzle. The sound of a shot rang out.

Harper flung himself head first towards the grass. In the moment he began his dive the bullet was already biting into his left thigh. When next he dared raise his head the man was disappearing down the steps of the station.

A mixture of whimpers and groans came from behind him. Harper raised himself upright, testing the leg gingerly. There was a sharp bolt of pain, but he could place his weight on the leg. He hobbled across the grass to the writhing jogger.

The lower half of the man's body lay in a pool of blood. It spread outwards as Harper watched. From the knees down, the legs were unrecognizable – reduced to a grisly pulp.

The man's upper body twisted and turned, the face contorted into a grim mask. Harper stared in disbelief

Senseless.

So much hurt. So much pain.

The jogger groaned again – a low, distant, guttural noise. It lacked the earlier strength and urgency. Mercifully, he was beginning to slip into unconsciousness.

Harper did what little he could. Took off his jacket. Laid it over the mangled flesh. Held the clenched hand.

When the man was no longer aware of the pain, Harper left his side and limped towards the road, shouting at the top of his voice.

A priest on his way to the cathedral was the first on the scene. Calmly, he assumed control, issuing instructions to the next person to arrive to call an ambulance and the police. As shock set in, Harper sat on the damp grass, shaking uncontrollably and staring at a sacrilegiously discarded hamburger container and polystyrene beaker. The priest put his arm around him and prayed. That was when Harper saw the light.

11

There were two ambulances: that, in theory, should have provided some relief for Harper. But theories can be like classic cars, beautiful to contemplate but too often breaking down in practice. He sat in the back of the second, trying to erase from his mind the vision of the jogger's pain-contorted face and legs of pulp: in the seat opposite, a detective from the municipal police leaned towards him, notebook in hand, forcing him to recall every little detail.

The short, swarthy Walloon, fluent in English as well as French, had been surprised at the detailed description of the build and clothes of the assailant, given the brief glimpse Harper had claimed to have had. Harper had told him, matter-of-factly, that he had a photographic memory, then added that at times like this he wished he hadn't. The Walloon, hair streaked with grey, eyes sunken into a face etched with lines of experience, nodded to show that he understood only too well.

'You were lucky,' the policeman said, his questioning completed.

Harper looked down at the blood-soaked pressure pad on his thigh. Shook his head.

'The bullet passed straight through your leg,' the policeman persisted, sweeping his left hand through the air as if to brush aside Harper's denial. 'You are lucky to be alive. You might have been shot in the head or the heart.'

'No,' said Harper. 'The attacker fired *before* I dived to the ground. And *after* taking careful aim. He never intended to kill me, only to stop me pursuing him.'

'He is a strange man, this man with the limp. Why use a tyre lever as a weapon when you have a gun in your pocket?'

'The noise of a gunshot breaking the still of an early morning?' Harper said, thinking out loud. Then he remembered the screams. 'No, not that. Something more complex.'

The Walloon, fluent also in non-verbal French, gave a Gallic shrug.

'Maybe when you can interview the jogger,' Harper said, 'he might be able to suggest a reason.'

'Maybe,' the policeman said, sounding unconvinced.

Harper looked at him questioningly.

'I know this jogger,' the Walloon said. 'His name is Charbonnier. He is a politician.'

'I see your problem,' Harper said, sighing sympathetically.

If there was one group of people more economical with the truth than admen, it was politicians.

Harper telephoned Klein from the hospital. Explained the situation. Received a sigh of annoyance rather than sympathy.

'You want me to stall them for a whole hour?' Klein had shrieked down the phone. 'What the hell am I supposed to do for sixty minutes? Comic monologue? Whistle a selection of best-loved classics? Act out Macbeth?'

'No, that might be bad luck.'

'I'll kill you for this, Harper.'

'And there's one other thing,' Harper had said, grinning sadistically to himself. 'I need you to go shopping.'

'Shopping? At a time like this? Are you mad?'

'Here's what you need to get,' he had replied, dictating a long list.

'You *are* mad, Harper,' Klein had said, slamming down the phone.

It's a possibility, Harper thought, self-doubt causing him to question the game plan. Had it really been a flash of inspiration, or was it a mirage brought on by desperation?

Hell, it was too late now. All he could do was to trust his intuition. Do the unexpected to stun everyone into listening. Stake everything on a very cheap trick.

The headquarters of AUC is situated on the corner of Westraat and Rue Froissart. Harper paid off the cab driver and stood on the pavement gazing up at the rich man's folly – an inverted pyramid. The apex and the lower four floors were buried deep in the ground; the upper sixteen stories rose slant-wise into the air so that the occupants of the offices at the very top could look down on the world.

One of a trio of security guards escorted him to the top floor, pausing to swipe a smart card through a slot each time their way was barred by electronic doors. As they moved along the final corridor, Harper hung back. He took three deep breaths and stepped into the lion's den.

*

The boardroom of AUC occupies the north-west quadrant of the top floor of
the pyramid, giving it the advantage of windows on two sides, each providing a different panoramic view across the city to the unobscured horizon in
the distance: from this height even the gleaming stainless steel globes and
white lattice struts of the Atomium three miles away could be clearly seen.

It was a grand room in all meanings of the word. Harper doubted that the
decor would win any awards for good taste, but it certainly did not lack originality. The interior designer responsible had taken as his theme the naval
background of the Chairman of the company. The internal walls and the
spaces below the windows were clad in mellow oak. In the centre of one of
the vast windowless walls was a four-foot-by-three portrait in oils of Sir
Angus Cameron. Powerful but benign was the image the artist had sought to
portray – one out of two isn't bad. To either side was mounted, in the same
brass frames as the picture, a slim display case: one contained Cameron's
dress uniform, complete with ceremonial sword of honour, the other his
gallantry medal in a circle of lesser decorations. On another wall was a map
of the world, its surface pock-marked by red dots showing the location of
every AUC factory and office. When the double doors to the room were
closed the two halves came together to form a ship's wheel, four feet in diameter. Even the wall lights were in the shape of brass bells.

The floor space of the vast room, apart from a six-foot-wide perimeter,
was dominated by a table thirty feet long and ten feet wide. The table was
made of the same honey oak as the wall cladding and had a continuous cylindrical decorative brass strip about three-quarters of an inch wide running
along the edge. Around the table were twenty-five deeply padded swivel
chairs in wood and antique brown leather. Concealed within the fabric of the
tabletop were set, anachronistically, computer terminals. Pressing a button
on the edge of the table caused a wooden cover to slide back and a screen and
keyboard to rise up ready for use, in the manner of those machines seen
peeking out of the desks of television newsreaders.

Harper took it all in with one sweeping glance, blotted out the belittling
environment and concentrated on the audience: faces bore expressions of
intrigue, eyes examined him, some drifting down to his leg for evidence of the
bullet – Klein would have played the situation for all it was worth, killing time
and scoring points for the agency simultaneously. He gave one all-encompass-
ing 'Good morning'. Charly rose from her seat and walked toward him.

She looked so different today, as if she had made a conscious effort to minimize her beauty so that no one present would be distracted from the business at hand. She was wearing a black pin-striped trouser suit complete with waistcoat, a white blouse with Belgian lace collar, and black suede low-heeled shoes. Her red hair was swept up and back, held in place by two tortoiseshell combs. A simple pair of jet stud earrings was the only jewellery she wore. As she stood close by his side, the air conditioning wafted a tantalizing flower-scented breeze past Harper's appreciative nose.

'It's your meeting, Charlotte,' said Sir Angus, 'but perhaps we could make a start.'

The portrait flattered Cameron. His hair was greyer and thinner at the temples; his beard less distinctive, its definition and contrast lost as the red hair had given way to shades of pepper and salt; his face was fatter, with three chins and flabby jowls; his eyes were a much lighter shade of brown, suggesting a coldness and hardness inside. Yet his physical presence had not been exaggerated. It was partly his huge size, but even more than this it was his aura: it radiated out like some fear-inducing pheromone. Harper took an instant dislike to Cameron, saving himself valuable time.

Charly briefly introduced everyone. Some of the audience represented the interests of various geographic market sectors (France, Germany, the Iberian peninsula, Eastern Europe, Asia and so on), while others were drawn from the different operating divisions (pharmaceuticals, industrial chemicals, agrochemicals and plastics). How, Harper wondered, did they manage to make decisions given this overlap of responsibilities? But then the answer came to him. This wasn't a decision-making unit; it was a toothless senate under an omnipotent emperor. Whatever the individuals said, with the possible exception of Charly, Cameron would have the final say and the power of veto. Lax called the shots.

Harper smiled and nodded at each person in turn. One, Andrew Evans, the recently appointed head chemist, gave him a broad smile. A stocky man with wayward dark brown hair, ruddy complexion and a small porcine nose, Evans wore an old, ill-fitting tweed jacket with brown leather elbow patches, and looked like he might be auditioning for the role of some eccentric, scatterbrained scientist. Or, maybe he had already landed the part.

Harper addressed the audience. 'Today,' he said, 'there will be no formal presentation. No charts. No long speech.' He paused. 'No point.'

Harper walked over to the representative for Spain and Portugal.

'Let me explain,' he said, 'by starting with just one word. Zaragoza.'

There was a sharp intake of breath around the room.

'Zaragoza,' Harper repeated for maximum effect. 'Hundreds of innocent people killed; thousands blinded; countless cancers generated; fetuses aborted; babies born deformed. An ecological disaster, animals and plant life destroyed, the land contaminated for decades. Need I go on?' He nodded his head. 'Oh, yes, I do.'

He moved with theatrical slowness round the table until he stood directly in front of his next victim, the man from agrochemicals.

'Nemesis,' he said.

The man flinched at the mention of the second taboo subject.

AUC, seeing the 'success' of Agent Orange in the Vietnam war, had 'perfected' their own more powerful, dioxin-enriched version of the defoliant chemical. And sold Nemesis across the globe to governments, juntas and military dictators who cared more about eliminating a few troublesome rebels than the destruction of vast swathes of forest.

'Nemesis,' he said again, leaving the word hanging in the air as he moved on once more to where Klein sat ashen-faced in shock and fear. Harper reached down and picked up the four carrier bags of shopping from the floor by Klein's chair. Walked back round the table until he stood directly in front of Sir Angus Cameron. One by one, he upended the bags and dumped the contents to form a tottering mountain.

A mountain of plastic.

Hamburger cartons, polystyrene beakers, plastic bottles, disposable cutlery, rolls of shrink-wrap and a variety of examples of elaborate packaging designed solely to disguise or glamorize the ordinariness of the products within.

Harper dropped the four plastic carrier bags on top of the pile. And, as a final gesture, he swept his hand swiftly from side to side, knocking down the mountain and scattering its contents across the length and breadth of the table.

All eyes turned to Cameron, waiting for the explosion.

Harper didn't give him a chance.

'Zaragoza, Nemesis and this,' he continued quickly, gesturing at the mess while locking eyes with Cameron. 'We can take your money, Sir Angus – spend an absolute fortune on award-winning advertising campaigns. But that would be to act in the same cavalier fashion as you. Self-important, self-centred, self-seeking and too damn self-satisfied. We can't change your image. No one can. Not while you refuse to take any responsibility for your actions and your products.'

From the periphery of his field of vision Harper saw a nod from Andrew Evans. He broke eye contact with Cameron and turned to the head chemist.

'Forgive my lack of scientific knowledge,' he said. 'But all these examples on the table are what you call polymers? Is that right?'

'Correct,' Evans said in one of those heavy Welsh accents where pauses are inserted into the mid . . . dle of words. 'In layman's terms, polymers are giant molecules made up of chains of other molecules.'

'And the raw materials for the original molecules are coal, cellulose – plant life – and, by far the most important, petroleum – that being a product of oil?'

Evans nodded and gave an encouraging smile.

'Coal, plants and oil,' Harper said, looking pensive. 'Precious natural resources, in other words. And to make matters worse it takes energy – from even more of those precious natural resources – to convert the short molecules into the giant polymer chains. What an utter waste! Virtually none of these materials are recycled. Huge volumes of these non-biodegradable plastics are dumped each year to pollute our planet in perpetuity. Ten per cent of all solid waste in industrialized countries. Millions upon millions of tons each year. And rising exponentially. In a few years, all the landfill sites will be full to the brim. What are we going to do then? Or will it not be relevant because there won't be the fuel to power the trucks that carry the waste? Does anyone here think of the future? The future of our children, and our children's children?' No one spoke. Harper shook his head in a mixture of sadness and condemnation. 'And you wonder why your image stinks.'

Harper sat down.

There was an oppressive silence from the audience.

Charly stared at him, seeing him in a new light, he hoped.

Evans stared at him with the raised eyebrows of interest.

The rest just stared.

'Never,' Sir Angus Cameron said, 'never in my entire life, have I been addressed in such a way.' Klein opened his mouth to apologize. Cameron raised his hand to cut off the interruption. 'At least someone round this table has got some guts.'

Klein gave a sigh of relief.

'Well then,' Cameron said, looking round the table, 'what are we going to do? Harper is right. We have much to atone for in our past. And, as regards the future, how can we convince the people out there that we have turned over a new leaf?'

'I don't think you can,' Harper said. 'Why, given your past record, should anyone trust you?'

'Are you saying that we face an impossible task?' Charly asked. '*Impossible* is not a word in the AUC dictionary.'

Cameron gave her a proud that's-my-girl smile.

'I am saying,' Harper said, 'that there is absolutely no reason why anyone should believe *you*. They might, however, believe someone else. Think of it as a kind of medieval joust. You need a champion from outside your organization to fight for you. Someone to speak for you. Someone with impeccable credentials when it comes to telling the truth and in his concern for the environment.'

'And who do you suggest?' Cameron asked.

'There is only one person,' Harper said. 'Your old rival. Jeremiah Drew of GreenWay.'

'Excuse me, Harper,' he said, 'but you seem to have simply replaced one impossible task with another.'

'I never said it was going to be easy. But think of the result. Jeremiah Drew has criticized you publicly for years for your stance on the environment. Members of GreenWay have demonstrated against the opening of your new factories – didn't they once attack one of your laboratories and release all the animals? If Drew tells the world you have changed, then no one can doubt it is true. You would, of course, need a very powerful argument to persuade him to act as your champion.'

'And what might that be?' Cameron asked.

'What have you done for the environment?' Harper asked.

Silence.

'OK, what might you be able to do in the future? All you need is just one thing. But something so strong that we can hang the whole campaign on it.'

'Who can give Harper what he needs?' Cameron asked, letting his eyes rove around the table before settling on Charly. 'Who can give me the solution to the problem?'

'The enzyme,' she said quickly. 'We launch the enzyme.'

'Brilliant,' said Cameron, smiling proudly. 'The perfect – the only – solution.' He nodded his head decisively. 'Andrew, you brief Harper on the enzyme. Harper, I want you back here next week with concepts.'

'You want a new campaign in a week?' Harper gasped.

'No,' Sir Angus said, grinning. 'I want two campaigns in a week.'

'Two campaigns?' Harper couldn't believe his ears.

'Aye. One long-term campaign designed to turn round our image – that is your responsibility, Harper. And one short-term campaign – that is Klein's. Both must break in exactly two weeks time. That is when I will announce a takeover bid for Laurelle. AUC is about to become the number one petrochemicals company in the world.'

'So what exactly is an enzyme?' Harper asked Evans, turning to a clean page of his pad and hoping he wasn't going to have to fill it with impenetrable scientific formulae made up of incomprehensible hieroglyphics.

They were alone in the boardroom. Evans was pouring coffee while biting pensively on his lower lip.

'It's really quite simple,' he said. 'An enzyme is just a complex protein which makes possible biochemical reactions. Each enzyme is basically a specific biochemical catalyst.'

'And this is what you regard as "really quite simple"?' Harper said, laying down his pen. 'Please warn me when you get to the complicated stuff.'

'Sorry,' Evans said. 'Now how can I put it? Think of your digestive tract.'

'I'd rather not,' Harper replied, not feeling too good as it was. His stomach was empty, his leg was throbbing and he desperately needed more painkillers.

'There's an enzyme in your digestive tract,' Evans continued, unheeding, 'that breaks down the large proteins, carbohydrates and fat molecules of foodstuffs into small particles. When that enzyme has done its job, other enzymes take over, passing the small molecules from the intestine to the bloodstream. Still others use those small molecules to build large and intricate molecular structures in the body and to control the release of energy. You see, Kit, all complex and integrated chemical reactions that take place in animals, plants and microorganisms are regulated by enzymes.'

Harper sighed. How the hell was he going to explain this to the creative team? They had mental blocks coping with the mechanics of antidandruff shampoo. But at least there they could fall back on the old standards of combs, giant white flakes and the threat of social ostracism.

'Enzymes,' Evans said, 'are used in the leavening of bread, curdling of cheese, fermenting wine, brewing beer and so on. They are very specialized and very specific, acting on only one kind of substance or group of related substances called the substrate. Each enzyme catalyzes only one reaction.'

'OK,' Harper said, only slightly the wiser, 'so what reaction does *your* enzyme catalyse? What does it do, Andrew?'

Evans smiled proudly.

'Basically,' he said, 'it eats plastic. Or, more accurately, encourages the plastic to biodegrade itself.'

'Jesus!' Harper said, visualizing the potential. 'This is absolutely brilliant.'

'And that's not all,' said Evans. 'When the enzyme has done its job, you can use the resulting product as a fertilizer.'

'And this works?' Harper said, remembering the old adage that if something sounds too good to be true, it usually is. 'It's not just an idea? It really works?'

'Oh, yes,' Evans said. 'We've been running large-scale field tests for six years now.'

'So why haven't you launched it sooner? This enzyme is a bloody miracle product. You not only solve the biodegradability problem but also effectively, although in a different form, put back into the earth what you have taken out.'

'There's a minor technical problem,' Evans admitted.

'Ah,' Harper said, suddenly feeling less hopeful. 'And what is this minor technical problem?'

'Catalysts, as I'm sure you know, permit or drastically alter the speed of chemical reactions. But they do not actually take part in those reactions. That means they do not get used up. And that is no good to a profit-centred organization like ours. We need to sell the product not just once but over and over again. In order for this enzyme to be a commercial success, we have to discover a compensating chemical which will act as a suitable retardant or inhibitor.'

'A compensating retardant or inhibitor?' Harper said, shaking his head. 'Andrew, what the hell does that mean?'

'In layman's terms,' Evans said, 'I suppose you could say that we, er, have to find a way of killing it.'

STAGE THREE

REACTION

12

Harper had been on many tours of factories in the past. They could be either mind-numbingly boring or absolutely fascinating depending not on the production processes or the products themselves, but on the enthusiasm of the guide. Evans looked like he would make it interesting, and who knows, Harper thought, he might pick up something useful that they could work into one of the advertisements.

The research laboratories, buried below ground level, occupied the penultimate three floors of the building: the lowest floor, Evans explained, was split into two, one half housing the security operation and the other the equipment that provided the offices with the technical services they needed and the air conditioning that made them habitable.

Evans swiped his card through the slot on the security module on the wall and ushered Harper inside.

'Jesus!' said Harper as the room hit his senses and he was forced to reassess all his expectations.

The air was clean and sweet – no lingering pungent aromas of chemicals smelling like rotten eggs or pickling vinegar. The low hum of the air conditioning provided a background to an enthusiastic buzz of bantering chatter from the white-coated chemists and technicians so that the ambience was like that encountered in an operating theatre in *MASH* or *ER*, a team of dedicated professionals working together rather than a group of boffins in silent isolation. The laboratory area itself was enormous, maybe fifty feet square, but then it had to be to accommodate what to Harper's untrained eye appeared to be every scientific device that a questing scientist could desire, and then a few more for luck. He could imagine his chemistry teacher at school having orgasms at the mere sight of it all. On the ceiling, banks of spotlights, strategically positioned smoke detectors and sprinklers, and six large turbines poised, Harper presumed, to suck out at the touch of a button any accidental leakage of noxious gases. Not that there should have been any, since against one wall was an airtight gas chamber: it was built of thick Plexiglas, its front section either able to be lifted up entirely for cleaning purposes or completely secured by two steel handles when in use. Also in the front were those circular holes filled with thick black-plastic armpit-length gloves more usually associated with messing about with fuel rods in nuclear power stations. Surrounding this central experimental section was a series of individual glass-fronted offices equipped with computer terminals with twenty-one-inch flat-screen monitors.

'What were you expecting?' Evans said, grinning at Harper's stunned expression. 'A room filled with hissing blue-flamed Bunsen burners?'

Harper nodded. 'And populated by men with concave cheeks from a lifetime of sucking pipettes,' he said. 'So this is your domain, Andrew.'

'A small part of it, Kit,' Evans said proudly. 'But the most important part, I admit. All the initial exploratory research work of the group is carried out on these three floors and the discoveries made are then allocated to laboratories in the most appropriate division for further development and commercial exploitation. This is the breeding ground, if you like.'

'A little like advertising,' Harper said with an ulterior motive. 'The creative team comes up with the concept – the overall idea, the copy, layout and rough visuals – and then others – photographers, retouchers, and so on – work on the execution. And, like you, we also test our product – market research among the target audience in our case. Tell me about the tests and trials you undertake.'

'Similar to your market research, but much more sophisticated. Everything taken to the nth degree. Same statistical disciplines, but with much lower margins of error. We work on 99.99 per cent confidence limits,' Evans boasted. 'Only a one-in-ten-thousand chance of being wrong.'

'Yet it still happens,' Harper countered. 'Like with thalidomide.'

Evans frowned, then shook his head slowly.

'Thank God I had nothing to do with that,' he said. 'I don't know how I could ever have coped with the responsibility. Wasn't one of our products, fortunately.'

'But,' Harper persisted, 'symptomatic of the industry, some would say? A rush to launch before adequate testing had taken place?'

'It wasn't like that,' Evans said, shaking his head more vigorously this time. 'No matter what you might believe, the testing was rigorous. You couldn't really fault the methods or the samples. They were unlucky.'

'*They* were unlucky? What about all the kids born without proper arms or legs? Or the mothers who, forewarned too late, went through the trauma of deciding whether or not to have an abortion?'

'That can never adequately be put right, Kit. But what you have to realize is that thalidomide is not the demon it is painted. It is *truly* a wonder drug. Alleviating morning sickness is the least of its beneficial properties. It is *now* the drug for curing leprosy, for relieving the excruciating pain of mouth, oesophageal and genital ulcers, and for the treatment of the wasting disease that usually accompanies AIDS.'

'You can't call thalidomide a wonder drug when it had such terrible side effects.'

'Maybe,' Evans said. 'But the industry learned a lot from thalidomide. I repeat, Kit, there was nothing fundamentally wrong with the tests or clinical trials. What no one appreciated at that time was the problem caused by time-windows. Thalidomide had no fetal side effects except, it later transpired, when taken during a very narrow time-window during the first trimester.'

'And that makes it all right?'

'No, Kit. But, armed with the new knowledge of time-windows, it makes it impossible for history to repeat itself. We can build them into our trials, cover every eventuality.' He gave a reassuring smile. 'If you knew what a pharmaceuticals company had to go through to get a licence for a new drug, you'd appreciate just how thorough the procedures are. That's not to say there are never any side effects, but any that do exist are known and prescribing doctors can pass on a warning – it's then up to the patient to weigh up the balance of risks and benefits. Someone suffering from leprosy, say, will have a higher risk threshold than someone with morning sickness.'

'So what tests have you conducted on the enzyme?'

'I'll explain that in a moment,' Evans said, spotting a tray of sandwiches and ice-cold beers being carried into one of the side offices. 'Over lunch. But there's something I'd like you to see first.'

He led Harper to a workbench where a blonde-haired woman was perched high on a stool peering down in deep concentration at a slide at the bottom of a tall microscope.

'Françoise,' Evans said, making the woman jump. 'Would you run a little experiment for Mr Harper? Show him the power of enzymes and give him a glimpse of the future.'

The woman lifted herself from the high stool, smiled knowingly at Evans and said, 'Come, Monsieur Harper.' She walked toward the gas chamber, her white coat hanging loosely on her thin body. She pushed a button on the outside of the chamber to activate the internal extractor fans, then inserted her arms into one of the sets of plastic sleeves. Picking up a tall cylindrical container, she poured a little of the contents into a steel vessel.

'This is oil sludge,' she said, as the thick viscous liquid dribbled slowly from one vessel to another. 'The lowest distillate of crude oil.'

'When oil is refined,' Evans began to explain, 'it is distilled in a huge column. The lightest, higher distillates give us petrol, diesel, kerosene and aircraft fuel; as we move down the column, the products are progressively heavier – petrochemicals, waxes, lubricants, greases and bitumen. This thick sludge is the residue left over.'

Françoise set the steel vessel on a halogen hotplate, flicked a switch and turned a dial to set the temperature to 50° centigrade. She measured out a tiny quantity of a white powder on a set of electronic scales and waited for the thermostat to indicate that the set temperature had been reached.

The indicator light on the thermostat glowed red. Françoise sprinkled the few grains of white powder on top of the oil. There was an instant fizz from the vessel and a light-brown crumbly substance began to form, puff up like popcorn and spread across the surface of the oil.

'The white powder is an enzyme,' Evans said. 'You can see how quickly it works given the right conditions – each enzyme functions best at a specific temperature.'

'Voilà,' Françoise said, scraping the light-brown substance into a wide-based glass dish. She tipped up the steel vessel to show Harper that it was completely empty.

'Very impressive,' Harper said. 'But what have you made?'

Françoise opened the front of the airtight chamber and withdrew the dish. She ran her index finger over the surface, some of the light-brown puffed-up crumbs sticking to her fingertip. Which she then popped into her mouth.

Harper stared at her with a mixture of incredulity and revulsion.

'Pure protein,' she said, smiling broadly at him. 'Would you care to try some?'

'Thanks for the offer, but I don't want to spoil my lunch.'

Evans grinned. 'Come into my office, Kit. You need a break. And you've seen enough here, I think.'

Evans opened the door to his office and waved Harper inside. On the desk was the tray of sandwiches, beers and mineral water.

'Sit down, Kit. Help yourself,' Evans said, sliding a plate and napkin over the desk.

Harper eased himself into the chair, the wound in his leg throbbing in complaint at too much standing and walking. He picked up a bottle of mineral water, slowly poured some into a glass while eyeing the sandwiches suspiciously.

'Don't worry,' Evans laughed. 'Just unadulterated smoked salmon, pastrami and chicken. No added ingredients, I promise.'

'You don't expect people to eat that stuff?' Harper said. 'The protein, I mean.'

'Eventually, yes. The plan is to introduce it initially into pet food, then to extend gradually to human beings – starving Third World countries first and, as the concept gains acceptance, moving on to vegetarians in the developed world. It's just like soya, really. But we're talking long term here. The discovery has only very recently been made. We've fed some mice, rats and monkeys on the protein, but it will still be a year or two before we start trials with humans. And then another five years before the tests are complete and we are granted all the necessary marketing licences.'

'I wish I wasn't so ignorant of science,' Harper said with a sigh. 'Then perhaps I wouldn't feel so uneasy about it.'

'It's not just you,' Evans said. 'It seems to me that half the population holds science responsible for all the past evils of the world and the other half believe it is the saviour of the future of mankind.'

'And which is the truth?'

'Neither,' Evans said. 'And both.'

'You read Classics?' Evans said with wide eyes.

They had set aside business and were making small-talk over lunch. Evans popped the remains of a pastrami sandwich in his mouth, propped his elbows on the desktop and stared with awe at Harper. 'I wish I'd read Classics,' he said wistfully.

'What is this?' he said, shaking his head. 'Role reversal? A little while ago I'm wishing I knew more about science, and now you're wishing you'd read Classics. Something seems to have gone wrong somewhere.'

'I had to study Latin at school,' Evans said. 'Jesuit place in Hereford, terribly old fashioned, mother's choice, I'm afraid. It was a real struggle – I couldn't master the language side of the subject, but I was hooked on the history. Loved it. All those heroic deeds – better than Roy of the Rovers for me. Three years at university reading about heroes would have seemed like heaven.'

'You might have been disappointed, Andrew. Half the time would have been spent on the Greeks, and their heroes were very different from the Romans. While the old Roman stories are mostly in praise of courage, the legendary history of the Greeks has heroes whose chief quality was cleverness. It was mainly the intellectual virtues that the Greeks admired. From the job you do now, it sounds like you finished up a Greek, not a Roman.'

'And how about you, Kit? Are you Greek or Roman?'

'I'd love to echo your words. To say "neither and both". But—' Harper trailed off, unwilling to admit, even to himself, that his chief Roman quality had been the absolute worship of Bacchus. 'Tell me about the tests on the enzyme,' he said, changing the subject.

'I'll do better than that,' Evans said. 'I'll show the results. Come with me to the centre of the AUC universe.'

Harper rose from his chair.

'You don't have to move,' Evans said, laughing. He pointed to the computer terminal on his desk. 'This terminal, and all the others in this building and in the AUC offices throughout the world, is connected to the mainframes that occupy the lowest floor of the pyramid. I call the computer *Deep Thought*.'

'After the one in *The Hitchhikers' Guide to the Galaxy*, I presume?' asked Harper. 'The machine whose task it was to answer the ultimate question of life, the universe and everything.'

Evans nodded, happy that someone appreciated his little joke.

'Through this keyboard there is access to every piece of work we have ever done.'

'Isn't that a bit dangerous?' Harper said. 'So much confidential material accessible to all and sundry.'

'That is the beauty of this system. Let me demonstrate.'

Evans pressed a button on the front of the VDU and the machine began to whirr and hum.

'My predecessor did not appreciate the benefits of the computer: Mueller was a bit of a Luddite; only used the terminal when he had to. Me, I love it.'

A text box shone out in deep blue against the grey background of the screen.

'First I need to give the computer my name and first-level password.'

Evans typed his surname and initials and responded to the next question on the screen by hitting a sequence of six keys. Harper watched the man's fingers attentively, and, turning his eyes back to the screen, saw that six aster-isks had appeared.

'Now I have access to all the standard programs for daily use – word processing, spreadsheets, graphics, statistical analysis and so on. However, if I want to delve the scientific records I have to give a second password.'

Evans beamed with pride, as if he were father to this electronic child.

The screen instantly demanded another password. Evans responded; another series of stars appearing in place of the letters he typed. There was a brief pause and the screen filled with a new page of options. 'All our records are sequenced numerically. Each project has a code number and, now that my access has been approved by *Deep Thought*, I can call up any of the files by simply inputting the appropriate number. Then the whole contents of the file are open to me. It's quick and easy. I can even choose whether to inter-rogate the file in date order from its beginning or to search by giving keywords, so that only subfiles containing the keyword will be displayed. The amount of time and effort it saves is incredible.'

'I don't want to rain on your parade, Andrew,' Harper said with a shrug, 'but what's to stop an embittered employee using the authority of his pass-word to lock off files from general view? Or, even worse, deleting whole sections from the memory. It seems a very vulnerable system to me?'

'O, ye of little faith,' responded Evans. 'The computer operators back up the data onto disk each night – the worse that could happen would be the loss of one day's input. And the system has firewalls and other sophisticated protective devices. Unauthorized access to this computer is impossible.'

'Everything is impossible until proven otherwise,' Harper said with a smile. 'An enzyme that eats plastic sounds impossible to me. Did you discover it, by the way, or was it your late predecessor?'

'I'm tempted to laugh,' Evans said. 'But I suppose one shouldn't mock the dead. Yet it's hard to feel much sympathy for Mueller, I'm afraid. I doubt if there is a single person here who will shed any tears over him.'

Harper raised his eyebrows questioningly, and encouragingly.

'He was a bitter man at the end,' Evans said sadly. 'Mueller hadn't made a significant discovery for years. He just took the credit from others. Excelsior was my discovery and so was the plastic-eating enzyme'

Evans pushed away his plate and took a long reflective sip of the ice cold beer. He shrugged. 'Do you want to see what it looks like?'

Evans reached into the bottom drawer of the desk and withdrew a stain-less steel box. Took off the lid and showed the contents to Harper.

Harper looked unenthusiastically at a dull grey powder.

'I was hoping,' he said, 'for something that would shine with rainbow hues, or that would glow in the dark. It's not the most visually stunning of substances.'

'Life isn't *Star Trek*,' Evans said. 'Even if Sir Angus does have a nasty habit of saying "Make it so".'

Evans replaced the box and caught sight of his watch as he did so.

'Is that the time?' he said. 'I'd better give you a lift to the airport. If I print out all the details of the trials of the enzyme, you can read them as we go along and ask me any questions.'

The drive in Evans's Citroen provided more evidence to force Harper to re-evaluate his initial impression of the man as a stereotypical boffin. Yes, the car was littered with the normal family detritus of sweet wrappers and comics, but out of the cassette player came, not some anonymous middle-of-the-road classical background drivel, but the jolly sounds of Gilbert and Sullivan. Evans sang along loudly to tunes from *The Gondoliers, Patience* and *The Mikado*. When they stopped at traffic lights, pedestrians and other drivers peered into the car to view the ruddy-faced man with the booming voice. And to shake heads and raise eyebrows.

Harper did his best to concentrate. But his best wasn't good enough. He resigned himself to having to read the lengthy document on the plane and then again at home. Contented himself with flicking through the pages, getting the general drift and seeking clarification – or more usually explanation – of some of the technical terms. As the car pulled up outside the airport and the last bars of 'Three Little Maids from School' faded from the speakers, he turned to Evans.

'Two questions,' he said.

'Only two?'

'For now, at least. Firstly, why Kazakhstan?'

'That was Mueller's choice, so I can only guess. A huge country – five times the size of France, I believe – so plenty of choice for the test and control sites; the test site being the one where the product of the enzyme is used as fertilizer, the control site where they continue with the standard agrochemicals. It also has the required mix of agricultural areas and nearby industrialized cities and towns where the waste plastic can be collected for processing. And, last but not least, I suspect, given the highly depressed economy of the country, we would not have had to pay them much to participate in the tests.'

'Not the most convenient of locations. It seems a bit isolated. How the hell do you get there?'

'The company's private jet,' Evans replied.

Silly me, Harper thought, feeling more than a little naïve.

'Second question,' Harper said. 'What are we going to call this enzyme? We need a name with meaning. Any thoughts?'

Harper knew he shouldn't really have asked the question – it was the job of the copywriter – art director axis to come up with brand names. But rarely could they work up much enthusiasm for what they considered to be a task unworthy of their 'wide-ranging strategic talents' and, frankly, their success rate was pretty dismal.

'How about Jupiter?' Evans suggested, returning to their earlier classical theme. 'Doesn't the name mean *shining father*? Father of a new future, perhaps. Sir Angus would like that.'

'Jupiter had a habit of lobbing down thunderbolts on his enemies,' Harper said. 'A little too close for comfort, perhaps.'

Evans nodded and laughed. 'Wouldn't want to encourage him, eh? What about Apollo, then?'

'God of prophecy – that has connotations of the future, I suppose – and of medicine. Not bad.'

Harper was just about to settle on the name when he experienced one of those strange flashes of intuition where your brain shouts at you the answer to a problem, but doesn't even whisper the reasons behind it.

'I've got it,' he said. 'Gaia. The personification of Mother Earth. And she was married to Uranus, god of the sky. Heaven and earth wedded together. And we might also tie it to Lovelock's *Gaia Hypothesis*, the planet as a single organism. It would appeal to the Green lobby, and that could prove useful.'

'Agreed,' said Evans. 'The Gaia enzyme it is.'

Harper shook Evans's hand and stepped out of the car. Before he entered the terminal, he turned around, waved back and smiled. But by the time he had passed through the doors, the smile had become a frown. Maybe it wasn't the best choice of name, after all. He gave an involuntary shudder. Just concentrate on Gaia, he told himself. Forget about what her children did.

13

Charly Mendoza sat at her desk, trying to work but finding that her heart really was not in it. How could she even begin to plan when she knew she was not to play any part in the future?

The door swung open.

'I think I owe you an explanation,' Sir Angus Cameron said.

'And an apology,' said Charly.

'May I come in?'

'Why not? What could you interrupt that isn't totally pointless from my point of view?'

Cameron walked slowly across the room, avoiding her gaze. Settled his bulk in the thickly padded leather chair opposite Charly. Looked at her with misty eyes.

'Do you trust me, Charlotte?' he said.

'More so than you trust me, it seems. Why didn't you tell me about Laurelle?'

'Because it would only give you more reason to stay.'

'And why do you want me to go? I don't understand, grandfather.'

'Throughout your life, Charlotte, I've always had your best interests at heart. Even when your mother insisted against my wishes on marrying that no-good barfly Mendoza and settling in America, I had people watching over you all those years. That's how I was able to be with you so soon after both your parents were killed in that car crash. And ever since then I've done everything I possibly could for you – the best private schools, Oxford, Harvard Business School, taking you on here and helping you climb the ladder of success.'

'Only to push me off when I was on the penultimate rung.'

'It's not like that, Charlotte. Just regard the move as a sabbatical, if you like. A sideways move. Take a couple of years out and broaden your experience.'

'In some two-bit advertising agency? That's not going to take a couple of years. Couple of months would be long enough to learn what they could teach me. I want to stay, grandfather. This is what I've worked for. And this is what I thought you were grooming me for. Wasn't I supposed to be the successor?'

'You're in planning, Charlotte,' he sighed. 'You know better than most that there are times when even the best plan has to be modified due to a change in circumstances. This is one of those times. I'm going to have buy loyalty from Laurelle. I need to give some of their people top jobs. And yours is one of them.'

'Thanks very much! Doesn't blood count for anything? Why me? Why am I to be the sacrificial lamb?'

'Because of who you are. Your presence would make the Laurelle people uneasy. Give them a while to settle in. Let them get acclimatized to you as the linchpin of our advertising agency. Then you can make a triumphal return. To a bigger job in a bigger company. Trust me, Charlotte. Your welfare, your future, has always been my biggest concern. And now more than ever. You must believe that. What I do, I do for you.'

'OK, grandfather,' Charly said. 'If it is what you really want, then I will go.'

'Thank you, my dear,' he said. 'I'm so glad it's settled.'

Sorry to disappoint you, Charly thought. But, as you said, there are times when even the best plan has to be modified. She gave a little smile. How ironic! In business you're always told to prepare an exit route in case things go wrong. But if there was no exit route, how could her grandfather make her go? She had a scheme – a wonderful scheme. Not that anyone else was going to like it. Especially Harper.

14

Harper finished the main advertising brief and the supplementary creative brief, produced some guidelines for choice of media, printed out ten copies of everything and entered the conference room with ten minutes to spare. The interior of the room had been designed by Jackson, the creative director, in what could only be described as mock-Mediterranean, although in Harper's judgement it was more mock than Mediterranean. The carpet was a deep blue, the walls pale blue but the shade progressively lightening as it neared the brilliant white ceiling. There were dazzlingly bright sun-yellow venetian blinds – more Adriatic than Mediterranean, surely? – on each of the windows. The table, currently laid with pens, pads and glasses for ten people, was made from a roughly hewn and sharp-cornered one-inch-thick slab of marble set upon two ornate dark-green wrought-iron pillars: for larger meetings matching side extensions could be added to each end. Along the wall to the right of the door was an ersatz-marble plastic sideboard, its top now bearing ten bottles of mineral water and ten cans of beer arranged in precise triangles like pins in two adjoining bowling lanes. Hanging from the wall to the left of the door were two huge monitors linked to DVD and video players: in each corner hung a speaker. Harper had been in this room on countless occasions, but his senses were still stunned every time he stepped through the door. Individually, each colour and item of furniture had something to say, but together it was like a residents' meeting in the Tower of Babel.

He walked around the table distributing copies and seeing in his mind's eye the occupant of each seat. Klein, as account director, always took the chair on the short side of the table to the right; the creative team, Philip and Ned, together with Jackson would sit with their backs to the window and be joined by Mick from Traffic (the department responsible for the coordination and progress of the campaign within the agency from concept through to fully finished advertisements); Harper himself would sit on the other long side with James, media director, to his right and Tony and Verity (media buyer and media planner respectively) to his left.

James, wearing an open-necked, short-sleeved shirt and an amiable smile, was the first to arrive.

'What do you reckon?' he said, looking thoughtfully at the windows. 'Blinds up or down?'

'Makes no difference,' Harper said. 'We'll be blinded either way. You choose.'

'I suppose we could always change sides,' James said mischievously, while pulling up the blinds and letting the light flood in.

'And transgress one of the basic proprieties of briefing meetings?' Harper said. 'Not to mention as a consequence having to sit facing a row of sulking faces for an hour. I don't think so.'

James took two bottles of mineral water from the sideboard, passed one to Harper and took his usual seat.

The others began to drift in. Philip and Ned were known as the odd couple. Philip, the copywriter, was quiet, thoughtful and gay: Ned, the art director, was like some throwback to Neanderthal times – the agency joke was that it wasn't Ned's salary that was the main expense but the need to constantly replace the carpets because his knuckles wore grooves in them as he walked. Finally, they were waiting for just Jackson and Klein. Those now present picked up the briefing documents and started to read through them. A buzz of excitement went round the room when they reached the part with the budget.

The door opened.

In walked Klein. And Charly.

What the hell was she doing here.

The effect of her entrance on the people already in the room was dramatic. The buzz died, leaving only an awkward silence. Eyes stared and brains transmitted the word *interloper*.

A few of the attendees – those whose politeness or male chauvinism overrode their shock – stood up.

'May I introduce Charly Mendoza,' Klein said. 'Head of corporate planning for AUC.'

'I'll get another chair,' Harper said to create a diversion.

He was more successful than he had intended, due to bumping into one of the sharp edges of the damned table. He hopped on one foot comically as the wound in his leg screamed vengefully at him.

'That won't be necessary,' Klein said, immune to the distractions of Harper's performance. 'Our creative director, unfortunately, can't make the meeting.'

Not *can't*, Harper thought, sitting back down and breathing hard as he tried to fight against the pain. *Won't*. Taking someone's customary seat at the table was a small offence when compared to the cardinal sin – hanging offence? – of permitting a client to sit in at a briefing meeting.

Charly stood there for a moment challengingly – and, Harper suspected, to let everyone take in the no-nonsense signals of the black linen business suit, white high-necked cotton blouse and long red hair scraped severely back and tied with a black silk scarf. Then she sat down at the head of the table.

Gasps were suppressed – just.

Klein, through clenched lips, somehow managed to make the obligatory formal introductions. Nods came from around the table. With the exception of Ned, that is: with his brain being unable to cope with the complex decision on whether to grunt or drool, he did both simultaneously.

'Perhaps we can proceed, Harper,' Charly said. 'The sooner you are finished, the sooner these people can get down to some work.'

Harper opened his mouth to speak, but was distracted: James had written the single word *bitch* in block capitals on his pad and was now busy underlining it.

Charly looked at her watch pointedly and drummed her fingernails on the table.

Harper shook his head in knowing disbelief and gave her a broad smile. She looked away and down at her pad, giving a good impersonation of someone concentrating hard.

'Let's go through the brief from the top,' Harper said.

'I would have expected everyone to have read the brief by now,' Charly interrupted. 'Why don't we go straight on to any questions.'

'We *could* do that,' Harper said, seeing clearly the game she was playing. 'Or, alternatively, if you would be so kind as to give me a moment, I could go fetch a knife.'

'Thinking of committing suicide?' Charly asked.

'It's not for me,' Harper said, looking into her deep-brown eyes. 'It's to cut the atmosphere.'

'Don't get smart with me, Harper.'

'Sure,' he said. 'You're the client. Whatever you say.' He paused, an expression of serious consideration on his face. 'So, Ms Mendoza, how dumb would you like me to be?'

'Just act natural, Harper,' she said. 'That should do fine.'

He glanced round the table. A couple of people were slumped back in their chairs, minds reeling; some others were sniggering; Philip was making notes so that he could reuse the interchange in the novel he was planning (and had been ever since Harper had first met him) and thereby claim the repartee as his own; Ned was frowning, still trying to work out the exchange before last, or the one before that maybe; Klein was not amused.

'I think you owe Ms Mendoza an apology,' he said.

'Only in private,' Harper replied, rising from his seat and walking to the door. He held it opened and gestured to Charly. 'After you, Ms Mendoza.'

They went outside, shut the door and moved along the corridor out of earshot.

'This charade is unworthy of you, Charly,' he said. 'Stop it now.'

'When I'm enjoying myself so much? No way.'

'I know what game you're playing.'

'I'm sure I don't know what you mean,' she said, managing to sound hurt.

'You're trying to scupper the takeover of the agency.'

'Scupper?' she said thoughtfully. 'Sounds like something my grandfather would say.'

'You think that by alienating everybody around that table there will be a red revolution and the takeover will be called off. And that will mean that you won't be forced to move here and become planning director. Well, let me tell you, it won't work. You don't know Klein. When there's money involved, he will take whatever crap you dish out and keep coming back for more. And he'll sack anyone who won't do the same. There are some good people here, Charly, and I don't want to see them sacrificed as pawns in your chess game with your grandfather.'

She opened her mouth but Harper raised his hand and continued.

'If you ruin this briefing meeting, no one will emerge as a winner. If we work together, maybe we can find a solution to your problem.'

'Is that the best you can offer? *Maybe?*'

'Carry on in the direction you've been taking and you have no chance. But do as I ask, and we keep your options open while we both search for the answer. Let's work together, Charly, not against each other. What do you say?'

'There's blood on your trousers,' she said.

'Hell, that's the least of my worries,' he replied. 'For what I said to you in that room, Klein is going to skin me alive.'

'You handle the briefing, Kit,' she said, breaking the spell. 'I'll take care of Klein.'

Charly, Harper began to realize, was a woman of extremes: whatever she did, she did with an unbridled passion; whatever she thought, she thought with utter conviction; whatever personality dimension one cared to measure, she was always at one end or other of the spectrum, never in the middle. In the space of a few minutes she went from growling tigress to purring pussy cat. She won everyone over, especially Ned.

As Harper expanded on the brief by going deeper into the detail and explaining the rationale behind the objectives set, she gave supportive nods. When someone asked a question, she smiled as if to say *how pertinent, how perceptive.* She listened without interruption unless called upon by Harper to contribute; gave reassurance that AUC, being a responsible company, would not launch the enzyme until an effective inhibitor had been found (although she was confident that would not be long); agreed, without taking insult, that the results from Kazakhstan showed only a marginal difference in crop yields in the test area compared to the control area which was still using conventional fertilizers.

'Yet any improvement in yields, however small,' Harper pointed out, 'is worth shouting about. The fertilizer resulting from the Gaia enzyme is produced without any oil-derived raw materials, and so represents a conservation of natural resources. But remember, the fertilizer properties of the enzyme are simply a by-product – the icing on the cake, if you like: the key benefit is the biodegrading of plastic.'

'And yet,' Philip said, 'you chose the name of Gaia. Mother Earth, didn't you say? Isn't that focusing on the secondary benefit rather than the primary?'

Harper, still unsure of why the name had leapt into his mind, could not disagree. But he didn't have to.

'Love it, man,' Ned said. 'Great name.'

From anyone else but Ned, Harper would have suspected a heavy deployment of irony.

'I can picture it now, man,' Ned said, a dreamy look on his face. 'Forty second TV commercial, extended to a minute for cinema. Typical rural scene; dark-skinned peasants toiling in the burning sun; light glinting over sparking rivers; camera pans—'

'On either side the river lie, long fields of barley and of rye,' Philip quoted wistfully.

'I think it's more wheat, rice and cotton in Kazakhstan,' Harper corrected, brushing aside the Lady of Shalott and catching a glimpse of the hidden agenda which Ned and Philip had in mind.

'Even better,' Ned said, swept along by his vision. 'Wheat, rice, cotton: couldn't be more perfect, man. When can we leave?'

'You don't have to commit yourself to an idea yet, Ned,' Harper said. 'You have the whole weekend to think. Anyway, there must dozens of suitable rural locations in this country.'

'Verisimilitude will not do,' Philip said.

Ned, not understanding, but trusting his partner, nodded his head in agreement.

'Kazakhstan or nothing,' he said.

'I'm not sure we have the time,' Harper said, knowing the shoot would be artificially stretched into a long all-expenses-paid holiday.

'I can make all the necessary travel arrangements,' Charly said helpfully. 'We could use the company jet and stay on the farm at the test site. Just let me know when you want to go and how many people and I'll take care of everything.'

'Brilliant,' Ned said, already imagining himself sipping champagne in the company jet. 'Although a hotel might be better. Wouldn't want to put these farmers to any trouble. I'll phone a couple of directors as soon as the meeting is over.'

'I think we should wait until we at least have a concept,' Harper said, trying to rein in the enthusiasm.

'No sweat,' Ned said. 'Trust us, Kit. When have Phil or I ever let you down?'

Do you want the answer, Harper thought, in chronological order, or by magnitude of disaster?

'OK,' Klein said, perhaps sensing what was going through Harper's mind and trying to forestall an embarrassing digression, 'we reconvene on Monday morning and at that meeting I want to see concepts, media schedules, full costings including production and a timetable.'

'If it helps,' Charly said – please, don't be more helpful, Harper thought – 'I can be available this weekend. If anyone gets stuck, or needs fresh input, that is.'

'Terrific,' Ned said.

'Me, too,' Harper said quickly. 'I'll stand by. All you need to do is phone my mobile and I can be here in twenty minutes.'

'I'm sure you've got better things to do,' Ned said, so considerately.

Klein rose from the table and the meeting began to break up.

'If you can give me a minute, Charly,' Harper said. 'I just need a quick word with Ned and Philip.'

'I'll be with Klein,' she said, giving him a conspiratorial wink.

'So, Ned,' Harper said, when the others had drifted away. 'Why do you want to go to Kazakhstan?'

'Good creative reasons,' he replied, being unwilling or unable to elaborate. Then he grinned. 'And I've always really fancied going to India.'

Harper let his head drop to the table, and groaned.

'You're off the hook, Kit,' Charly said as she came out of Klein's office.

'Thanks, Charly,' Harper replied.

'Don't thank me too soon,' she said, biting her lip. 'There was a price to pay.'

'Don't tell me. I'm to spend all weekend here holding Ned's and Philip's hands? I think Ned rather had you pencilled in for that job, but Philip won't complain about the swap.'

She shook her head. 'Klein doesn't want to go to Kazakhstan.'

'Who in their right mind would?'

'You?'

'Oh, no.'

'Oh, yes. Klein claims he can't be spared, what with the takeover so imminent and all his other work commitments. So *you* are to go to Kazakhstan in his place and act as a restraining influence on people and budget.' She lowered her eyes. 'Sorry, Kit. I know it's going to create problems for you at home, but I felt we had to give Klein something as a trade.'

'You said *we?*'

'I told Klein I'd go along too. That should make my grandfather happy.'

'And if Sir Angus is happy, Klein is ecstatic.'

'I ought to go now,' she said.

'How about dinner tonight?'

'I don't think that would be a good idea, Kit.'

'Tomorrow?'

'No,' she said firmly.

'Sunday lunch?'

'I am *not* coming to your house for a cosy family Sunday lunch. That is totally out of the question.'

'Not *my* house,' Harper said quickly. 'A friend of mine. Saul Drummond. Every Sunday at his place it's open house: bring a bottle of good claret and everybody's welcome. You'll like Saul. And he might be able to help us find a way out of your dilemma – planning director here or staying at AUC, I mean. Saul is the most brilliant strategist I know. It can't do any harm, Charly. What do you say?'

'God, you're persistent, Kit.'

'My only virtue,' he said, smiling.

'Yeah,' she said. 'OK. You've beaten me down. When and where?'

Harper gave her the details and watched as she moved with swaying hips towards the lifts. Then he rushed to his office.

'Saul,' he said into the mouthpiece of the phone, 'I've got a big favour to ask. How are you on Sunday lunches?'

15

In Kazakhstan it was early afternoon. Piotyr Ivanov watched as the smoke from the pit curled up into the air and drifted on the breeze toward the shores of Lake Balqash. Then he looked up at the sky questioningly as if God might pop his head from out of the thin layer of cloud and reveal all. Somewhere there had to be an answer – a reason why even He had abandoned them.

'These things happen,' came the muffled voice of the local manager of AUC through the handkerchief clamped tightly over his nose and mouth. 'Cows get sick, cows die. It is the way of the world. Farming is a hard life.'

'But it has its compensations, eh?' said Leonid, chuckling. 'Come, Piotyr,' he said, speaking now to his grandson, 'we must go inside and provide our visitor with some iced tea. There is business to conduct.'

Piotyr picked up his shirt from where it lay on the ground next to the empty petrol can and wiped the glistening sweat from his muscled body. He turned away from the pit and walked silently toward the whitewashed farmhouse, leaving the foul smell behind. The burning hair and hide wasn't so bad: he had got used to that, and it was not so very different from the acrid smoke of the harsh black tobacco of Leonid's hand-rolled cigarettes. It was the next stage when the fat bubbled and popped in the flames that turned his stomach every time. Still, the stench from a pig was worse, the rich aroma of hot grease more condensed, more powerful and seeming to linger in and around the pit for days.

The AUC man gestured at a group of farm hands huddled conspiratorially by the giant silo. 'Get them back to work,' he ordered, his gold tooth flashing in the light of the sun.

Easier said than done, Piotyr thought. His fellow Russians were generally cooperative, but the Kazakhs were a proud and stubborn race, difficult to reason with at the best of times. They were also moody, troublesome and superstitious. Their strange Turkic language was simultaneously lyrical and incomprehensible to Piotyr, but he sensed what they were saying. Yet he could not let it be known that he agreed with them.

He spoke to them in Russian – a language they had been forced to learn by necessity and tyranny many years ago – and broke up the mutinous gathering by a mixture of threats and bribes. As a precaution, he despatched the workers singly, sending each to some isolated duty in a far flung corner of the sprawling farm. When he arrived back at the house, the man from AUC was already climbing into his jeep and gunning its engine.

'He did not stay long,' Piotyr said, entering the main room of the house and standing by the window. The stream of dust created by the spinning wheels was already receding to the distance as the jeep sped away towards the road to Semey.

'Long enough,' Leonid replied, waving a thick wad of money triumphantly in the air. 'This is real money, boy. Dollars, not damned Kazakh roubles that will be worth half as much in a month's time. He paid for the cow *and* gave us a special bonus. The trial is over, boy. No more figures to collect. We can concentrate on the farm now.'

'For all the good it will do,' Piotyr grunted. 'This land is cursed, old man. We should never have come here.'

'Have you forgotten Russia already?' Leonid scolded. 'Did they teach you nothing at university? Count your blessings, boy. You are wrong. The land is rich. We are rich.'

'But at what price?' Piotyr asked, pointing out of the window to the nearby village church with its row of wooden crosses in the graveyard.

'Riches and death,' Leonid shrugged. 'They always go together.'

16

Harper looked up at the wall clock and stared in disbelief. There was something about the presence of children that produced abnormalities in the delicate fabric of the space–time continuum: take one five-year-old and the normal laws of physics cease to apply, all motion takes place as if occurring in a sea of molasses and yet time passes as if its engine is turbocharged and running on neat Benzedrine. If Einstein had had a couple of kids around when he was working on his theory, he would have come up with a whole new slant on relativity.

'Come on, Cassie,' he urged, removing the frying pan from the washing up water and balancing it precariously in a small gap in the congested draining rack. If the clock was to be believed it was half past ten and they were due at Saul's at eleven to help with the preparations for Sunday lunch. 'It's time you got dressed.'

Cassie picked another piece of crust-free, lightly-toasted bread from the small wicker basket, stuck her knife in the butter (transferring to it a large smear of strawberry jam) and, having spread it on the toast, helped herself to jam (adding both runny butter and toast crumbs to the contents of the jar). And all this in slow motion.

'I am dressed,' she said, taking a minuscule mouthful and examining the resulting tooth mark with all the deliberation of a forensic surgeon seeking the vital clue to nail Hannibal Lecter.

Technically, Cassie was correct. She was dressed in a pair of short purple leggings, a light-blue T-shirt with a transfer of the moon and stars on the front, long white socks and a pair of once-white trainers with fluorescent pink laces. But to Harper's critical eye it looked as if she had chosen her outfit by spraying herself with contact adhesive and walking through her wardrobe.

'I thought you would wear your party dress,' he said. 'You know, the black velvet one with the red silk collar?'

'It is *not* a party, Daddy,' Cassie said, giving him a withering look.

'But it is a special lunch.'

'I like these clothes. They're my very favourite in the whole wide world.'

'But, Cassie, a young lady has to make the right impression. She should *never* be seen in the same outfit twice. Uncle Saul has seen you in those clothes before.'

'When?' she asked, screwing up her brown eyes and squinting at him suspiciously.

'Don't you remember, Cassie?' he said, shaking his head.

'Yes,' she said doubtfully. 'Of course I do, Daddy.'

'Then go and change, eh? And brush your hair.'

She looked at him as if he had suggested she jump in a pit full of snakes.

'Bring me the brush and I'll do it,' he offered.

She now looked at him as if he had suggested she jump in a pit with snakes at the bottom and big hairy spiders all around the sides.

Oh, well, you can't win them all. Harper sighed and shrugged his shoulders.

'Daddy,' she said. 'Are *you* going to change?'

'Why?' he said, thinking of the time he had spent deliberating before finally settling on the sand-coloured chinos, matching short-sleeved shirt and tan boots.

She sighed and shrugged her shoulders.

'OK,' he said. 'Let's both be quick.'

It was to be another half an hour before they climbed into the old Saab, (Cassie wearing the black dress, short white socks and black patent shoes; Harper in black jeans and a white shirt; two bags of books, videos, games and toys on the back seat; three bottles of claret wedged upright on the floor behind the driver's seat) and a further fifteen minutes before they arrived at Saul's.

'Good morning, Kit,' he said, wiping his hands on the blue-and-white striped apron. 'I would say you are late, but I detest being repetitive.' He bowed low at Cassie and extended his hand. 'Hello, Cassie. How pretty you look.'

'What can we do to help?' Harper said.

'You can set the table, Kit, and Cassie can help me in the kitchen. Come inside, the pair of you.'

Saul stepped aside and the tantalizing aroma of roast beef drew them into the corridor. Harper handed Saul the wine he had brought and peeled off to the left to enter the dining room. The long mahogany table shone brightly and a smell of beeswax hung in the air.

'You'll find everything you need on the sideboard,' Saul said. 'Set the table for twelve, please.'

'Who's coming?' Harper asked, as Saul and Cassie moved towards the kitchen.

'Whoever was available at such short notice to provide you with an alibi,' Saul shouted back.

There was cutlery on the sideboard for seven adults and five children, together with thick place mats and coasters, delicate wine glasses, brightly coloured plastic beakers, two silver cruets complete with pots of English mustard, ramekins filled with horseradish and crisp white linen napkins. Harper set the table so that the adults were at the end near the window and the children near to the door, convenient for going in and out, and in and out and. . . . The task took him twice as long as it should have done since he kept stopping to look at his watch and to listen out for the doorbell. When he finally emerged into the corridor he saw Cassie kneeling on the carpet, picking up crisps and blowing on each one before putting them back into the bowl. She smiled up at him sheepishly, stood up and carried the bowl into the sitting room.

In the kitchen, where steam billowed from saucepans and every worktop was littered with vegetable peelings and dirty crockery, cutlery and chopping boards waiting to be washed up, Saul was sipping a very large gin and tonic and consulting a sheet of paper.

'What do you think that says?' he asked, pointing to a word on the paper.

'Who wrote this?' Harper asked.

'My cleaning lady. A very good cook, so she immodestly says.'

'It's a shame her talents don't extend to writing,' Harper said. 'As far as I can make out, it says either *strain* or *drain*, not that it makes much difference, I suppose.'

'I'll take your word for that,' said Saul, sighing heavily. He removed a dirty saucepan from the sink and looked around for somewhere to put it. 'Hold that, for a minute,' he said, passing the pan to Harper. 'Why didn't you ask her for tea, Kit? It would have been so much simpler to make a few sand-wiches and buy a couple of cakes and sticky buns.'

Saul drained the potatoes and then went back to the list to find out what to do next. Harper started running hot water into the sink, preparing to clear the dirty dishes and tidy up the kitchen. Cassie reappeared, crisp crumbs on her lips. She surveyed the chaos critically.

'Nanny Trent says that you should clear up as you go along,' she said.

'Does she now?' said Saul, gritting his teeth and wringing his hands on the apron as if it were Nanny Trent's neck.

'Yes, Uncle Saul,' Cassie said, 'Nanny Trent says a tidy—'

'Perhaps, Cassie,' Harper interrupted, 'you could put all the rubbish in the bin and then I can wash up the chopping boards. And hadn't you better get the potatoes in the oven, Saul? That's the big black box-like thing with the glass door, by the way.'

'What does Nanny Trent say about sarcasm, Cassie?' Saul asked.

The door bell rang.

'I'll get it,' Cassie shouted enthusiastically as she abandoned scraping potato peelings into the bin with her fingers and ran from the room.

She reappeared leading Charly by the hand.

'Oh God, I'm early,' Charly said, seeing Harper up to his elbows in soapy water and Saul trying to fit a very large dish into a very small space in the oven.

'Nanny Trent says you should say *Gosh*,' Cassie said with a suitably chastising frown, letting go of Charly's hand.

'Nanny Trent,' Saul explained with a warm smile, 'is the font of all wisdom, my dear. She is also infuriatingly infallible.'

'Sounds like someone else I know,' Charly said, glancing at Harper while she looked around for something on which to wipe her sticky hand.

'Allow me to introduce myself,' Saul said, handing her a dishcloth. 'Saul Drummond. So glad you could come along to my open house.'

'Which you do every week,' she said, eyeing the sheet of paper by the hob.

'I find it helps to have a schedule,' Saul replied.

'I can see that,' she said. 'Such organization.'

'But at the expense of courtesy, it seems. What can I get you to drink, Charly?'

'I've got lemonade,' Cassie said, sitting herself down on one of the chairs at the table. 'It's very good. The bubbles tickle your nose.'

'How can I go against such a glowing recommendation?' Charly said.

'Perhaps some grown-up's lemonade,' Saul said, taking a bottle of champagne from the refrigerator.

Harper dried his hands and looked across at her. She was wearing a sand-coloured suit, the jacket single-buttoned and tailored to her slim waist, the skirt three inches above her knees, and knee-high brown suede boots. Her hair was loose and tumbled down in long waves on to the shoulders of the jacket. Her make-up was minimal – or, maybe, just very skilfully applied to appear so – a light dusting of shadow over the deep-brown eyes, a touch of blusher on the high cheekbones, a trace of gloss giving a hint of wetness on her full lips.

Cassie looked at him strangely. He felt himself flush with embarrassment and prayed to Gosh that she wouldn't say, 'Don't stare, Daddy, it's very rude.'

'My real name is Cassandra,' she said to Charly instead.

'And mine is Charlotte. But I like Charly better.'

Harper tensed himself for *but Charly is a boy's name.*

'Me too,' Cassie said to his relief. 'Nanny Trent calls me Cassandra when I've been naughty. But my teacher calls me Cassie 'cos there's a girl in my class called Sandra and it saves a muddle.'

The door bell rang again.

'Shall we answer it, Charly,' Cassie asked, already leaping up from the table.

Charly looked at Saul.

'If you would be so kind,' he said. 'Perhaps you would take whomever it is through to the sitting room. We'll join you in just a moment.'

'It's very unnerving,' he said to Harper when they were alone. 'She looks so like Heather.'

'A very different personality, though,' he said.

'Maybe that is just as well, Kit.'

Lunch passed as uneventfully as is possible when there are five children aged under seven and four adults – five if you included Charly – who seemed a little puzzled at being there. Harper wondered at first if Saul had accosted people in the street and paid them to turn up, but the other guests turned out to be neighbours and after a couple of glasses of claret these nodding acquaintances began to relax.

Both couples were in their early thirties. One was a man who was something vague in the City – Harper never quite established exactly what – and his heavily pregnant wife; the other was an estate agent and her heavily drinking husband. All professed to adore very rare roast beef and vegetables that dissolved on the plate – al dente, in the opinion of the estate agent, was so overrated.

'So what does a planner actually do?' the estate agent had asked Harper, after it had been his turn to declare an occupation.

'A planner,' Saul cut in, seizing the opportunity to educate and pontificate simultaneously, 'is a little like God. Or should I say Gosh, Cassie?'

Cassie, quite used to being teased by Harper, had ignored him and carried on comparing notes with a freckle-faced girl on the top hundred things wrong with boys. The estate agent had seemed, not unnaturally, a trifle puzzled.

'François-Marie Arouet,' Saul had said, impishly not clarifying matters except to any students of French literature who happened to be present. 'Voltaire,' he had added after a pause, only slightly more helpfully. 'He wrote, "If God did not exist, it would be necessary to invent him." You see, when I started out in advertising, there were no such animals as planners. But each and every agency – and there weren't very many of them – had at least one account director who could only be described as an advertising *natural*. Someone who could intuitively feel what was right and what was wrong.'

The estate agent had frowned, presumably regretting asking what she had imagined was a perfectly simple question.

'As the industry grew,' Saul continued, 'there were not sufficient *naturals* to go around. Ideas became weaker, great campaigns became merely good. So, perforce, it became necessary to invent planners. Substitute opinion surveys for intuition and focus groups for instinct. What was once, to see in action, as beautiful as any form of art, was turned into a science.'

'Science has a lot to answer for,' said the heavily-pregnant woman.

'Really?' said Charly.

'Take the atom bomb, for instance,' the woman said.

'Is this a dagger which I see before me,' Saul bellowed, holding his knife in the air.

The adults stared, the children nudged each other and giggled.

'Is it a deadly weapon?' he asked. 'Or a mere tool to make one's life a little easier?'

'It depends on who is holding it, I suppose,' the woman said, having been led to the conclusion like a lamb to the slaughter. 'And the intended purpose.'

'Exactly,' said Saul. 'There is nothing intrinsically wrong with science. It is *scientists* who carry the responsibility for how their discoveries are used or abused, as the case may be.'

The doorbell rang – to the rhythm of 'shave and a haircut, two bits'!

'That will be for you, Cassie,' Saul said.

Cassie, followed by the other children, ran to answer the door.

'It's a magician,' they cried in unison.

'Everyone off to the sitting room,' Saul ordered, clapping his hands. 'I will join you once I have cleared the table. Do I have any volunteers to assist? Kit and Charly, one pace forward, please.'

'Did you mean that about planners?' Charly asked Saul as the procession, arms laden with dirty dishes, filed along the corridor to the kitchen.

'About planners, yes,' he said, almost apologetically. 'But, at the risk of dangerously hyperinflating an already overblown ego, not about Kit. *He* is a natural, and that is why I have nurtured him since the day we first met. I would trust his intuition, his instincts, with my life, if that is not overdramatizing what is essentially a rather specialized talent. But enough of such trivia, Charly. Kit tells me you are impaled on the horns of a dilemma.'

Charly explained her problem while Saul poured two large glasses of armagnac.

'So you expected,' Saul said with wide eyes, 'on your grandfather's retirement, to be elevated to the position of running a multinational enterprise?'

'Not single-handedly, no. But I did expect to be made managing director alongside a suitable chairman.'

'By which, I presume,' Saul said, 'you mean non-executive. A mere figurehead for the benefit of providing reassurance to the City and the institutional investors.'

'I was led to believe by my grandfather that that was his plan, yes.'

'And, for clarification purposes only, you understand, we can assume that you are capable of such a position of power and responsibility?'

'I believe so,' she said. 'My grandfather has groomed me since I first joined the company. I have been very thoroughly prepared.'

'And yet he appears to have had a change of mind, or heart perhaps. Which you believe is due to some behind-closed-doors deal with Laurelle to smooth the path for the takeover.'

'That is what my grandfather tells me. He does have a reputation for cutting such deals.'

Among other things, Harper thought.

'Moving on,' Saul said, 'so that we may at some stage move back with eyes alight with vision, tell me about this image campaign that everyone is working on, Kit.'

Harper explained the background, the problem and progressed to routes to its solution, including the hoped-for but highly unlikely endorsement by GreenWay.

'The focus,' he said, 'will be the Gaia enzyme. By concentrating—'

'Gaia?' Saul interrupted. 'Who thought of that name?'

'Actually, I did,' Harper said proudly.

'What's wrong with it?' Charly asked, seeing the frown on Saul's face.

'Everyone agrees that it is a great name,' Harper said defensively, but with a lack of conviction that surprised even himself. 'Very fitting,' he added.

'I'm sure it is,' Saul said. 'And how did you come to think of the name Gaia?'

'It just came to me,' Harper shrugged. 'Would you accept a flash of inspiration?'

'Most certainly not,' Saul said. He paused. 'Well, is no one going to ask me why not?'

'OK,' Charly said. 'I'll be the patsy. Why not?'

'There is empirical evidence,' Saul said, 'to show that the human brain generally works at only about five per cent of its full capacity. Imagine the synaptic gaps which open and close to carry the electrical impulses to the brain – well, the vast majority of the time only one in twenty of those hundreds of thousands of little switches are functioning. But, the hypothesis is that on very rare occasions all the circuits function at the same time. And it is the product of these moments of maximum efficiency that we call insight, intuition or a *flash of inspiration* – all convenient terms to explain away what we do not really understand. The brain, at full capacity, has solved a problem, but has worked at such a level and at such a speed that it could not get around to supplying the logic behind that solution.'

'And what has this to do with Gaia?' Charly asked.

'There are perhaps more sinister reasons,' Saul said with a raising of his eyebrows, 'why the name Gaia might have popped into Kit's convoluted subconscious. You have absolute confidence in this enzyme, Charly?'

'Yes,' she said. 'It's tried and tested. But why do you ask?'

'Because, I suspect,' Harper said, 'Gaia has other connotations apart from Mother Earth. She was the mother and wife of Father Heaven, Uranus.'

'Are you talking about incest or something?' Charly said.

'No,' Harper said. 'The problem was their children. Gaia, according to Greek mythology, was the mother of the earliest living creatures. Unfortunately, these were such little darlings as the Titans, the Cyclops and the Hundred Headed Ones, notably Typhon who was believed to spew forth the molten lava from Mount Etna.'

'And lava destroys everything in its path,' Saul said. 'Worrying, is it not?'

'Not to me it isn't,' said Charly. 'I have never heard such a load of undiluted clap-trap in my life.'

'Ah, but you have never worked in advertising,' Saul said, smiling.

'And I sure as hell never want to,' she said. 'More so by the minute, too.'

'By which circuitous route we arrive back at the point where we started,' Saul said. 'Fascinating journey, though.'

Charly looked at Harper and shook her head in a mixture of disappointment and disbelief.

'So this,' she said, pointing at Saul, 'is the person who is the most brilliant strategist you know? And this is the person who is going to solve my problem?'

'On the contrary,' Saul said. '*You* are the person who will solve your problem.'

'I don't think I can take any more of this "riddle wrapped in a mystery inside an enigma" stuff.'

'You quote Churchill at us,' Saul said. 'How are you on Napoleon?'

'Limited to "An army marches on its stomach", I'm afraid.'

'I wasn't thinking of that,' he said. 'Especially after the rather dismal lunch I served. No, I had in mind "In war, moral considerations account for three-quarters, the balance of actual forces only for the other quarter." You, Charly, believe that right – birthright? – is on your side. So the battle, therefore, is already three-quarters won.'

'But what you need, Charly,' Harper said, feeling the synaptic gaps open-ing and closing as if about to overload, 'is a total victory.'

'And what will that be?'

'What is the hardest part of this campaign?'

'The creative solution?' she ventured.

'That's down to sheer luck,' Saul said.

'Aided by a superb brief,' Harper said.

Saul waved his hand dismissively in the air.

'The hardest part, Charly, will be getting GreenWay to endorse the Gaia enzyme, and thereby rubber-stamp the new caring image of AUC.'

'And how are we going to do that?' Charly asked.

'Not *we*, Charly, 'Harper said, 'but *you*. *You* will persuade them. *You* will deliver GreenWay on a plate to AUC. And, by so doing, you will have your outright victory. Then who can deny that to the victor belongs the spoils?'

'But how?' she said. 'How am I going to sign up GreenWay.'

'Hell,' said Harper, 'don't ask me. I'm on planning, you're on execution.'

'See you in the morning,' Harper said as they dropped Charly off outside her hotel.

'See you, Kit. Bye, Cassie. It was good to meet you.'

'Charly?' Cassie said, biting her lower lip.

'Yes, Cassie?'

'Will you show me how to do my hair like yours? Please, Charly. Will you?'

Charly hesitated.

'Kids,' Harper said, embarrassed, but hopeful. 'What can you do with them?'

'Don't ask me,' she said. 'It's not my specialist subject.' She turned to Cassie. 'Maybe another time, huh?'

'Yes, Charly,' Cassie said, disappointed with an adult *maybe* – in her expe-rience it was always synonymous with *no*.

'Why did you ask her that?' Harper asked as they drove away.

'Because I like her,' Cassie said. 'And I want to see her again.'

'That's a very good reason,' he said.

'Daddy?'

'Yes, Cassie?'

'Will you marry Charly one day?'

'No, Cassie. She's out of my league.'

'What does that mean, Daddy?'

'It's like not having the opportunity to be with someone at school because they are in a higher class, because they're better at everything than you are.'

'You told me that it doesn't matter if someone is better at something than you, just as long as you try your hardest and do your best.'

'That's true,' he said, thinking hard of what to say next.

'Good,' she said.

17

Monday, late morning

Jeremiah Drew finished reading the document and sat staring at it, deep in thought. Slowly, he leaned back in the chair and looked across the room to the far wall. There was a mist of sadness in his eyes as they settled on the large framed photograph – the handshake with Boutros Boutros Ghali at the opening of the United Nations Environment Programme conference on global warming. For the first time, he noticed how the rays of the sun had faded the colours. The high point for himself and GreenWay suddenly seemed such a long time ago.

When he had founded GreenWay, Drew had believed that anything was possible. That you could change the world, put a stop to the folly of mankind through a combination of awareness, education and reasoned argument. Now he had been forced to recognize the truth. His words had been lost amidst the constant clamour of big business and the oft-repeated empty plat-itudes of governments – those at economic or political risk from the actions he advocated; those who feared the imposition of taxes on energy or the remodelling of industry; those who resorted to scaremonger stories of a return to some Luddite-ruled Stone Age where the wind was the sole source of power and the wheel was only to be seen on bicycles. If he were to stand any chance of being heard, he must metaphorically shout his message.

He pressed the button on the intercom and said to his secretary, 'I'm ready to see Ms Mendoza now.'

Charly breathed deeply and stepped into the office. One glance around was enough to boost her confidence: the old, utilitarian, dark wood desk and chairs, the discoloured emulsion on the walls, the disposable pens and grey recycled pads on the desktop all pointed to someone who was lacking in cash rather than a sense of interior design. She gave Drew's hand an elongated shake while mentally sizing him up. The solidity of the large body and broad shoulders wrapped in the cosy brown woollen cardigan; the gravitas of the silver hair; the look of concern in the grey eyes framed by the dark eyebrows above and worry lines below. He would be the perfect spokesman for AUC, the perfect vehicle for the launch of Gaia. If she could persuade him, that is.

'It's good of you to see me,' she said.

'Not really,' Drew replied. 'After your patience and persistence in waiting two hours, it seemed like the only way I was ever going to get rid of you.'

'I've come here to talk about the future,' she said. 'A better future.'

'For whom? You, AUC, me, the world?'

'All of those,' she said.

'That I find hard to believe,' Drew said. 'Since when have the future interests of AUC ever accorded with mine, let alone the world?'

'Since we discovered an enzyme which rapidly biodegrades plastic into an environmentally friendly fertilizer,' Charly said casually, noting Drew's response of raised eyebrows.

'You best sit down, Ms Mendoza. Some coffee, perhaps, while you tell me all about this miracle product? I must say I am more than a little interested.'

Over a pot of weak, cheap, instant coffee, Charly explained the history of the development of the enzyme, the mechanics of how it worked, the resoundingly positive results of the trials and the imminent launch of the product across Europe before rolling out to the rest of the world. The only thing she omitted was the inconvenient absence of an inhibitor – that, until Drew had agreed to her proposition, was irrelevant.

'I congratulate you,' Drew said, when she had finished. 'But why are you telling me all this? Why has the mountain come to Mohammed? Where do I fit into the grand scheme?'

'In the past,' Charly said, 'your organization and my company have never seen eye to eye. We have always been on opposite sides of the fence. There have been unfortunate things said, unfortunate deeds done – your attack on our animal laboratories, to take just one example—'

Drew raised his hand to cut her off. 'I take no responsibility,' he protested, 'for the misguided actions of an unauthorized group of what may or may not have been members of GreenWay. I have always denied any knowledge of what they planned.'

Charly nodded her head understandingly, but made a mental note that he had said nothing about disapproving of their actions.

'The Gaia enzyme,' she said, 'is a perfect opportunity for us to bury the hatchet, to wipe the slate clean and start afresh. To demonstrate unequivocally to all concerned that we have stopped fighting each other; that, from now on, we are willing to work together for the larger common good. We want you, Mr Drew, to tell the world about Gaia.'

'Ah,' he said, a smile on his lips, a gleam in his eye. 'I see it all clearly now. You don't want me to spread the news about Gaia, you want my endorsement of it. In short, Ms Mendoza, you want to buy credibility.'

'And,' she said, 'we imagine that will not come cheap.'

'*If* I am willing to sell.'

'Let me show you what we have in mind.' Charly opened the art bag and took out the story boards for the commercial. Each board showed a separate scene, and in virtually all of them, Drew was prominent. 'This will be the spearhead of our advertising for the launch of Gaia.'

'I will have to give this some serious thought,' he said.

'But I haven't told you yet what we are prepared to pay you as a fee.'

'I already have a figure in mind,' he said. 'If I agree to endorse Gaia by appearing in the advertising, I will only do so on my terms. But before I can make any decision I will need access to all the research and to the results of the trials. Unabridged, unedited, warts and all.'

Charly cursed under her breath. If she supplied Drew with what he wanted, then he would find out about the lack of an inhibitor. 'There are no warts,' Charly said.

'I would like to establish that for myself.'

'I could only release such information to you if you signed a confidentiality agreement.'

'I will agree to that condition,' he replied.

She cursed again.

'Very well,' she said. 'I will arrange for everything you need to be flown over and delivered to you later today.'

'There's no rush,' he said.

Charly shook her head. 'I'm afraid there is a time problem,' she said. 'I need your answer by Thursday. The campaign is scheduled to break in a fortnight and there is a film crew lined up to fly out to Kazakhstan on Friday to shoot the commercial. You would need to make yourself available for, say, five days.'

'As with all things,' Drew said, 'the devil is in the detail.'

'Thursday is the deadline for your decision, Mr Drew. No later.'

'Rest assured, Ms Mendoza. I read quickly. And I learn quickly. You will have your answer in time. One way or another.'

18

Tuesday afternoon

Ronnie Stoker stood on the pavement outside the European Commission building, camera in hand. He was wearing brown leather sandals over red woollen socks and a brightly coloured Hawaiian shirt outside of a pair of electric blue slacks – Bermuda shorts would have been more fitting for the unsubtle disguise, but these he had been forced to reject for the view they would have given of his scarred leg. A large guide book to Brussels jutted conspicuously from the front pocket of the rucksack on his back. He raised the camera to his right eye and focused on the main entrance, watching for his mark to appear. His mark would exit the building in exactly two minutes time: the man was a creature of habit.

No, make that *habits*, Stoker thought, chuckling out loud and attracting sideways glances from the homeward bound pedestrians hurrying along the street to the metro station. He shot a couple of pictures, then moved a couple of feet to his right as if considering the artistic merits of a different angle.

The door revolved and a small group of people emerged; two secretaries in light summer dresses and strappy sandals, three *stageurs* in suits that had sufficed in university days but now looked worn and unfashionable and would have to remain so until salaries rose at the end of their probationary period or they moved on to better things, and a tall slim man in an immaculate light-grey suit, white shirt and navy blue tie.

A very smart man, Stoker thought. But a very stupid man. Weak, too. A dangerous combination of personality traits. The man had everything – a huge salary (that he did not even have to touch because of the overgenerous expenses that came with the job), a pretty wife and two kids (safely tucked away at home in the outskirts of Hamburg), excellent prospects for promotion to the top of the tree and the head of the pecking order – and yet he seemed prepared to jeopardize it all in the compulsion to pursue self-indul-gent pleasures. Forbidden fruit? Maybe that was it, the illicit nature of the liaisons, the risks involved and the catastrophic consequences of being caught red-handed all adding to what might otherwise be dismissed as cheap thrills.

Stoker shook his head, thinking of how easily the man had fallen into the honeytrap. He lowered the camera, let it dangle on the strap around his neck, reached for the guide book and set off on an intercept course.

'Excuse me, sir,' he drawled Texan-style, his thumb on the turned-down page in the book, 'but I need some help. Maybe you could just take a look at this.'

Stoker spread the pages of the book and thrust it towards the man. He watched sadistically as the face turned ashen and the eyes opened wide as they stared at the photograph pasted inside.

It wasn't a particularly good picture, Stoker had to admit – wouldn't win any prizes for the subtlety of lighting or originality of subject matter – but the focus was sharp and it was sufficiently well-composed to show clearly both faces and the look of ecstasy written large on each. There were others in the series that contained more detail – the pealing wallpaper behind the head-board, the plastic tooth-mug tumblers of schnapps on the bedside cabinets, the long blonde hair, scarlet fingernails and standard textbook seduction costume of black basque, suspenders and high-heeled, thigh-length boots – and the man could study them all at his leisure later. But only when he had paid the price.

'What do you want?' the man whispered, casting nervous glances about him. 'How much?'

'I'm not after money,' Stoker said, shaking his head. 'It's like I told you, I need some help. A small favour. The kind that only you can provide. It's all very simple, and quite painless. Providing you do exactly as I say. Otherwise, well . . . Why don't I just leave that to your vivid imagination.'

19

Wednesday afternoon – Brussels

Harper stepped off the plane and on to *terra firma*. He headed for the near-est smoking section and, rare for him, lit a cigarette with shaking hands. It wasn't just the result of the turbulent forty-minute flight from London: far worse was the thought of spending *six whole hours* suspended precariously in the air miles above the earth's surface when he flew to Kazakhstan on Friday. Knowing it was an irrational fear didn't help to overcome it: that was the very essence of phobias – it was impossible to rationalize them and negate the paralyzing effects of terror and panic.

It was two o'clock when he checked in at the Royal Windsor, a good three hours before the rest of the team were due to arrive and a dress rehearsal for the presentation of the creative work was scheduled. Harper had heard nothing from Charly since Monday. The concept boards had been delivered back to the agency, together with a brief note to the effect that Drew would not commit either himself and GreenWay at this stage: time was needed to check the facts and consider all the implications. If Drew refused, they were all down the tubes: Charly would have no victory; the agency had nothing up its sleeve but the old standby of featuring the client, albeit a photogenic Charly, as presenter; Sir Angus Cameron would go apoplectic if he recognized the desperate measure and its deficiency of both creativity and credibility, and they'd be lucky to keep their heads, let alone the account; Klein would lash out in defeat; Harper would have staked everything and lost. He checked in, deposited his bags in his room and the huge roll of dollars that had been provided to finance 'incidentals' on the shoot in the hotel safe, and jumped into the waiting taxi organized by the bell desk.

The hospital was in Tervuren, just past the *beaux quartiers* in the southeast of the city. It was a two-storey brick and smoked-glass building arranged in the shape of a capital H, the crossbar housing administration on the ground floor with operating theatres, X-ray and other central facilities above, and the two long sides containing suites of private rooms. The visitors' car park was full of shiny status symbols from Ferraris through Porsches and down to Mercedes. Inside, doctors in white coats and nurses in short white dresses walked around with intensely efficient looks on handsome and beautiful faces like the opening title sequence in some Hollywood drama. If you were sick, Harper thought, then this was the only place to be: if they couldn't cure you, then you died a happy man, gazing up into blue eyes and holding a manicured hand.

He entered the building, walked past a waiting area kitted out with antique tables and purple velvet settees that might once have come from Napoleon's boudoir and up to a dark-haired receptionist who looked as if she would be more at home behind a cosmetic counter at Harrods.

'Kit Harper,' he said. 'I'm hear to see Monsieur Charbonnier. I telephoned yesterday: they said it would be all right.'

'He has a visitor at the moment, monsieur,' she replied, critically analyzing Harper's jeans and leather jacket and frowning as they failed to come up to anywhere near the required standard. She shook her head thoughtfully, decided that the tone of the waiting area should not be lowered by his presence and said, 'Perhaps you would like to go straight through and wait outside his room.'

Harper followed her instructions along the corridor until he found the designated room. He slouched up against the wall, arms folded across his chest, thinking of what he now knew of the jogger and the impossible-to-ignore irritating itch it had created in his problem-solving brain. He was here to scratch at the surface and see whether it made the condition better or worse. He found his mind wandering back to the vision of Cassie with tears in her eyes as they said farewell that morning and was grateful when his attention was grabbed by the sound of raised voices from inside the room. The door opened and a blurred figure burst through, in its haste tripping over Harper's extended feet and landing on the carpet.

'Sorry,' Harper said in that peculiarly English way that decrees it is imperative that you get your apology in first, even when it isn't actually your fault.

He bent down, reeled back momentarily as the strong citrus cologne assaulted his nostrils and helped the man to his feet.

'My fault,' the man said in a heavy German accent, managing to smile at Harper.

The man was tall and what could be described as dapper. He stood there dusting invisible specks from his hand-sewn suit, making minute adjustments to the angle of the knot in his silk tie and using his fingertips to check that not one strand of his light-brown, perfectly coiffed hair was out of place.

There followed one of those comical little dances where the man and Harper both moved to the same side of the corridor to clear the path for the other, switched simultaneously to the other side and then back again. Eventually the man stood his ground and waited for Harper's next move.

'Sorry,' Harper repeated, knocking on the door of the room and entering at the curt summons of an irritated 'Oui?'.

From behind him, Harper heard the soft padding of loafers on the carpet and smelt the aroma of acres of orange and lemon groves receding. Not that that was much relief, since it hung in the air of the room, throwing a challenging gauntlet in the face of the air conditioning system.

Charbonnier, wearing blue satin pyjamas, was propped up in bed, both heavily plastered legs suspended from the ceiling at an angle of forty-five degrees. There was a moment of recognition in his eyes.

'You must be Harper,' he said. 'Before you sit down, would you please do me the service of opening the windows. Otherwise my deputy's presence will linger. And I am being tortured enough without that.'

Harper, who had worked on a fragrance account, understood the problem. If someone is totally loyal to a particular perfume or cologne, then the prolonged everyday usage leads to them becoming desensitized. Since they can no longer smell the scent, more is used at each application until the effect is overpowering for those whose sensitivities are intact. He raised the roman blinds, slid across one half of the double-glazed windows, gratefully sucked in air and turned to face Charbonnier.

'It was good of you to agree to see me,' he said.

'Time, like my legs, hangs heavy,' Charbonnier said with a shrug. 'And how could I refuse? Thanks to your intervention I will someday walk again. Who knows what would have happened if you had not come along? The rest of my life spent in a wheelchair, at best. The end of my life, at worst.'

Harper sat down on a chair by the bedside. Examined Charbonnier's face. The healthy glow of the jogger had disappeared, replaced by the paleness of pain and the etched expression of suffering that he remembered so vividly. He shivered involuntarily.

'Shut the window, if you are cold,' Charbonnier said.

'No,' Harper said. 'It's not that.'

'Ah, hospitals,' Charbonnier said. 'I have noticed they can have that effect on people. Death seems just around the corner.'

'Monsieur Charbonnier,' Harper said, anxious to change the subject, 'can I ask a few questions?'

The Gallic shrug again.

'I don't like unsolved mysteries,' Harper continued. 'Have the police come up with anything that might suggest a motive for the attack on you?'

'None. As I told them, I have no enemies. At least, that is what I had thought.'

'I have no right to pry into your private life—'

'Nor my business life, Monsieur Harper.'

'But, with your indulgence, that's what I would like to do? As I understand it, you work for the European Commission.'

'Not the best-loved organization in the world,' Charbonnier said. He made a passing gesture over his legs. 'But I doubt that the ill-feeling towards the Community would generate this type of response.'

'You are the Commissioner in charge of concentrations. The person who has the final say over acquisitions and mergers. Is that correct?'

'I make a recommendation on such matters, yes.'

'I have an hypothesis. There is something I need to check, if only for my own peace of mind. There is an acquisition about to be announced.'

'There are always acquisitions about to be announced,' Charbonnier said, eyebrows raised.

'This is a very big one.'

'Is it, Monsieur Harper?'

'If my hypothesis is correct, you know which one I am talking about.'

'You will have to be specific.'

'I can't,' Harper said. 'That would be a breach of confidence on my part.'

'As would any comment from me.'

'What if we both say the names of the companies involved simultaneously?'

'Then we might both give away a different secret. That would be two sins committed in a single breath.'

Harper pondered. If his hunch was right, uttering the names AUC and Laurelle would be no surprise to Charbonnier. If, however, he was simply chasing shadows with no substance, then he would have leaked information of potentially great value. An unscrupulous person could make a fortune by trading in the shares of the companies.

'Can you call a nurse,' he said.

Charbonnier tilted his head in puzzlement.

Harper took out his diary and removed a sheet of paper. He tore it in half.

'I am going to write down the name of the acquiring company,' he said. 'I'd like you to do the same. When the nurse comes, we ask her simply to tell us if the two names we have written are the same. If they are different, I will leave you in peace. If they are the same, then we can discuss matters further without each of us having breached confidentiality.'

'You intrigue me, Monsieur Harper,' Charbonnier said, pressing a buzzer fixed to the bedside and stretching out his other hand for his half of the sheet of paper.

The nurse came, listened to Charbonnier's instructions, raised an eyebrow and read the two pieces of paper. '*C'est la même chose*,' she said.

'Would you have been in favour of the takeover?' Harper asked when they were alone again.

'I do not know,' Charbonnier admitted. 'I would have followed my normal procedures. Carried out a full investigation on the likely effects of the acquisition and announced my recommendation in due course. One month, two perhaps.'

Not a time-scale that would suit Sir Angus Cameron, Harper thought. He would prefer a rush to judgement – as long as the verdict went his way.

'And you have no preconceptions?' he said.

'What does that matter? My investigation would have been fair to all sides.'

'And now that you are no longer in charge?'

'My deputy, it appears, equates thoroughness with procrastination. He sees a delay as likely to cause uncertainty and, therefore, damage to the businesses concerned.'

'Thank you, Monsieur Charbonnier,' Harper said, rising from the chair. 'You have been most helpful.'

20

The good news was that Drew had agreed to appear in the advertising. The bad news was that there were conditions. The even worse news was that he would not state those conditions except to Sir Angus Cameron in person. So no one knew in advance of the presentation whether they would be acceptable. All Harper could hope was that Drew, having appreciated the golden opportunity, wouldn't get greedy.

'If you want me to present the creative work,' Harper said to Jackson, as the first of the two taxis containing the JKL contingent travelled to the AUC building, 'then I quite understand. It was my idea to try to set up a victory for Charly and spring it on Cameron and Klein.'

'As creative director,' Jackson said, 'it's ultimately my responsibility that we have nothing better as an alternative campaign than the tired old standby of putting the client in the advertising. And, beautiful though Charly is, who is going to believe her?'

'Me, for one,' Harper said.

'Exactly,' said Jackson. 'You, for a grand total of one. Thanks all the same,

Kit, but I'll risk it. We play it just as we rehearsed yesterday evening after Klein had left the room. Let me have my bit of fun. Let me string along Cameron for a while before he owns me lock, stock and barrel. And, more to the point, I've never forgiven Klein for what he did to Saul. I want to see him squirm for a change.'

'Why do you put up with him?' Harper asked.

'Klein and Lottersby each own forty per cent of the shares: I have a useless twenty. All Lottersby wants is a quiet life and the cushion of a wad of cash on which to retire. He lets Klein run the show. I soon found out that rocking the boat only leads to being outvoted. Klein doesn't interfere in the way I handle the creative department and in return I go along with all the major decisions. It's a gentleman's agreement that works in practice.'

'That would be fine if Klein was a gentleman,' Harper said. 'And if he had a good track record of honouring agreements.'

'You're an idealist, Kit. You would do well to learn the art of compromise.'

'I can't afford to compromise my principles. I don't have much self-respect in what I do as it is.'

'Nothing in life is perfect.' Jackson shrugged at Harper. 'Maybe for me it's easier. I'm an artist and a showman; advertising gives me the opportunity to practise both my skills. If yours is a permanent rather than a temporary condition, perhaps you should put it to the acid test; ask yourself – is it good enough to stay or bad enough to go?'

'If we lose the AUC account today, the decision could be out of my hands.'

'Quit worrying. The due diligence on the sale of the agency is being carried out as we speak. The takeover will be finalized in another couple of weeks. Cameron would be cutting off his nose to spite his face if he took away the account.'

'Not necessarily,' Harper said, rubbing at his scar. 'You didn't see the look in Cameron's eye when he was talking about acquiring Laurelle. That's his number one priority – all-consuming, maybe. He'd ditch us like a shot if that was the only way to get the campaign he needs to help climb the last rungs of the ladder to number one in the market.'

'Don't disillusion me as well,' Jackson said. 'Don't even sow the seed that the only reason you're doing this is some unconscious desire to avoid the issue until it is settled for you. From my point of view I couldn't give a toss about the AUC account – it's a creative nightmare with a tyrant in the starring role. But for Klein, it's money. And if he loses money, he'll look for a human sacrifice to the god of Mammon. How are you at being tied to an altar?'

'The knife's been up against my jugular for a long time now.'
'Just pray it isn't today that you finally see the point.'

The room was the same: an overpropped nautical set with its showcase of dress uniform and ceremonial sword in homage to the great Sir Angus Cameron. The audience was the same, too: bit players with non-speaking roles, there to fill out the stage. The atmosphere was different though: you could almost sense the electricity in the air. They were here to see a show, and that's what Jackson intended to give them.

Charly was seated at one end of the long table, her mobile phone on the table ready to send the summons to her secretary at the appropriate cue. She nodded at Harper and gave a nervous smile.

Jackson moved to the centre stage presentation position. He stood there immobile for what seemed like an age, maybe giving any students of semiotics in the audience a chance to decode the meaning of his taupe collarless suit (it's a suit, alright; satisfied?), the olive-green, open-neck silk shirt (ties are passé, and interrupt the flow between heart and brain) and the light-brown suede thick-soled boots (for comfort and kicking): or maybe it was simply a ploy to build the tension. When Jackson finally judged the moment to be right, he took out a set of story boards from the giant art bag and placed a cassette player on the table. Harper, Ned, Philip, and Klein had settled in vacant chairs, Ned assuming a matching vacant expression. Sir Angus Cameron waited as coffee jugs circulated around the table and then gave a nod to signal the start of the proceedings.

Jackson took a sip of coffee to clear the crippling dryness that invades the throat in the moment before the voice must kick into action, stripped off his jacket to show he meant to get down to business and looked Cameron directly in the eye.

'We have an image campaign for you,' he said. 'An image campaign that has passed the test of research with flying colours.' Harper gave a supportive nod. 'But I don't believe in research.' Jackson walked across to Cameron. 'Why should we, Sir Angus, delegate our judgement to a bunch of middle-class citizens who have never taken a major decision in their pathetic little lives?'

Cameron's eyes narrowed in confusion. Harper could tell that he wanted so very much to agree with Jackson, yet did not want to commit himself for fear of falling into a well-laid trap.

Klein sat very still, trying hard to work out what was going on and hoping that the deviation from script was a last-minute ad hoc clever ploy.

'You and I, Sir Angus,' Jackson continued, 'can smell a good idea and sense a sound strategic move a mile away. *We* don't need research. *We* have gut feel. Instinct – that's what separates the successful from the also-rans. And my instinct,' Jackson said, lowering his voice and shaking his head sadly, 'tells me that you deserve better than what I am about to show you. AUC should have the best: I can only offer you a very poor second.'

Klein clutched the arm of his chair. Had Jackson gone completely mad? Had he caught the advertising equivalent of BSE from Harper?

Jackson let his gaze momentarily wander away from Cameron in order to drink in the intoxicating delight of the hoped-for panic on Klein's face.

Cameron's face became dark and his eyes narrowed. 'I want the best,' he squealed, like a little boy denied his dessert of sticky treacle tart. 'I *demand* to see the best.'

'Very well,' Jackson sighed, taking a second set of story boards from the bag, 'but it won't make any difference. You still won't be able to have it.'

The first board – close-up sketch of the earnest face of Jeremiah Drew – knocked them back in their seats. Sir Angus and Klein gaped open-mouthed.

Jackson pressed the play button of the cassette machine: over a few muted bars of the *Pastoral Symphony* a very passable imitation of Drew's voice came loud and clear through the speaker. As sentences or phrases were completed, Jackson turned over boards to synchronize action and words.

The audience listened in silence and watched in awe. They heard the authoritative voice not only endorsing Gaia, but actually praising it; they saw the index finger, normally used to stab awkward accusing questions at the fat cats of big business, pointing at the green landscape of Kazakhstan and show-ing the abundant fruits of the scientific discovery. There was the recycling process being demonstrated and explained, here was the plug for the conser-vation of resources and the answer to the problem of dwindling capacity at landfill sites. Finally the AUC logo and the strap-line, 'Discovering a better future – for you, your children and your children's children'.

When he had finished, Jackson simply said, 'If only,' and shook his head regretfully.

'What do you mean *if only*?' barked Cameron.

'If only we could have persuaded Drew to appear in the commercial. We tried absolutely everything, but failed.'

Harper saw Charly press a button on her phone – *enter*. She stood up. Eyes turned towards her.

'Then you must have tried the wrong approach,' she said. '*I* have persuaded Drew.'

The door opened on cue and in walked Jeremiah Drew, his silver hair shining bright against the sober jet-black suit. He strode over to Charly and shook her hand.

'May I sit?' he said, addressing Cameron.

A speechless nod in reply.

'I must congratulate you, Sir Angus. I have studied the files on Gaia most thoroughly. You have a truly remarkable product. One with which I will be proud to be associated.' He paused. 'Under certain conditions, of course. And to save us all time, I must emphasize that these conditions are non-negotiable. As I see it, you need me to give credibility to your product and your new image. For that I must exact a heavy price.'

'Name it, Drew,' Cameron replied.

'Firstly,' Drew said, almost apologetically, 'I will not have anyone put words in my mouth. I will write my own script.'

Philip bit his lip and held his tongue.

'You have no objections, I assume, Klein?' Cameron said.

'No, sir,' said Klein, ever willing to defend to the death the vital role of the agency.

'Agreed,' said Cameron.

'Secondly, the fee required for appearing in the advertising is one million pounds. Half up front today; the balance when the commercial goes on air.'

'So,' said Sir Angus, a wry smile signalling that he was pleased to see Drew dragged down to his level, 'even the protector of the good of mankind has his price.'

'It is not for me personally, Sir Angus,' Drew said, 'but for GreenWay. We need funds to carry on our good work. The end justifies the means.'

'Whatever,' Cameron said. 'Agreed.'

'Finally, seeing that you claim to have turned over a new leaf, you will demonstrate your new-found commitment by conducting a full-scale ecological assessment on all your operations in every location across the globe. *And* rectify any threats to the environment that are found.'

There was a pause while Cameron calculated the cost. He gave a little wince. 'Agreed,' he said for the third time.

Get it in writing, Harper thought. This is a man you cannot trust, Drew.

'Then I am happy to shake your hand,' Drew said, standing up and moving across the room to where Cameron was now rising to his feet.

There should have been a photographer present. It was a momentous scene; the two old adversaries shaking hands to seal the end of enmity and the dawn of a new era.

A brave new world? Harper wondered.

Maybe.

Then again, in the light of his conversation with Charbonnier, maybe not.

21

Harper was brushing his teeth in preparation for a pointlessly early night. He knew from past experience that sleep would either be non-existent or fitful, a series of brief catnaps punctuated by nightmares of falling from the heavens out of which he would wake in a cold sweat. The flight to Kazakhstan was due to take off from Brussels airport at nine in the morning and, Klein had stressed, it was now his responsibility to make sure everyone from the agency and the film production company was assembled – tallest to the left, shortest to the right? – and ready to leave the hotel by half past seven. Harper assessed the chances of that happening as pretty slim – Ned and Philip were not renowned for being up with the lark, always brushing aside any criticisms as irrelevant since, they claimed, all their best ideas came late in the day. He was dreading any delay. Not because they would miss the flight – it was a private plane and wasn't going to leave without them – but because it would mean a postponement of the nerve-racking take-off. If something was inevitable, he preferred to get it over and done with.

His bags were packed and lay open on the second single bed in his room. One large suitcase filled to the brim with a range of clothes from lightweight trousers and T-shirts to sweaters and jackets to meet every eventuality of an unknown climate; one medium-sized rucksack containing essentials for the journey – mobile phone, diary and notebook, paperback novel, spare cigarettes, spare lighter, spare spare lighter and so on. He came out of the bathroom and, in an act of displacement activity, fiddled with the top layer of clothes while thinking back over the events of the day.

After the main event of Jackson's presentation of the image campaign the remainder of the morning and afternoon had been spent with the minutiae of details regarding the shoot, the production timetables, media schedules, costs and then the campaign to announce the takeover bid for Laurelle. The more Harper heard, the more bored he became. The only change in his mood was when anxiety took over. The production timetable was so tight that it necessitated the videos of each day's filming being flown back to London for overnight editing. That alone would have been bad enough for someone who was in charge of his first shoot. What triggered a red alert was the answer to a question from Cameron.

'What's the track record of this director?' he had asked.

'Patrick has never shot a bad commercial,' Ned had replied, before quickly changing the subject to some detail of the biodegrading process and whether time-lapse photography would need to be used.

Never shot a bad commercial. Harper knew what that meant. Never shot a good one either. It was Patrick's first shoot, too – the blind leading the blind – and that explained how Ned had been able to get a director and crew who could drop everything – i.e. nothing – and start with just a couple of days' notice.

Jackson had departed (taking with him Harper's suit, the only item of clothing he was sure he would not need in Kazakhstan) and was already thinking of possible creative solutions for a new improved washing powder which produced exactly the same results as the old version at a slightly higher price. Charly had taken Harper aside, thanked him for his part in her victory and then left with a disappointing 'see you in the morning'. After a battle, it is always the general that takes the credit and the footsoldiers that lick their wounds. And Klein had inflicted a few of those. While reminding Harper that he was holding him totally responsible for the success of the shoot – on time, on budget, or else – he also made it clear that he had held him equally responsible for risking the AUC account by keeping him in the dark about the Drew-endorsed concept for the image campaign. Another nail had been hammered into his coffin. How many more to go before Klein was satisfied that the lid was securely on and the occupant could be buried?

A knock on his door interrupted the contemplation of his fate and raised his spirits.

'Who is it?' he shouted, rushing across the room.

'Us.'

'Oh,' a deflated Harper said, before opening the door to Philip and Ned.

The pair of them stood there with knowing grins on their faces.

'Aren't you ready yet?' Ned said, his voice slightly slurred.

'Ready for what?' Harper asked.

'Didn't you get the message?' Philip said. 'We're going clubbing.'

Wonderful! The last thing he wanted was to spend half the night in some noisy nightclub watching other people get drunk, and the other half rounding up everyone for early morning assembly in the lobby. No way!

'Charly's going to be there,' Philip said.

'Who said?'

'She did,' Conrad chipped in. 'She rang earlier this evening.'

'Why didn't she speak to me?'

'She couldn't get through to you,' Conrad explained. 'You were engaged, apparently – phoning home, I presume. Anyway, she said we all deserved a celebration. We're to meet her inside at eleven o'clock. Come on, Kit, get your skates on.'

'I don't know,' said Harper.

'You wouldn't want to disappoint Charly, would you?' Philip said.

'If he doesn't want to come,' Ned said, 'let's not waste time trying to persuade him. All the more for me, I say. And I don't just mean drink. That Charly's really something. Every time I look at her my—'

'Give me five minutes to change,' Harper said.

Harper hadn't been to a nightclub in years. Now he remembered why.

The heat generated by the two hundred or so bodies crammed into this one claustrophobically small room made the temperature inside ideal for glazing pottery; the walls glistened with droplets of condensed hormone-rich sweat; the air was so thick with smoke that, within an instant of entering, Harper found it hard to breathe; the music so loud that conversation was impossible, so repetitive that he couldn't tell when one record had stopped and the next had started, so mindless in its simplistic rhythm that he wondered whether all the hysterically leaping and gyrating occupants had come straight from the operating theatre after total lobotomies.

Strangely, no one else seemed to mind. Maybe it was the anaesthetizing effects of the bottles of beer they were all sipping through wedges of lemon. Or maybe he was just getting old.

'I can't see Charly anywhere,' he shouted, after scouring the dance floor with streaming eyes for a conspicuous mane of fiery red hair.

'Must be downstairs,' his lip-reading companions shouted back in unison.

They wove their way on a line of least resistance zigzag path through the crush of bodies until they had gained the sanctuary of the stairwell.

'Downstairs,' Ned said. 'In the basement. 'Don't know why we didn't try that first.'

Presumably, Harper thought, because the basement would be even hotter and more claustrophobic than the upstairs kiln from which he had just escaped. And, it appeared from the two leather-clad, chain-bedecked, muscle-bound bouncers guarding the door, because they were expecting trouble.

Not that Harper, through the low-lit gloom, could see why. It seemed much more civilized down here: less crowded, less smoky, a shade cooler, the music slower and softer, couples dancing cheek to cheek rather than competing in some gymnastic contest. Even the clothes worn by the women were more formal, the crop tops, boob-tubes and miniskirts of upstairs being replaced by long slinky figure-hugging dresses in soft shiny fabrics. Among those men not in business suits, tight black jeans were almost a uniform, most often teamed with glistening white sleeveless T-shirts.

'I need a drink,' Ned said.

'Walk this way,' Philip said, wiggling his way towards the long bar where two blondes, a brunette and a black-haired woman sat on high stools sipping brightly coloured cocktails and smoking long thin cigarettes.

Harper followed, peering into the stygian shadows in a vain effort to spot Charly. There were a few who were tall enough, others with long red hair but none with both characteristics.

'I can't see Charly here either,' he said. 'Are you sure we're in the right place?'

'She's probably just late,' Ned said. 'Never known a woman who wasn't.'

Philip passed a beer to Ned and a non-alcoholic equivalent to Harper. Apart from the fact it was flat and had a synthetic metallic taste, it was just like the real thing.

'If she's not going to show,' Harper said, 'I'm going back to the hotel.'

'Give her a chance,' Philip said. 'Finish your beer first. Maybe even have a dance. We're here to have some fun.'

'Right on,' said Ned, chuckling.

Philip sidled up to the brunette and whispered into her ear. She took a long hard look at Harper, slid off the stool, trip-trapped up to him on four-inch stilettos, grabbed his hand and pulled him forcefully towards the dance floor.

Before he knew it, the brunette was clutching him tightly against her and had planted her head on his shoulder. Harper began to panic. What if Charly walked in now and saw him locked in a clinch? Curtains, that's what. And not the net variety either. The full, heavily draped set with pencil pleats, matching pelmet and tiebacks.

He pulled away, but the brunette placed a hand on his bottom and pushed him back again.

'Don't struggle,' she said huskily in his ear. 'Relax. You know you want me.'

He looked over her shoulder, scanning the room for Charly. All he saw was Ned and Philip creased up with laughter.

The brunette nestled closer to his face. Her hair was course and scratchy against his skin. Her left hand was still clamped on his bottom, her right began to wander from his shoulder down past his waist to his leg. She stroked his thigh with her palm. Her tongue licked, her teeth nibbled and her lips sucked at his neck.

Don't make a fuss, he told himself. Finish this one dance, then the instant the music stops and the vice-like grip loosens, jump back, thank her politely and run for your life to the safety of the bar.

The thigh stroking turned to nail raking. Her body pressed tighter. He could feel her breasts punching holes in his chest and the hardness of her pubic bone rubbing up and down and side to side against his body. She was enjoying herself, evidently. He could hear her breath coming in short heavy bursts.

Then the anatomically impossible happened.

She seemed to have developed two pubic bones, one digging into his crotch, the other into the side of his leg.

Then the penny dropped.

Harper broke out in a cold sweat.

He raised his hands to place them between their bodies. Pushed at the rock-hard silicone-implant breasts. Broke the grip. Shoved her away. Correction, shoved *him* away.

He fled from the dance floor, striding quickly – and manfully – up to Ned and Philip.

'You bastards,' he said, his face flushed with embarrassment. 'You bloody set me up. Charly's not coming is she?'

'Neither is your partner any more,' Ned said, hysterical almost to the point of helplessness.

'Very funny,' Harper said.

'Wassa matter?' Ned slurred. 'Can't take a joke? You played such a good one on Klein, we thought you deserved one in return.'

'You're pathetic,' Harper said.

'Don't call me pathetic,' Ned said loudly.

Harper, with his back to the bar, could sense from the artificial silence around him that people were beginning to stare at them. It was time to leave. He tried to get past Ned.

'Bloody planners,' Ned said, blocking his path. 'No sense of humour. No sense, full stop, come to that.'

'Out of my way,' Harper said.

'Giving orders, that's all you're good for,' Ned said, pushing angrily at Harper with both hands.

'You're drunk,' Harper said.

'I'll show you how drunk I am,' Ned said, swinging a fist in a wide and heavily telegraphed right hook.

Harper swerved his head out of the way.

He was still congratulating himself on the speed of his reactions when the straight left hit him on the mouth, splitting his lip in the process. He staggered back under the weight of the punch and finished up in the lap of one of the two blondes – no, blonds – sitting at the bar.

The stool, with its high centre of gravity tilted under their combined weight, overbalanced and toppled to the floor. They landed together in a heap, Harper on top, the blond, wig askew, beneath. She – he – took one wide-eyed, startled look at Harper and using arms and legs rolled him over. Harper was left spread-eagled on the floor, swathed in a hot mist of scent, as the blond raced towards the exit as quickly as the oversized high heels would allow.

Harper took a deep breath and jumped to his feet. 'Let's get out of here,' he said. 'Quick.'

The blond was already at the door, talking urgently to the two bouncers. Money appeared to be changing hands. The bouncers looked across at Harper and started to move purposefully in his direction.

'Trouble,' Harper said.

'I'm not afraid of them,' Ned said scornfully.

'Well, you should be,' Harper replied. 'They're twice your size and three times as mean.' And, he omitted, probably four times as intelligent.

The two bouncers, it seemed, surrounded the three of them.

Philip, playing conciliator or maybe just realizing he could speak their language (lingual and body), stepped forward and said, 'It's all right, we're leaving, loves.'

'Not until we say so,' said the slightly more muscle-bound of the two bouncers.

The power of the threat, Harper thought, was diminished somewhat by the slightly high-pitched and lilting delivery.

Maybe Ned felt the same.

Or maybe it was just that time of the evening when Ned had to finish up in the casualty department of the nearest hospital otherwise the whole day would have been wasted.

Ned threw a punch at the nearer of the two bouncers. Missed, lost his balance and collapsed to the floor. In retaliation, a boot was planted in Ned's ribs. The other bouncer shaped up to do the same.

Philip stood there transfixed with shock. Harper quickly debated with himself as to the right course of action: pitch in or leave Ned to the lesson of a kicking. But Ned was a slow learner – he'd be back within half an hour of being thrown out of the place for another try.

Harper bent down and picked up the high stool from the floor. With a leg in each hand he swung the chair and hit one bouncer in between the shoulder blades. The bouncer pitched forwards, hit his head on the bar and sank to the floor.

The other bouncer gave Ned a final kick, this time on the side of the head, and turned his attention towards the new threat. Harper swung the stool again, connecting with the bouncer's midriff and sending him backwards with the force of the blow.

The bouncer caught his breath and took stock. He placed a hand in his trouser pocket, pulled out a shiny metal knuckleduster and slipped it on the fingers of his right hand.

Harper jabbed with the stool like a lion tamer, keeping his adversary at bay. He began to edge back towards the door, drawing his quarry with him. Philip started to help Ned to his feet. If they could only reach the exit, maybe they could outrun the muscle-bound bouncer.

Harper prodded again with the stool. The bouncer grabbed the seat with his left hand, yanked it from Harper's grasp and threw the stool aside. He squared up to Harper, legs apart and balanced on the soles of his feet. He drew back his right fist ready to send the knuckleduster with all his force into Harper' face.

'Behind you,' Harper said.

It was the oldest trick in the book and the bouncer was determined not to fall for it.

Instead he fell for Ned's kick in the groin. And then to the floor.

Harper, Ned and Philip ran to the door, up the stairs and out of there.

Harper nursed his split lip in the bar of the Royal Windsor. Ned, sipping a large brandy for purely medicinal reasons, didn't seem to be nursing anything – a case of where there's no sense there's no feeling.

'Brilliant,' Ned said. 'I haven't had as much fun for ages. What a great evening.'

'Do me a favour,' Harper said to Ned.

'No more jokes?' Ned asked.

'Not a bad idea,' Harper replied, 'but that wasn't what I was thinking. Do you remember the blond I knocked off the stool?'

'Sorry, can't help,' smiled Ned. 'Didn't have time to get the phone number.'

'But did you get a good look at her – him?'

'While you were dancing, yes.'

'Can you do me a drawing?'

Ned shook his head. Not in the negative, but in puzzlement.

Harper borrowed a pencil and a white paper napkin from the barman. Handed both to Ned. 'Just the face will do.'

Ned sketched away with skill and speed.

'There you go,' he said, passing the finished product to Harper.

Harper inverted the pencil and, using the eraser on the other end, began to rub away at the long blond wig. Then he thinned the heavily lipsticked mouth, rubbed out the eye shadow and rouge and sat back in his chair to see what he had left.

The face that now stared up at him was just as he had expected. But then there couldn't be many men who used so much of that very singular orange-and-lemon scented cologne.

STAGE FOUR

END PRODUCT

22

The airport at Semey in Kazakhstan was a small single-storey building that looked as if it had been put together by an untalented eight-year-old from an oversized and badly stocked construction kit: none of the angles seemed quite square, the glass was smeared with greasy fingerprints and the concrete panels, polluted by the fumes from the heavily industrialized city, were a grubby grey-black. Harper led the baggage-laden group through the single swinging door and came face-to-face with a member of the *militsia* in a cream-coloured top with a semi-automatic machine gun clutched tightly against his chest.

The military policeman waved the gun in the direction of a queue which stretched far back from a barrier: immediately in front of it was a wooden cubicle over which hung a sign that read *Immigration* in Russian and English. At Harper's side, Charly groaned.

'This is the last thing I need,' she said.

Harper knew exactly how she felt. He was hungry and tired. OK, so it wasn't actually nine o'clock in the evening biological time but, after a seven-hour flight – how can sitting down for so long be so exhausting? – the last two hours of which they had spent bumping about in turbulence as they crossed one mountain range after another, and now the added disorientation of a six-hour time difference, all he wanted to do was have something hot to eat and then curl up in bed and sleep. The only positive aspect of the flight, unless one was a dedicated fan of sandwiches that dried up instantly in the pressurized atmosphere, was that Philip and Jeremiah Drew had worked together on the script for the commercial and finally agreed a version that met the demands of both truth and persuasive advertising prose (the three key words of which are *you, new* and *free*).

'Someone was supposed to meet us,' Charly said. 'Where the hell is he?'

'Maybe he's gone to the wrong airport,' Evans said.

'Thanks for cheering me up,' Charly said.

'I only meant that there may have been some confusion, since our plane will be flying on to Alma-Ata.'

Although Alma-Ata, the capital of Kazakhstan, was the nearest airport to the test site where they would be filming, Evans had decided that while they were coming all this way he might as well inspect the control site as well. So, once they had cleared the airport, they would have around a hundred miles to travel to Lake Zaysan. After an overnight stop at the control site there would be a further three hundred and fifty miles to cover the following day before arriving at the test site at Lake Balqash. Meanwhile, the plane was scheduled to fly to Alma-Ata so that the videos of each day's filming could be delivered every evening and flown back to London for the labour-intensive and time-consuming editing process.

'We are a good forty minutes early,' Harper said, mentally giving thanks to the tail wind that had pushed them along for the latter half of the journey. 'He's probably not arrived yet. Still, I'll go and scout around.' He dumped his heavy suitcase and rucksack on the grimy plastic-tiled floor and pushed forward to move deeper into the throng of people.

The air was thick with aromatic Turkish tobacco and the sour smell of sweat from the crush of bodies. On the low ceiling, three fans twirled lethargically, momentarily cutting the clouds of smoke into thin wisps before they reformed around the flickering fluorescent lights. Harper took off his lightweight jacket, rolled it into a tight ball so that his bulging wallet was well away from groping hands and edged forwards. At the front of the queue a trio of Korean businessmen was arguing vociferously and ineffectively with an implacable, stone-faced official who kept repeating the word *visas* in a deep, bored voice and gesturing to a pile of grey forms on a wooden counter.

Harper tried to peer past the barrier but all he could see was another sea of bodies. He collected a stack of the forms and trudged wearily back.

'No sign of a reception committee,' he said to Evans and Charly.

She rolled her eyes and sat down on her suitcase.

'What's the hold-up?' she asked.

'Seems like they want to see visas,' he replied, handing each of them a form. He kept one for himself and passed the rest back along the straggly line of the group. 'Or maybe they just want the hundred and eight dollars of hard currency that seems to be the price of each one.'

The queue shuffled forward a couple of feet. Charly got up, kicked her suitcase along the floor and sat down again. Harper gazed down at her. There were patches of perspiration on the shoulder blades of her khaki cotton blouse. Her matching jeans, heavily creased from the long plane journey, were tucked into calf-length brown leather boots that were making Harper feel even hotter just from looking at them. He undid his shirt another couple of buttons and wiped the sweat from his neck.

'Welcome to bloody Kazakhstan,' he said.

It took thirty minutes before they arrived at the head of the queue. Harper had collected all the passports and visa application forms and handed these over. The official scanned them briefly and grunted, 'Hundred twenty dollar each.'

'But it says here one hundred and eight,' Harper said.

The official picked up a pen, amended the figure on the form and shrugged at Harper. 'Hundred twenty dollar,' he repeated.

'Just pay up,' Charly said. 'The sooner we get past him, the sooner we get out of this hell-hole.'

Harper took out his wallet, counted out fourteen hundred-dollar bills to cover the cost of eleven visas and laid the money on the narrow ledge of the cubicle. The official re-counted the bills untrustingly, stamped their visas and waved his hand as a sign for them to go through.

'Don't suppose there's any chance of some change?' Harper asked.

'No understand,' the official said.

'Now, how did I guess you were going to say that?' He sighed, turned to the group and said, 'Come on, the next queue beckons.'

They entered a larger area; to the right was a sluggishly moving carousel, to the left a series of X-ray machines set before a long counter where baggage was being searched. The Koreans were arguing again, gesticulating madly, shaking heads and shouting loudly, and all with the same nil effect as last time.

'What is it now?' Charly said.

Harper was just mentally preparing himself to set off on another sortie when a tall dark-haired man dressed in a black suit pushed his way toward them.

'My friends,' the man said, smiling widely and proudly giving them a flash of a gold tooth centre-stage in his wide mouth, 'I am sorry I was not here to greet you when you stepped off the plane. You are early – such an event rarely happens in Kazakhstan.' He bowed to Charly. 'Ms Mendoza, I presume. Allow me to introduce myself. I am Kazam, humble representative of AUC Kazakhstan.'

Charly shook his hand, introduced Harper – 'he's in charge of the shoot' said almost through gritted teeth – and Evans and gestured at the remaining members of the group: Drew, Philip, Ned, Patrick and the four members of the director's film crew.

'It's good to meet you, Kazam,' Harper said. 'Yours is the first smile we've seen since landing.'

'Too many years of Soviet rule,' Kazam shrugged. 'Too many years when there was nothing to smile about. The people of this country have forgotten how to smile.'

'How long before you can get us out of this dump?' Charly asked.

'Just as soon as we have gone through the ritual of customs.' Kazam produced more forms. 'Each of you must fill in one of these. It is a joint customs and currency declaration. You must put down the amount of all currency you are carrying and make a list of all valuables – watches, jewellery, cameras and so on.'

There was a loud groan from the film crew: they wouldn't need a form but a whole pad to catalogue the three video cameras, the boxes and boxes of videos, the portable lighting rig, the sound equipment and whatever else was in the four large steel containers.

'They will X-ray your baggage,' Kazam continued, 'and then search it. One tip – if they ask for something, say no.' Kazam shrugged again. 'Don't make life easy for them – if they really want it, they will take it anyway.'

'Any way to short circuit proceedings,' he said to Kazam.

Kazam sucked air past the gold tooth while he contemplated the situation. 'There is a phrase you will hear often while in Kazakhstan. "*Dollar yest?*" It means, "Do you have dollars?" So, Mr Harper, *Dollar yest?*'

'How much will it cost?'

'It depends on the mood of the customs official. And how much he has made already today.'

'Is everyone here on the take?' Harper said.

'Of course,' Kazam said, looking at Harper as if he were the village idiot. 'They have to be, otherwise how could they pay for the privilege of having their job?'

'They have to pay their superiors so that they can work here?'

'No, Mr Harper. You do not understand. They have to pay a percentage of their unofficial earnings to the local mafia. When the Russians moved out after giving Kazakhstan its independence they left behind a power vacuum. The *mafiosniki* stepped in. Now they control everything that goes on in this country. They make the wheels turn. Providing,' Kazam laughed, 'that they are greased.'

Harper wondered whether Mueller, who had chosen Kazakhstan for the testing of the enzyme, had been on the take too: there had to be a reason for what seemed an increasingly bizarre choice. In a land where nothing seemed to function without payment of a bribe, accounting for monies spent would be impossible and, therefore, no one would be any the wiser if a little extra was skimmed off the top.

'Give me five hundred dollars,' Kazam said. 'I will sort out the problem.'

'I suppose he really is your company representative?' Harper said to Charly and Evans. 'It wouldn't surprise me if he simply vanished and we never saw him again.'

But, fifteen minutes later – and five hundred dollars lighter – after only a cursory examination of their baggage, Kazam led them safely out of the airport.

Harper, glad to be free of the oppressive heat of the building, took a deep breath of the cool night air – and coughed.

'Sulphur dioxide,' said Evans, wrinkling his nose. 'Probably some oxides of nitrogen, unburned hydrocarbons, ozone and maybe a little hydrogen cyanide too.'

Yuk, thought Harper. Sounded even worse than it smelt.

Evans pointed to the illuminated skyscrapers on the outskirts of the city. Harper rubbed his already stinging eyes and stared into the distance. A haze of smog clung around the lights from the windows.

From behind him there was a roar of engines. He spun around to see a fleet of vehicles – four jeeps and a truck – pulling up to the kerb. Kazam clapped his hands and the drivers leapt out and started to load the luggage on board the truck.

As if by some unwritten agreement, the group divided themselves up and climbed into the jeeps. Harper sat in the back of the lead vehicle, Charly at his side and Evans in the front.

The convoy set off, slowly negotiating the traffic inside the perimeter of the airport before speeding up on joining a straight, fast road. The road signs were all in Cyrillic with no English equivalents, but Harper, because of the strong similarities with the Greek alphabet, could make a fair stab at the place names. This seemed to be the main road to Alma-Ata (large script), passing through a place called Georgievka (much smaller). The diesel engine of the jeep throbbed loudly and erratically, the heater wheezed asthmatically as it emitted a slow stream of warm air, the hard suspension exaggerated every slight indentation in the road's surface so that it was like being on a small boat in a heavy sea. In spite of – or maybe because of – the noise and the motion, Harper felt Charly's head sink down onto his shoulder and heard her breathing become slower and deeper. He wriggled his arm free and placed it around her, telling himself it was purely to cushion the effects of the jeep's bumpy progress on her sleeping body. The soft strands of her hair began to tickle his nose – it was such a long time since he had experienced that feeling – and after a while he moved his head to one side to make it more difficult for memories to be triggered.

To the left of the road, from time to time, he saw the lights of isolated houses flash by: to the right, nothing except the occasional glimpse of a red sign on a high steel electrified fence. He felt his eyelids grow heavy and heard as if in the distance the drone of Evans and Kazam talking in low voices.

Suddenly he was jolted awake and forward in the seat. The jeep was stopping.

'Are we here?' Charly asked sleepily. 'Get your arm off me, Harper,' she added, realizing the position she was in and quickly sitting up straight.

Kazam chuckled. 'Just a checkpoint,' he said. 'I can handle it.'

'Don't tell me,' Harper said. 'More dollars?'

'Only if you don't want a long delay while the truck is searched.'

'How much this time?'

'A hundred dollars should be acceptable.'

Harper handed over a hundred-dollar bill as half a dozen *militsia* fanned out along the line of vehicles. Kazam climbed from the jeep and hurried off to intercept the officer in charge. They vanished into the shadows behind the headlights to conduct their business.

Harper opened his door and stepped outside. He lit a cigarette and walked up and down stretching his cramped long legs. From behind him he heard the crunching of roadside gravel.

'Cigarette?' said one of the military policemen. He was thick-set and unshaven, looking like a reject from the Dirty Dozen (too psychotic to pass the selection process), but pointed the muzzle of the machine gun downwards in a friendly – or at least not an overtly unfriendly – gesture.

Harper extended the packet. The man, using his free left hand, slid out a cigarette and placed it between his lips. Then the hand reached out again, this time closing around the packet. He locked eyes with Harper, at the same time raising the gun slightly to waist level. Harper released his grip and watched the packet disappear into the soldier's breast pocket. The soldier reached out a third time, carefully took the cigarette from Harper's lips, used it to light his own while intently watching Harper's reaction, opened his fingers to let it drop to the gravel and ground it out with the thick sole of his boot. Then he stood there challengingly, exhaling a long stream of smoke towards Harper's face. The body language crossed the communication barrier. 'I take what I want,' it said. 'And what are you going to do about it?'

'Get in, Harper, for Christ's sake,' Charly hissed from inside the jeep.

The soldier turned and noticed Charly for the first time. His eyes widened, then narrowed thoughtfully, and finally gleamed. He licked his lips, sending a shiver down Harper's spine, and stepped closer to the jeep. *I take what I want.*

'Hey,' said Harper, tapping the soldier on the shoulder.

The soldier spun round, instinctively raising his gun. He stared at Harper, grunted something unintelligible, and probably unprintable, in Russian and then directed his attention back towards Charly.

'Cigarette,' said Harper, moving around the soldier to block his path. 'Cigarette,' he repeated, spreading his hand and gesturing to his lips.

The soldier looked deep into his eyes.

Harper backed toward the jeep and shut the door. He leaned back against it, obscuring the view of Charly, folded his arms across his chest and said a third time, 'Cigarette.'

The soldier slowly shook his head from side to side. Then he laughed, tapped his head with one finger and said, '*Soomashedshi.*'

'Now would be a very good time to get back into the jeep, Mr Harper,' Kazam said, appearing out of nowhere and opening the door. 'Quickly, please.'

Harper climbed aboard and stared straight ahead so that he would not have to see the grinning face of the soldier. Kazam jumped inside, gunned the engine and let slip the clutch. The jeep lurched forward.

'What the hell did you do that for?' Charly shouted angrily at him. 'Didn't you see the look in that soldier's eyes?'

'Yes,' said Harper. 'And better than you.'

'He called you Crazy Man,' Kazam said, laughing now they were safely on the road again.

'Shrewd judge of character,' Charly said. She tossed her head. 'And all for a cigarette!'

'Yeah, all for a cigarette,' Harper said.

Evans joined in the laughter.

'What's so goddammed funny?' Charly said.

'Well, Charly,' Evans began, 'what Kit was—'

'Leave it, Andrew,' Harper snapped, slumping down in the seat and closing his eyes. 'I'd appreciate some peace and quiet. I'm going back to sleep.'

'Huh! Just like a man,' Charly said.

'Just like a crazy man,' Kazam giggled.

After what he estimated as about half an hour, Harper felt the change in the surface under the tyres as the jeep left the road and turned on to a rough track. They made slow progress for another fifteen minutes and then the vehicle finally pulled to a halt. He opened his eyes and saw the dim glow of lights in the downstairs windows of a two-storey farmhouse, and, framed in the doorway, the silhouette of a tall man, his arm waving to beckon them inside.

'At last,' Charly said, jumping out of the jeep and striding toward the door.

The others followed hard on her heels and they entered a large whitewashed room lit by oil lamps and with a big open fire blazing at one end. The group congregated around the fire, jockeying for that best position that is close, but not too close, to the heat. The man approached, bowed his head very slightly and spoke at length.

'What did he say?' Harper asked.

'He said that his name is Rak,' Kazam answered.

'That was a long speech for such a short name,' Harper said.

'He also recited his ancestry. His father's and mother's names, their parents before them and so on back to times long past. In this country it is said that if a man cannot name his ancestors for seven generations, then he is no Kazakh.'

'Tell him we are proud to meet a true Kazakh,' said Harper, bowing at Rak.

While Kazam was translating, a short, round woman of about forty dressed in a blood-red smock and wearing a white turban on her head entered the room. At her side was a pretty young girl of sixteen or seventeen with long black hair and dark eyes. They each carried a pitcher filled to the brim with a cloudy white liquid.

'And also to meet a true Kazakh's daughter,' Ned added, smiling at the girl and making her blush coyly.

Rak led them to a rectangular wooden table suitable for eight people, if they were very close friends and didn't have any hang-ups about invasion of body space. The table was surrounded by an eclectic collection of chairs, low milking stools and packing cases. As the group sat down, Rak's wife and daughter filled earthenware mugs with the white liquid and handed these around.

Harper sniffed warily at the drink. 'What is this?' he asked Kazam.

'Koumis,' came the unhelpful reply. 'It is our national drink and a great source of pride among us Kazakhs. Families compete for who can make the best koumis. Rak honours you by providing koumis.'

Harper held his mug in the air and gestured politely at Rak, then at his wife and daughter. Ned followed suit – but lingered on the eyelash-fluttering daughter. The others joined in the toast. The family stood there expectantly, smiling at their guests.

Raising his mug to his lips for an experimental sip, a very strong, very sour odour entered Harper's nostrils. Maybe, he told himself, it wouldn't taste as bad as it smelt. He was right – in a way. It was ten times worse. The taste was as if some highly innovative sadist had diluted warm, rancid butter with petrol. Harper felt his stomach turn and his throat gagging.

Rak, with a capacious grin on his lips, said something to him.

'Good?' said Kazam.

'Tell Rak that I've never tasted anything like it in my life,' Harper said, forcing a smile and looking around to see puzzled expressions on ten faces. 'What exactly is it?'

'Fermented mare's milk,' Kazam said.

The faces around the table grimaced.

'We don't wish to offend Rak, Kazam,' Harper said, 'but can you explain that we are all much too thirsty to appreciate fully the koumis. Some water would help us savour its unique flavour. And if there is any food, that would be very welcome too.'

Rak listened to the translation, nodded his head and the family hurried out.

Soon there came the sounds of something sizzling and a variety of smells, not all of them unpleasant, began to waft through from the kitchen.

'I could eat a horse,' Ned said, sniffing the air.

'I wish you hadn't said that,' said Charly. 'How about you, Crazy Man,' she said, turning to Harper, 'are you hungry?'

He shrugged. 'Maybe I'll content myself with a cigarette.'

'Stop sulking,' she said.

The drivers entered before he had a chance to say 'Who me?' or 'That's rich'. The good news was that they homed in on the koumis, enabling the group to pour the contents of their mugs surreptitiously back into the pitchers. The bad news was that they had unloaded the contents of the truck: now, on the floor beside their bags and the camera equipment, was a long line of rolled-up sleeping bags.

'I'll never forgive you for this,' Patrick grunted at Ned.

'Look on the bright side,' Ned replied, leaping up to take two heavy platters from out of the hands of Rak's daughter. 'Maybe you're right,' he said, seeming to have had rapid second thoughts, judging not only from the words but also by the shocked expression on his face.

Ned placed the food on the table.

'Oh my God!' said Charly.

Harper stared down: one dish contained a mountain of rice with unidentifiable yellow cubes and fatty scraps of meat spread across the top; the other, a vast mound of noodles as thick – and about as appetising – as boiled sisal.

Rak's wife placed a bowl of greasy stock on the table and signed that they should spoon it over the noodles. With noodles like that, Harper thought, it was the least they deserved.

The feast (!) was completed by a plate of kebabs – the fat-to-meat ratio being about three to one – lying in a pool of grease and draped with raw onion, rounds of unleavened bread and jugs of water.

'I hesitate to ask,' Harper said to Kazam, 'but can you tell us what we are about to eat.' And may the Lord make us truly grateful – and immune to gastric side effects.

'*Plov*,' Kazam replied, pointing to the rice dish that now sounded as good as it looked. 'Turnips and mutton,' he explained. 'And this is *shashlyk* – mutton kebabs – eat them with the noodles, *laghman*, and sauce.' – *Sauce*, thought Harper. You cannot glorify that bowl of rapidly congealing grease by calling it sauce – 'The bread is *lepeshka*. Enjoy.'

For half an hour they drank water thirstily, ate bread hungrily and picked unenthusiastically at the least offensive bits of the other dishes. The drivers shovelled great spoonfuls of rice and noodles into their mouths, swallowed lumps of meat – fat and all – and washed everything down with more koumis.

'Any chance of some coffee,' Harper said, ignoring the rumblings of his stomach and going over to his rucksack to retrieve a new pack of cigarettes.

Kazam shook his head.

Harper felt his spirits sink to a new low.

'Coffee, I'm afraid, is an expensive delicacy here in Kazakhstan,' Kazam explained. 'But there will be glasses of refreshing *chai* – tea – and *spirrt*. Coffee would only keep you awake,' he shrugged. '*Spirrt* will make you sleep.'

'Then whatever it is,' Harper said, thinking of a hard floor and a thin sleeping bag, 'bring it in.'

He walked over to the fire and sat down on one of the cushions that had been laid out by Rak's wife in a wide semi-circle; lit a cigarette and waited while the others drifted across to join him.

'Will the test site be like this?' he asked Kazam.

'Oh, no. The test site is run by Russians,' said Kazam, seeming to spit out the last word. 'You will find that everything there is very different.'

'Then roll on tomorrow,' Ned said, voicing everyone's thoughts.

'And there was I,' Harper said, 'thinking that tonight was the only thing on your mind. With the addition of Rak's daughter, that is.'

Ned shrugged. 'Wouldn't be right, Harper. And anyway—'

He was interrupted by the arrival of tea – thick, black and unsweetened – together with Rak struggling under the weight of a huge flagon. He poured a clear liquid, presumably the promised – threatened? – *spirrt*, into tiny glasses and passed these around.

Ned took a sip and rapidly followed this by swallowing the rest of the glass. 'Wow,' he said breathlessly. 'Rocket fuel,' he elucidated. 'But bloody good rocket fuel.' He held out his glass for a refill.

Rak looked at Harper expectantly; nodded at the glass in his hand. Charly was watching him too.

'Tell him I am sorry,' Harper said, 'but I cannot drink alcohol.'

Kazam translated and Rak shook his head in pity and incomprehension.

'Should we be sitting this close to the fire?' Harper said, gesturing at the *spirrt*.

Kazam laughed. 'It is ninety-six per cent alcohol,' he said. 'I told you it would make you sleep.'

Later, Harper would wish he had swallowed a glass or two.

Harper lay wriggling uncomfortably in his sleeping bag and listening to the groans coming from the direction of Ned. Charly and the only female member of the film crew had been led upstairs, Kazam and the drivers had gone off to one of the barns, leaving Harper and the rest of the men to spread themselves out on the stone floor of the main room. It was hot and stuffy due to a combination of the warmth of the fire and the exhaled breath and radiated heat from their bodies.

'Oh, my head,' Ned complained loudly.

'It's your own fault,' Harper said unsympathetically. 'You shouldn't have had four glasses of *spirrt*.'

'This is a nightmare,' Ned moaned. 'A bloody nightmare.'

'Don't keep saying *mare*,' someone said in the darkness.

'And, if the food and drink wasn't bad enough,' Ned said, 'this place is a like a scene from *Deliverance*. Any moment now that daughter is going to appear playing bloody *Duelling Banjos*.'

'What the hell are you going on about?' Harper said.

'Inbred as hell, they are.'

'Just because they're simple peasants doesn't make them inbred,' Harper sighed.

'Didn't you notice?'

'Notice what?'

'The daughter had six fingers on each hand.'

23

Harper had spent the night tossing and turning and formulating a theory. So far it was like watching a film slowly develop – only the very darkest shades were becoming visible and these were of little help in revealing the overall picture. He slid out of the sleeping – what a joke! – bag, grabbed his shoes and clothes from the day before and picked a careful path among the bodies spread across the floor. Closing the door quietly behind him, he stepped outside.

From the angle of the sun already shining warmly on his face, Harper guessed that it was half an hour or so after dawn. In the yard running back from the farmhouse there was a standpipe with a old-fashioned pump handle. He splashed water over his face, cupped his hands to drink a little and slipped on his clothes. Looking into the distance he could see a crescent of snow-capped mountains running north to east. A mile or so away the waters of Lake Zaysan sparkled in the low, slanting light. Immediately surrounding him was a sorry collection of dilapidated buildings – two barns, some stables, a granary, a milking parlour – with crumbling stonework (very recently cosmetically enhanced by whitewash) and patched roofs. Apart from the plaintive lowing of a small herd of cows, he could hear nothing. Everywhere was eerily still and silent.

Harper set off towards the lake, passing a recently harvested field of wheat stubble and an orchard of apple trees. Picking an apple from a tree, he polished it on his T-shirt and took a bite. A little sharp perhaps, but clean and refreshing at this time of the morning and especially after the greasy meat of the night before.

He reached the lake and sat on a bank near the shoreline. Tossing the apple core into the water, he watched the water lapping over the reeds in the shallows. After a little while, a shoal of small fish came to investigate the floating core, swimming around it and then nibbling happily until frightened away by something larger. Pike? Perch? Whatever it was, its movements were erratic as if it was having difficulty steering through the reeds. Harper got down on his stomach and crawled slowly toward the fish to get a better look.

The fish circled the apple core in a clockwise direction, stabilizing its body with rapid movements of its pectoral and lateral fins. Through the clear water Harper could make out the gill covers opening and closing: tiny bubbles of expelled carbon dioxide floated up to ripple the surface of the lake. Suddenly a long shadow was cast over the water. The fish, startled, changed direction and sped off. Harper stared at it intently, disbelievingly, until it disappeared from view. Only then did he roll over.

'So here you are, Mr Harper,' Kazam said, frowning down at him. 'We wondered where you were.'

'Just enjoying the peace and quiet of this beautiful morning. And watching the fish in the lake. There seem to be plenty of them. What sort are they?'

Kazam shrugged – it was becoming an annoyingly repetitive gesture that was beginning to grate on Harper's frayed nerves. 'I know nothing of fish,' he said. 'We Kazakhs are nomads by tradition and upbringing. We are meat eaters – sheep, horse, goats.' He waved his hand in the air as if there was an endless list of flesh in their carnivorous repertoire. 'Fish is not to our liking. Too many bones and nothing to sink your teeth into.'

Harper shrugged. Maybe with time and sufficient shrugs he could break Kazam of the irritating habit.

'Come,' Kazam said, turning away and starting to stride off. 'We must go back to the farmhouse. We have a long journey ahead of us. Breakfast is being served. You must eat.'

As he followed Kazam back past the orchard towards the house, Harper noticed that workers had now appeared in the fields and that cattle were being led into the milking parlour. The farming day had finally begun.

'Hello, Crazy Man,' Ned said with a broad smile as Harper entered through the door. He was sitting at the crowded table next to – very close to – Charly, Evans opposite him. 'Andrew has been telling us all about your little brush with the law.'

'So the age of chivalry is not dead,' Philip said.

'It just smells that way,' the stubble-haired female member of the film crew said disdainfully.

'Would you like my seat?' Andrew said, somewhat shamefaced. 'Kazam is taking Jeremiah and me for a quick tour of the farm.' He smiled at Harper, then added as a placatory afterthought, 'Of course, you're very welcome to join us, if you like.'

'Thanks for the offer, Andrew, but I have something to do before breakfast.'

And, he might have added, I doubt very much that the tour will be enlightening in any way.

Harper walked over to his bag, rummaged around and, jacket in one hand and a pack of cigarettes conspicuously in the other, went back outside.

He stood by the pump, examining it as if he were wondering what it was and how, if at all, it worked, and waited for Kazam, Evans and Drew to emerge. When they were safely inside one of the barns, Harper hurried to the back of the other. Unwrapping his mobile phone from the jacket, he switched it on, keyed in his pin number and said, 'Come on, come on,' impatiently under his breath while the phone searched laboriously for a local node and a network. Punching out the familiar numbers, he checked his watch and prepared an apology.

Saul answered on the fifth ring. 'Yes,' he mumbled, his voice sleepily slow but tinged with anxiety.

'It's Kit,' Harper began.

'Kit?' The tone of Saul's voice changed to surprise and annoyance. 'Do you know what time it is?'

'About half past one in the morning your time, if my calculations are right,' he said. 'I'm really sorry to wake you, Saul, but this is very important and I haven't got much time. I'm in the backwoods of Kazakhstan and I don't know when I'll next get an opportunity to charge this phone.'

Saul sighed. 'Well, my boy,' he said, 'what do you want?'

'I looked at some facts and figures on Kazakhstan last week when I was preparing the brief. Regretfully, I didn't get past the first few pages. But something did stick in my brain. Can you check out a few things for me.'

Harper explained exactly what he needed to know, and then added that anything else Saul considered interesting would be useful too.

'Can I ask the reasons for this strange – and highly antisocial – request?' Saul said.

'Would you accept intuition? A hunch?'

'Yes, but I'd prefer something a little more concrete so that I can get back to sleep when I put down the phone.'

'How about a girl with six fingers and a fish with an extra pectoral fin?'

'I saved you some breakfast,' Charly said.

Charly, dressed in a pair of loose-fitting white trousers, dark-brown crop top and unbuttoned white blouse, was the only one left at the table. The others were either packing, standing in a queue waiting to wash at the kitchen sink or were outside somewhere getting a breath of fresh air.

'That was kind of you,' Harper said, sitting down opposite her.

'It's the least I could do,' she said. 'In the circumstances.'

Harper looked down at the plate she had placed before him. There was a round of *lepeshka*, a slice of cheese – let it be from a sheep, not a horse – and an apple. Hardly worth hurrying back from the lake for.

'Circumstances?' he said.

'Ooh, Harper,' she said, clenching her fists, 'you are insufferable.'

'What's in the glass?' he asked, peering suspiciously at an unappetizing blood-red liquid.

'Don't change the subject.'

'What subject?'

'You know very well what subject.'

He looked at her innocently.

'Andrew explained,' she said.

'And?'

'What do you want from me, Harper? A little fawning, perhaps? Bended knees? Tears trickling from my eyes? I am sorry. I misinterpreted your actions – your motives, too. You were creating a diversion. Drawing attention away from me. And letting that soldier know you would not stand idly by. I am grateful, Harper. OK? Are you satisfied now?'

'Partly.'

'*Partly!*'

'Well,' he said, smiling at her, 'you still haven't told me what's in the glass.'

'It's called *kompot* – the juice of red and black berries. It's OK. And, by the way, I hope it chokes you.'

'So do I take it, from those well-expressed and touching sentiments concerning my future, that the apology is over?'

'Oh, yes,' she said. 'And the strangulation is just about to begin. You can be a real sulky sonovabitch at times.'

'You're right,' he said.

'Wonders will never cease. The great Harper – Crazy Man as was – says I'm right.'

'Yeah. The juice *is* OK.'

Charly punched him hard on the shoulder, and burst out laughing.

'You know something, Kit?' she said, shaking her head at him. 'I've never met anyone like you before.'

'And, given a hundred years or so, you might even get to like me?'

'No, Kit,' she said, smiling sweetly. 'I wouldn't say *that* soon.'

It was an hour or so before Evans and Drew, wearing bored expressions, returned from their inspection trip. The luggage, film equipment and some food for the trip had already been loaded into the truck, everyone was washed and dressed and raring to go. Final goodbyes were said – and good riddances left unspoken – and the convoy pulled away a little after nine o'clock.

For the first leg of the journey Kazam chose a slow and bumpy cross-country route – maybe to avoid further incidents at *militsia*-manned check-points, but Harper doubted it – heading south-west to Ayaguz. From there they made better, and more comfortable, progress along the westerly highway towards Qaraghandy, and then it was back on minor roads of crushed gravel or bone-shaking, rutted tracks of baked earth.

They stopped for a short break at midday, stretching their legs before cowering in the shade of a small thicket of pine trees to drink warm water and eat cheese-filled *lepeshka*. Anyone with an ice-cold Coke and a Mars Bar could have held an auction and retired a wealthy person. To say morale was low would have been a massive understatement – something unknown in the world of advertising. The initially attractive scenery of low mountains and lush green steppes had long since lost its charm and now passed by unnoticed.

The heat, as unremitting as the view from the windows of the jeeps, was draining. But worst of all, the relief they had felt on leaving the control site at Lake Zaysan was now replaced by dread at what they would encounter at the test site at Lake Balqash.

During the afternoon, each mile seemed to take longer and each hour to pass more slowly. In Harper's jeep there was little conversation, Kazam being focused on negotiating potholes and Andrew and Charly locked in inner thoughts. The ride was too jerky and jarring for dozing and it was too hot to do anything but wriggle sore backsides in seats and wipe sweat from brows. Harper spent his time extending slightly his theory and calculating when his phone should ring. He looked at his watch and sighed: still only two-fifteen.

At three o'clock they stopped again, the vehicles pulling into the fringes of a wood of elm and poplar.

'Fifteen minutes,' Kazam said sadistically.

'How much longer before we get there?' Charly asked, rubbing aching limbs.

Kazam shrugged.

If he does that one more time, Harper thought, I'll kill him.

'Five hours,' Kazam said.

There was a chorus of groans.

'Six maybe,' Kazam amended, risking a lynch mob.

The group began to break up, individuals wandering off into the trees to seek a little privacy.

'Stay close,' Kazam shouted. 'This is wolf country.'

On faces could now be seen intense looks of concentration as people tried to work out how long their bladders might hold out or, alternatively, how quickly they could relieve themselves and regain the safety of numbers.

The drivers took jerrycans of diesel from the truck and refuelled the vehicles. Flasks of water that you could have almost boiled eggs in were passed around. Harper sat himself under a tree, telephoned home and spoke briefly to Nanny Trent and at length to Cassie. She wanted to know everything that he had done since they had last spoken on Thursday evening and, in turn, to recount every moment of her Friday. It was a conversation that put all the thinking about his theory into perspective, and yet, at the same time, increased its importance.

'Come home soon, Daddy,' Cassie said. 'I miss you.'

'I miss you too, Cassie.'

'Is Charly there, Daddy?'

'Yes,' he said, wondering what was going through his daughter's mind.

'May I talk to her? Please?'

'I suppose so,' he said, even more puzzled. 'Hold on.'

He walked over to where Charly was sitting. She had removed her blouse and was using it as part cushion and part barrier against grass and earth soiling the white trousers.

'Cassie would like a word with you,' he said, screwing up his face in apology. 'Would you mind?'

She took the phone from him. 'Hi, Cassie,' she said.

Charly listened while Cassie spoke. She gazed up at Harper, nodded her head to herself and gave him a weird look. 'OK, Cassie. I'll try,' she said, handing the phone back to Harper.

'What was that all about?' he asked Cassie.

'Girl talk,' she replied. 'Bye, Daddy. Love you.'

'Love you too, sweetheart. I'll phone again soon. I promise. Bye.'

'Well?' he said to Charly, preparing to repeat the unanswered question. 'What was that all about?'

'She just wanted to give me some advice, that's all.'

'My daughter – a five-year-old – wanted to give *you* some advice?'

'Yep.'

'Go on. And?'

'She said,' Charly fought back a smile, 'that I wasn't to let you tease me like you do her.'

'Is that all?' Harper said, relieved.

'Maybe,' she replied, getting up and walking back to the jeep.

'Hey,' he cried, chasing after her. 'You can't leave it like that.'

'Why not?' she said, grinning impishly. 'Isn't that exactly what a tease would do?'

'*Touché.*'

The call came through at a quarter to five. Harper immediately asked Kazam to stop for a moment, claiming that all the steel inside the jeep was shielding the signal. He walked out of earshot and sat down, pen poised over notebook.

'Sorry I took so long,' Saul said. 'But, in view of what I found, I thought it best to be thorough and double-check everything.'

'Hit me with it, Saul.'

Harper wrote furiously, making notes of dates, facts and figures: he wanted this in writing so that he would not forget any single detail. Later, when alone, he would set fire to the notes knowing that they would be burned on his memory.

'Thanks, Saul,' he said, having filled three pages of his notebook and closed it quickly as Kazam began to walk toward him. 'I'll explain another time.'

'You don't have to, Kit. But do something for me, eh?'

'Anything.'

'Well, if you're thinking what I'm thinking, make sure you take good care of yourself, my boy.'

'You can bet your life on it,' Harper said.

'It's not my life I'm worried about, Kit.'

<h1 style="text-align:center">24</h1>

'Chalk and cheese,' Evans said, smiling broadly, as were all the other members of the group.

They had arrived at the test site shortly after eight o'clock, passing two men with shotguns who were guarding the entrance, and had been greeted by a tall muscular man, Piotyr, in his late twenties, his wizened grandfather, Leonid, and, far more importantly to everybody's minds, a mouth-watering smell. Everything had been unloaded from the truck apart from the sleeping bags – joy on joy, there were beds *and* bedrooms for everybody – and now they were sitting on proper chairs around a vast dining table wolfing down *blinis* with sour cream and drinking chilled vodka.

The only person in the room who seemed uneasy was Kazam. Kazam the Kazakh, Harper thought. Piotyr and Leonid were Russians and it was as if some age-old racial tension had surfaced in their chaperon and guide. When Kazam translated for them he was curt and there was a hard edge to his voice. Harper got the distinct impression that the Kazakh couldn't wait for the filming to be over so that he could return to his own kind.

Harper leaned back in his chair, sipped apple juice and looked around while thinking of chalk and cheese. Instead of the oil lamps of the control site farmhouse, this room was lit by generator-driven electricity, one sign among many of permanence. The furniture was sturdy, built to last and to stay in place; there were photographs on the walls and rugs on the floor; the fire had a heavy grate and wrought-iron tongs and shovel. This was a place of homesteaders, not a makeshift shelter of nomads.

Two women, either of which by their age might have been Piotyr's grandmother, entered with bowls of rice and dishes of what was unmistakably beef stroganoff.

'It's such a change,' Harper said to Kazam, 'to have something that doesn't necessitate asking you what it is.'

Kazam translated and Piotyr and Leonid nodded.

'Tell them that this is bloody good,' said Ned, through a mouthful of food.

'*Charoshi*,' Kazam relayed laconically.

Harper took his first taste. It wasn't bloody good, it was terrific: succulent beef, flavourful sauce with the right balance of paprika hotness, rich and creamy without being greasy. He turned to Kazam. 'Tell them,' he said, 'that we have come over six hundred kilometres today. That the journey was very tiring, very hot and very uncomfortable. But all that we have endured, over every single kilometre we travelled, was worth it for the warmth of their welcome and the excellence of their food.'

Piotyr smiled.

Kazam translated.

Leonid's smile joined that of his grandson.

'What's the plan for tomorrow?' Charly asked.

'Sorry,' Harper said, suddenly realizing she was looking at him. 'I was miles away.'

'What's the plan, the schedule, for tomorrow?' she repeated.

Harper turned to Ned enquiringly.

Ned turned to Patrick.

The director had nowhere to turn.

'We're up against it as far as time is concerned,' Patrick said, 'so we have to make the maximum use of our resources, running in parallel whenever possible. We split up and scout around for the best locations. We start filming at ten sharp. We'll only have a couple of hours at the most before the heat builds and the sun bleaches the colours. In that time I want to shoot all Jeremiah's speech in one segment in one location. That way we have something in the can and have the option of a voice-over for later shots should we run out of time. Let's break for lunch between one and four. Is that OK, Kazam?'

Kazam confirmed the arrangement with Piotyr and Leonid.

'In the afternoon,' Patrick continued, 'we'll move from location to location, shooting background shots and close-ups of Jeremiah repeating his speech, but this time in tight little scenes. We'll rehearse the script over breakfast so that you all know the content as a whole as well as the individual shooting segments: when you're scouting, try to match each location to what you believe is the most suitable segment. We'll carry on filming' – *Carry on Filming* sounded very appropriate to Harper, who had understood very little so far – 'till the light fades, then review progress over drinks and dinner. All clear?'

There were reassuring nods from Ned, Philip and the crew. Thank goodness for that, thought Harper.

'Just one small problem,' Kazam said. 'This is a working farm. In some places there will be heavy machinery – dangerous machinery. And remember the wolves. I have guards posted, but I would be happier if we all stick together.'

I bet you would, thought Harper.

'I don't know if we can afford the extra time that will take, Kazam,' Patrick said.

'I am here to smooth your way,' Kazam replied, 'not to put obstacles in your path. I know this farm well. I already have many possible locations in mind. When I hear the script, I will select the most appropriate for us all to visit. It will save you much time, I am sure. Your schedule will not be affected, I promise.'

'Well,' said Patrick, unconvinced and unwilling to relinquish control to a mere interpreter, but at the same time wondering about the insurance cover and whether there was a waiver in tiny print concerning attack by wolf (singular or plural, male or female), 'I'll compromise. You show us the main location, Kazam, and we'll start shooting while everyone else scouts out the other options. Can you cope with two parties.'

'Have no worries, Patrick sir,' Kazam said, smiling. 'Leave everything in the hands of your humble servant. I will arrange for a second guard to protect the other party.'

Harper yawned loudly.

'Sorry,' he said. 'I didn't mean to be impolite, but it's been a long hard day. I'm turning in. Kazam, perhaps Piotyr could show me to my room?'

Harper rose from the table and went across to collect his luggage while Kazam went through the translation. Piotyr gestured to the stairs with one hand and stretched out the other to indicate he would help carry the bags.

At the top of the stairs Piotyr waved his hand to the left and then overtook Harper, walking quickly to a room at the end of a long corridor. Opening the door, he flicked on the light and ushered Harper inside. Placing Harper's suit-case on the bed, Piotyr nodded and turned to leave.

'Where did you learn English?' Harper asked.

'*Vinavat?*'

'I know you understand me, Piotyr. When I complimented you on the warmth of your welcome and the excellence of the food, you smiled. *Before* Kazam translated.'

'Say nothing, please,' Piotyr said anxiously. 'I cannot talk now or Kazam will wonder why I have been so long. Tomorrow, maybe.'

'Tomorrow, definitely,' said Harper.

Piotyr reached the door.

'One last question,' Harper said. 'Are there really wolves around here?'

'Only the kind that have gold teeth.'

Harper was woken by the stuttering of tractor engines kicking into life. He checked his watch, saw it was still only half past six, rolled over and pulled the covers over his head. It was a day where it was more important to be late than early.

He got up at nine o'clock, washed, shaved, dressed – all without hurrying – and went downstairs at ten minutes to ten. Drew was seated in a straight-back chair in front of the window so that the light shone upon him; the make-up artist was bending over him, applying a light foundation to conceal the redness around the freshly plucked eyebrows and also every single line and blemish that gave Drew's face character. Drew was frowning. So was the make-up artist. Neither was helping the other. Harper walked past the film crew, busy assembling and checking their equipment, loading film into Polaroid cameras and generally exhibiting all the signs of prematch nerves, and sat down at the table where Charly, Evans, Philip and Ned were finishing breakfast.

'Good morning everyone,' he said.

'Good morning, Kit,' Charly said, licking jam slowly and pleasurably from her index finger and inadvertently making Ned's 'visualizing' eyes glaze over.

Charly looked totally refreshed after her night's sleep and ready for anything the day might throw at her. She was dressed in a loose-fitting pink vest, navy-blue shorts, rolled-down cream socks and ginger suede walking boots. Her hair was tied back with a white scarf, freckles peppered her fresh face and her chocolate-brown eyes sparkled. Harper, like Ned, was having trouble dragging his eyes from her.

'Haven't you heard that it's the early bird that catches the worm?' she said.

'Only in the land of sound-bites,' Harper replied. 'Where's Kazam?'

'Out with Piotyr and Leonid,' Charly said. 'Scouting, I presume.'

'Be prepared,' he said. 'Is that coffee I can smell?'

Charly nodded. 'Seems like no expense is spared here. There's a pot keeping warm on the stove in the kitchen. It's probably a little stewed by now, though. Still, that's the price a sluggard pays for lying in bed half the morning.'

Harper got himself a large mug of coffee, took the only clean plate left on the table and filled it to overflowing with hunks of freshly baked bread, slices of cold meat, cheese and a rosy-red tomato. He sipped the coffee and leaned back in the chair, smiling from ear to ear.

Kazam entered, a shotgun slung over one shoulder, with Leonid, Piotyr and a thick-set man clutching a machine gun. He clapped his hands to get everyone's attention and announced that they were ready to leave.

Harper groaned loudly. Looked down wistfully at his breakfast and said, 'This is too good to rush. I'll catch you up.'

'You should not wander about on your own,' Kazam said, tapping the stock of the shotgun. 'Remember the wolves. Perhaps,' he said, turning to Patrick, 'we should wait a little while.'

'And be behind schedule before we even start?' Patrick said. 'No, let's get going. Someone show us the location for our main shot of Drew, the rest of you get scouting. Be back here at one o'clock sharp to compare notes.'

Kazam detailed Leonid and the guard to take Drew, Patrick, the cameraman and the sound engineer to the site that he had chosen and marshalled the others outside into a group to be led by himself and Piotyr. Both Kazam and Piotyr, for very different reasons, looked back at Harper before departing.

Harper drank some more coffee, made a doorstep sandwich of the bread, meat and cheese and walked to the window. The scouting party was heading west towards a distant field of golden wheat. Harper, sandwich in hand, slipped out of the door and made off in the opposite direction.

To his right – due south – were the blue waters of Lake Balqash: there the similarities with the control site ended. He could see boats on the lake; on the nearer shore were the outlines of the buildings of the small town of Balqash; immediately surrounding the stone-and-brick farmhouse, there were a large number of barns, all in good repair; in the fields, tractors were moving purposefully, reaping or sowing or ploughing according to the crops the fields contained; workers, stripped to the waist and wearing wide-brimmed straw hats, were busy on those hundred-and-one tasks that Harper had always imagined were necessary if a farm were to provide rich pickings rather than simply a scratched living. He took a bite of the sandwich and savoured the flavour of the cheese.

Harper headed towards the largest of the barns, pausing briefly to check inside the others – either neatly stacked with straw or bags of grain, or home to various types of heavy equipment. As he approached the big barn, he saw that a conveyor belt led up to the top. At the foot of the conveyor was a low-loader bearing an open-top steel container. He climbed up onto the wooden platform of the low-loader and peered inside the container. A mound of plastic, ready, Harper assumed, for the biodegrading process. This he had to see.

The high double doors to the barn were wide open. On the hard earth in front of them, a haze shimmered. As he stepped inside, the heat hit him like a speeding truck. In the centre of the barn was a very tall stainless steel silo emblazoned with the AUC diamond logo. There was a ladder on the side, leading up to the top of the silo to the point where the conveyor belt fed directly inside. A dozen twenty-five kilogram bags of dull grey powder, the Gaia enzyme, were stacked in two piles by the right-hand wall. On the ground behind the silo Harper could see three turbine fans wired up to a generator: the generator thudded, the fans whirred, achieving little except to direct a stream of hot air from the very lowest levels of the silo towards him. He looked up and saw that someone had removed a section of the corrugated roof to let heat rise upwards and outwards. The nearer he got to the silo, the hotter it became. He reached out his hand, then drew it back quickly when only inches from the steel. Too hot to handle.

He left the barn and stood outside in the relative cool, wondering what to do and where to go next. The lake. If he was to put his theory to the test, it had to be the lake. Still carrying the sandwich, now dry and curled up at the edges from the heat inside the barn, he set off southward.

Within ten minutes Harper could feel the baking sun on his face and his shirt sticking to his back. An apple orchard stood invitingly on his left and he decided to detour for a while to take advantage of its shade. As soon as he entered under the shelter of the trees he ditched the sandwich – better it was found here than in or near the barn. He walked along the fringe of the orchard, keeping the lake in view so that he would not lose his bearings.

Harper had only gone a little way when he came to a thick swathe of flat-tened grass. Something heavy had been dragged inside the orchard – recently too, otherwise the grass would have bounced back. He turned left and tracked the path of whatever had gone before him.

In the middle of the orchard was a clearing. In the middle of the clearing was a mound of freshly dug earth. The track stopped here.

Harper bent down and used his fingers to dig down into the mound. A few inches beneath the surface the earth was warm, a few inches further down he discovered blackened fragments. And then he found the bone.

An expert in anatomy would have told him that, by its length and thick-ness and the distinctive ball and socket joints at each end, this was the thigh bone of a cow. But Harper wasn't an expert. Yet he didn't need to be. The only relevant fact was that someone had burned an animal here, and that, in itself, was what was unusual. Farmers didn't burn animals – they were too valuable. Unless, that is, they had died of something that made them unfit for sale and consumption. It was all beginning to slot together: the jigsaw picture, that theoretical photograph in the developing fluid, was becoming clearer.

Harper filled in the hole he had dug, smoothing it over and sealing the smell of burnt flesh. Burning? There was something else important about burning. What was it? Damn! He remembered now. He had never got round to burning the notes he had made of Saul's phonecall. That must be his first task when he returned to the farmhouse – destroy the record of the conver-sation before Kazam was off duty and had an opportunity to snoop around his room. So, he resolved, quickly to the lake and hot-foot it back before the one o'clock deadline.

Retracing his steps, Harper jogged to the edge of the orchard and then slowed to a brisk walk. The lake didn't look more than a couple of miles away, but distances, as with so many things in life, can be very deceiving. After half an hour the buildings on the shoreline still seemed as far away. He was just beginning to wonder whether visiting the lake was a smart move when he heard a sound – and then he knew for certain that he had made the wrong decision.

Harper had heard enough of the irregular rhythms of diesel engines over the last couple of days to last him a lifetime and, more pertinently, to be able to recognize instantly the sound. A jeep – and fast approaching. To his left and right there were open fields; no patch of cover in which to hide. It looked like his run of luck had finally come to an end. There was nothing to do but brazen it out. He swivelled to meet the oncoming vehicle, stuck out his thumb and waved it in the air.

The jeep slowed and pulled alongside him. Harper opened the door, and heaved a sigh of relief. 'What are you doing here?' he asked Piotyr.

'Looking for you,' he replied, his voice low and solemn. 'I have been thinking. We do need to talk. Get in, we go to Balqash. There is something I must show you.'

'How did you get away from Kazam?' Harper said.

'I told him that we needed supplies. He was not happy, but what could he do?'

'Nothing, except order you to keep your mouth shut.'

Piotyr nodded. 'Kazam does not like you,' he said. 'He calls you Crazy Man, but I think he fears you. Why is that?'

'Maybe because a crazy man doesn't have the sense to leave well enough alone.'

'Then I am crazy too,' Piotyr said. 'That is what my grandfather thinks.'

The jeep sped over the rough ground, coming close to the shore and veering to the left towards the town.

'Are there fish in the lake?' Harper asked, feeling the necessity, like Saul, to double check everything.

'Of course. Very big lake – fresh water here, salt water in the east – very big fish.'

'And you eat the fish?'

'Why not?'

'Precisely.'

Balqash was more a settlement than a town. It reminded Harper of how movies portrayed Californian mining towns during the gold rush: the houses, shops and railway station were constructed mostly of wood, the streets were compacted earth with boardwalks, and the people were the kind who either avoided looking one directly in the eye or made a point of doing so challengingly.

Piotyr established an alibi by buying some provisions from a general store and five large fish for the evening meal. No one spoke to him, other than was absolutely necessary in order to make the transactions. Maybe, Harper wondered, it was because of his presence, the mistrust of obvious strangers not being an uncommon phenomenon around the globe.

'We have time for a drink,' Piotyr said, leading Harper to a bar on the waterfront.

They sat outside under a matting shade. Piotyr had a beer, Harper an ice-cold apple juice.

'Kazakhstan is the land of apples,' Piotyr said, making small talk as if having to build up to what was really important. 'Alma-Ata means Father of Apples. In Kazakh the name is Almaty, but the meaning is much the same.'

'But Kazakhs and Russians are very different, aren't they?'

'History has taught the Kazakhs to hate Russians,' Piotyr said.

'So why did you come here?'

'Money,' Piotyr said, shaking his head. 'Is that not what drives men?'

'There are other reasons for doing something. Love, perhaps. And sometimes simply because an action is morally right, or inaction is morally wrong.'

'In our case, money – greed – lured us here. My family have been farmers for generations – before the revolution on their own land, then on a collective farm and finally back to having their own land again. I went to university – that was where I learnt English – to study agriculture: the old Soviet Union, because it desired to be self-sufficient in wheat, took farming very seriously. If I had never been to university,' he said with a heavy sigh, 'then none of this would have happened. Not to *my* family, at least.'

Piotyr looked down into the depths of his beer glass. Harper sipped his juice and waited patiently for the continuation of the story.

'On my graduation day, Kazam and a man called Mueller came to the university. They talked to me and the members of my family who were there to see their dear little Piotyr graduate top of the class. Kazam and Mueller had a file on me. Knew all about me, my family and its history. They told us about Kazakhstan – the rich, fertile land, the cheap Kazakh labour, all the good things that a farmer loves to hear – and offered us an interest-free loan to buy this farm at half its market value. And lots of money if we would help them with their experiment – biodegrade the plastic, use the recycled product as fertilizer and supply them with facts and figures on crop yields and so on. It was an attractive proposition.'

'Too good to be true?'

'Leonid says that we are rich and that we should count our blessings, but—'

Church bells rang out. Harper, with the total disruption of his normal routine, had forgotten it was Sunday. He shook his head at his own stupidity.

Piotyr raised his glass and downed his beer in one long swallow. 'Come,' he said. 'It is time to visit the church.'

He led Harper along the main street to a small wooden building complete with short spire, little bell tower and dull bronze cross. There was a picket fence around the church. A line of people was filing inside.

'I'm hardly dressed for church,' Harper said, embarrassed by his jeans, dirty from kneeling down and digging at the mound, and his sweat-stained shirt.

'We do not go inside,' Piotyr said, leading Harper along the side of the church and to the back. 'This is why we have come to Balqash. This is what I must show you.'

Harper stood on the brink of the graveyard, frozen to the spot while memories of another graveyard in another time took control of his brain. Dimly aware of Piotyr walking over to a row of twelve graves set aside from the rest, he made an effort to pull himself together, brushed away a tear and followed. He looked along the row of graves.

'These are workers from our farm and members of my family,' Piotyr said, walking alone the line before stopping at the end and looking down sadly. 'And this is my wife. Help me, Mr Harper. Help me rid our land of the curse.'

They walked back to the jeep in silence, each of them reliving the past – the good times that made the deep-down pain of the bad so much harder to bear – and neither of them willing for the moment to contemplate either the present or the future.

'I know how you feel,' Harper finally said as the jeep bumped back towards the farmhouse. 'I lost my wife too. Cancer.'

'Then you will help?'

Harper nodded. 'You have my word,' he said solemnly. 'But, Piotyr, in order to help I need to ask you some questions. Forgive me for any hurt I may cause.'

The questions he asked were only for confirmation, merely adding the last touches of colour to the details of the picture that had now developed fully in Harper's mind.

'Drop me off at the orchard, Piotyr. I'll walk back from there. We can't take the risk that Kazam might see us together.'

'What will you do?'

'I have a theory. One that explains your curse. I need to talk it through with Andrew and Charly.'

'Can you trust them?'

Harper paused before answering. Both Evans and Charly, for their own and very different reasons, would find their loyalties tested. But, for his own and very different reasons, Harper needed to trust them both.

'There is no alternative,' he said.'

They had reached the first of the apple trees. Piotyr pulled to a stop.

'Can you come to my room tonight?' Harper said, climbing out of the jeep. 'Be there to provide some evidence when I talk to Andrew and Charly?'

'What time?'

'Midnight. When, hopefully, Kazam will be fast asleep. Make sure he drinks lots of vodka tonight, just in case.'

'I will leave that to my grandfather,' Piotyr said with a wicked smile. 'Leonid has the cunning of an old man. He will find a way.'

Harper turned to go, then extended his right arm back into the jeep. He shook Piotyr's hand, sealing his promise to help.

'Till tonight,' he said. 'In the meantime, watch out for wolves, Piotyr.'

'And you too, my friend,' Piotyr replied.

Wolves were one thing, Harper thought as he strode back. But the guns that were carried to shoot them was an entirely different matter.

It was ten minutes to one when Harper arrived back at the farmhouse. He walked up the stairs to his room. His suitcase and rucksack were where he had left them. His notebook wasn't. Instead of being tucked down the side, it was on top.

Careless!

Careless of Kazam not to replace it in the exact same position.

Careless of himself not to have burnt the notes at the first opportunity.

And now, he realized, there wasn't much bloody point.

25

Killing time – that was the phrase running through Harper's mind. Lunch, the afternoon's shooting sessions, the evening meal were all minor acts to be sat through before the main attraction came on stage at midnight.

The two groups – with the exception of Kazam, who wandered in a little later carrying a Polaroid camera instead of the shotgun – arrived back on the dot of one o'clock, hot and tired. Jeremiah Drew went straight upstairs to wash off what little was left of the make-up after the combination of heat and sweat had taken its toll. Everyone else flopped into chairs around the table and reached desperately for the pitchers of water or the bottles of beer. Only when thirsts had been slaked did anyone contemplate eating. And even then most had second thoughts. *Bortsch* (beetroot soup) and *kotlyet* (the Russian high-cholesterol version of a hamburger) were not the greatest stimulators of saliva glands.

'So what have we got in the way of locations?' asked Patrick.

A large number of Polaroid photographs were spread across the table in front of him.

'The field of corn looks favourite,' said Ned. 'Shooting Drew in front of it at sunset would be what I'd go for.'

'Thanks, Ned,' Patrick said, wanting input from the group, but not that much. 'I think you can leave the final selection and timetable to me.'

'They're planning to start harvesting tomorrow,' Ned pressed. 'We could shoot that at sunrise. Make a good contrast.'

'Since you intend to film the biodegrading process,' Kazam said, 'I wondered whether you might like to do that at sunrise.'

When the day is at its coolest, Harper thought cynically. And when the fans have had another day working away at reducing the heat inside the barn.

'I took some pictures of the location,' Kazam said, handing over a couple of Polaroids showing the silo and conveyor belt.

'Thank you, Kazam,' Patrick said, hardly bothering to look. 'I'll bear that in mind.' He examined one of the photographs on the table. 'What's this white stuff?'

'Cotton,' said Philip. 'Rather pretty, I thought.'

'I like white,' Patrick said, nodding to himself. 'White is symbolic.'

'Really?' Harper teased.

'All things good,' Patrick explained with a serious expression on his face. 'Crusaders, nights in white satin, doves, you know? I don't suppose we have any doves around here, do we, Kazam?'

Harper looked round the table to stop himself groaning. The film crew were nodding sycophantically. Evans seemed as if he was trying hard not to pinch himself to check whether he was having a bad dream. Charly rolled her eyes at him. Kazam – spoilsport – shook his head. 'I can arrange most things, given time and money,' he said, 'but not white doves.'

'Pity,' Patrick said.

'We could paint some pigeons,' Harper said, suppressing a grin.

'I like it,' Patrick said, smiling, but very briefly. 'No, it wouldn't work,' he sighed. 'I mean, how would they fly?'

Charly gave Harper a warning glance. Must have known that he was thinking of suggesting they fix the wings open with splints and propel the birds in a low glide over Drew's head from a catapult out of camera shot.

'What else have we got then?' Patrick said.

'Sheep. Cows,' Ned said, shrugging his shoulders unenthusiastically.

'Animals are important,' Harper said, for no better reason but to see Kazam's reaction.

No change on the stony face.

'We better have some of them then, I suppose,' Patrick said. 'Right. Here's how I see it. Cotton, first and foremost. Then sheep. I want to postpone a decision on the cows until I've seen them in person,' – in person, thought Harper? – 'they can look pretty threatening, some cows. Finally, we do the corn. Take an hour off, Jeremiah, then we need to put you through make-up again. And don't forget to change into another clean white shirt for continuity purposes.'

'And tomorrow?' said Kazam.

'We wrap it all up by shooting the harvest, the biodegrading and recycling process and Drew with a handful of the enzyme stuff, showing it to camera and smiling down lovingly.'

'I will make the arrangements for us all to leave on Tuesday,' Kazam said, relief showing on his face. 'And for the operator to stand by the conveyor first thing in the morning.'

'Time to make some phonecalls,' Patrick said, stifling a yawn. 'See you back down here at four.'

Harper followed everyone upstairs, making a mental note of the positions of Charly's and Andrew's rooms. Once in his room he phoned home and then lay on his bed for ten minutes until everything was quiet. Tiptoeing along the corridor, he stopped first at Charly's door, knocked gently and waited, casting watchful looks to right and left and ears pricked for any creaking of the stairs.

'Who is it?'

'Kit,' he whispered.

'Go away, Harper.'

'Open the door. Please.'

'What do you want?' she said, poking her head through a minimal crack in the open door.'

He pushed his way inside and shut the door behind him. Tried not to look at Charly or her bare legs as she stood there wrapped only in a blouse.

'What do you think you're doing?' Charly said. 'Get the hell out of here.'

'Keep your voice down. I only want to talk to you for a moment.'

'Then say your piece and go,' she said, backing away.

'I want you to come to my room at midnight tonight.'

'Forget it, Harper. I won't feel any different at midnight to the way I do right now.'

'Sorry,' he said. 'I suppose I could have put that better.'

'And that too, I hope.'

'This is serious, Charly. There is something very wrong here—'

'You can say that again.'

'Shut up, Charly, and listen,' he said with such a stern expression that she took another pace backwards. 'And it would help if you trusted me from the outset for once, rather than only after the event. Just because everyone else you've ever known has always had an ulterior motive, it doesn't mean to say that I am the same. I *had* hoped you would have learnt that by now.'

'I *was* beginning to trust you, Kit,' she said. 'And then you come bursting into my room. Tell me, what am I supposed to think?'

'I got carried away,' he said. 'Didn't think. This is very important, that's all. I have a theory. A theory that, if it holds water, will blow AUC apart. I can't explain right now. I need to talk it through with you and Andrew. So, will you come to my room at midnight or not?'

'Andrew will be there?'

'Yes,' he sighed. 'Andrew will be there. Although I haven't asked him yet.'

'OK, I'll be there,' she said. 'But if you don't mind, I'll make the arrangements with Andrew.'

'So much for trust,' he said.

'A girl's got to take care of herself.'

'And men too. If I'm right, we could all be in grave danger. Say nothing about this to anyone. And tell Andrew the same. I am trusting *you*, Charly. Trusting you with all our lives, perhaps. Don't let me down.'

Harper turned his back on her and marched out of the door. A touch melodramatic, he appreciated, but he had made his point. Maybe even two points. And if he could choose only one of trust and life-and-death importance, which would it be?

★

If Harper had ever been under the impression that shooting a commercial was glamorous, then the afternoon would have been a totally disillusioning experience. The boredom was mind-numbing in its magnitude: he could feel his brain cells atrophying by the thousand with each slowly passing second. Take after take, each seemingly identical, of the same scene until Patrick declared himself satisfied and they moved on to repeat the process in a different location. Drew had said the same words – not always perfectly, granted – so many times that he was beginning to sound more wooden than Pinocchio. Sometimes they used three cameras simultaneously, shooting from head on, the side and even, Sergio Leone-style, from the hip. Harper wondered whose job was the most skilful: Patrick and his camera operators who, like monkeys sitting at typewriters, could have so many attempts that one shot was bound to be of Shakespearean proportions, or the editor, who had to review every inch of miles of footage, pan out the few nuggets from the mass of dross and weld the gold together so that the joins did not show. The artist would get the credit, the artisan the hard graft.

As soon as they had returned to the farmhouse, Patrick handed over the day's videos to one of Kazam's drivers and they were sped off to the airport at Alma-Ata so as to be on the editor's desk first thing in the morning. It was, in Patrick's words, a *symbolic moment* and the signal for everyone to relax. Cold beer was downed, then people drifted off to their rooms to wash and change for dinner. A dinner that, against all Harper's expectations, would turn out to be a celebration.

'Great news,' Evans shouted excitedly as he entered the room.

The faces around the table turned to him in expectation of something really terrific, like a takeaway Chinese meal.

'Laurelle have got big problems,' he said. 'UN inspectors in Iraq have apparently found a large supply of nerve gas – all in bright, shiny Laurelle canisters, if the report is accurate.'

The faces took on a bored expression: half of them had probably never even heard of Laurelle, let alone its planned acquisition by AUC.

'Is that it?' Patrick said, verbalizing the thoughts of the many.

'No, there's something even better,' Evans said, his eyes shining brightly. 'We've found the inhibitor.' This time the news was greeted with total incomprehension. '*We* have *found* the bloody inhibitor,' he said, doing a little dance of joy.

Harper turned to Charly. 'Have you made the arrangements for tonight?' he whispered. 'Does he know yet?'

She shook her head. 'Haven't had a chance.'

'Then you better do it quickly before he ruins everything by spending the entire evening getting blind drunk.'

'I checked my email before coming down here,' Evans said. 'There was a message from Françoise. She's found the inhibitor. Isn't it wonderful news? The final obstacle to launching the enzyme has been removed.'

Harper kicked Charly under the table. 'Do it now,' he said in her ear. 'And, while you're alone with him, get him to send a message asking for a sample of the inhibitor to be picked up by the plane and sent over for us to test *in situ* before we leave.'

Evans walked over to stand proudly by Charly.

'Sorry, Andrew,' she said, seizing the moment and his hand, 'but before you sit down, can you let me use your laptop and mobile? You've reminded me that I need to check my email to see if there are any messages from my grandfather.' She stood up and manoeuvred Evans towards the stairs. 'It won't take a minute. Then we can raise a glass or two without interruption.'

They disappeared briefly upstairs and Harper imagined the rain pouring down on Andrew's parade. He watched Leonid circulate among them with an ice-cold bottle of vodka and felt little red demons tempting him. But, like Kazam, he forced himself to settle reluctantly for a glass of apple juice.

A few minutes later, Charly and Evans, his eyes shining less brightly now, reappeared.

'Congratulations, Andrew,' said Drew. 'Like you, I'm very much relieved by your news. I would have hated to think of AUC wasting all this money on an advertising campaign that could never be used because the product could never be marketed. Cheers.'

Glasses were raised in the air. 'Cheers,' was echoed. Drinks were sipped. Harper thought he saw a puzzled look on Kazam's face; but their guide gave a customary shrug and took a longer, and more appreciative, gulp of his apple juice.

The party atmosphere grew and helped the meal pass more quickly. The fish, baked with herbs and served with boiled potatoes and plain rice, was the best, and healthiest, thing Harper had eaten in days. The drink flowed and faces began to flush. By the time Harper, Charly and Evans, one by one at discreet intervals, left the table, either no one noticed their departure, or they were all past caring. Kazam was no exception. Harper's last vision of the room as he turned to go up the stairs was of the Kazakh smiling with unfocused eyes into the bottom of his fifth glass of Leonid's specially spiked apple juice.

★

'Why Kazakhstan?' Harper said. 'That's what I asked you, Andrew, when you were giving me a tour of the laboratory. And that's what I've been asking myself ever since. It didn't make much sense then; it makes even less sense now.'

Evans was sitting stiffly in the only chair in the room; the table lamp, partially covered by a T-shirt, dimly showed the sulky expression on his face. Harper was perched on the window ledge, Piotyr standing with his arms crossed and Charly semi-reclining on the bed, her back resting against the wall and her legs drawn up underneath her.

'Is this going to take long?' Evans asked. 'You have already spoilt my evening. I'd rather you did not do the same with my night's sleep.'

'Sometimes in advertising,' Harper said, ignoring the testiness of a man who could see defeat about to be plucked from the jaws of success, 'we test a new campaign in as real life a situation as is possible. We run the new advertising in one region of the country and measure the effects against a control region: if one can keep all the other marketing variables the same – the level of distribution in shops, any sales promotion activity, special offers and so on – then any increases in sales of the product in the test region relative to the control region must be due to the new advertising. Isn't that pretty much what you are trying to do in Kazakhstan with the Gaia enzyme?'

'Yes,' Andrew said a little uncertainly, 'but I fail to see your point.'

'Let me put it another way. Think about when you are conducting a drugs trial. You follow the same procedure. Your test group is administered the new drug and your control group is given a placebo – a pill which is, say, just powdered sugar – because the mere fact of receiving treatment can psychologically make the patient feel better. The patient expects his condition to improve, and so in some cases it does. For you to assess the benefits – or the side effects – of your new drug, you compare the results of the two groups, test and control.'

'Sheer repetition of your argument, Kit, will not make it any stronger.'

'The point I am making is that any comparison is only valid if the two groups are identical, apart from the treatment or pill they receive. All other variables must be strictly controlled so that the two groups are an exact match, otherwise you can't be certain that any effect is due to the drug and not a difference in some other variable. For the trial of the Gaia enzyme you set up the same type of experiment, the test site uses the biodegraded product of the enzyme, the control site carries on with its conventional fertilizers. Any differences must therefore be due to the enzyme.'

Evans gave a grudging nod. 'That is the logic behind the methodology, yes.'

'But,' Harper continued, 'the experiment only works – the logic only stands up – if all the other variables are the same. Now, think back, Andrew. What was your first reaction when we arrived at this farm?'

'I can't remember. Relief that the journey was over? Ecstatic that there were no stomach-churning smells of *plov* or welcoming glasses of *koumis*?'

'No, Andrew. Your first words – your gut reaction – were "chalk and cheese". Now do you see what is wrong?'

'It was a figure of speech, that's all. We have two farms, both in the same country, both on the shores of a lake, both growing the same crops.'

'And there the similarity ends. All other variables are different. This is a flawed experiment. But, much worse than that, it is a *purposely* flawed experiment.'

Charly sat bolt upright and stared at Harper. 'If you are telling us,' she said, 'that AUC has wasted five years and countless sums of money on this trial, then I hope you have damned good evidence to support this theory.'

'Unfortunately, yes,' Harper said, no trace of self-satisfaction in his voice, only an anxious look on his face. He rubbed the scar subconsciously. Charly, reading the sign, frowned. 'If we are talking of chalk and cheese,' he continued, 'then lets start by comparing Kazakhs and Russians. And here, Piotyr, you must correct me if I am wrong or interrupt if I miss out anything of importance.

'Russians have a history of farming – and this family more than most – and they have a permanent relationship with the land: Kazakhs are basically nomads, independent of the land itself, moving as they do from place to place with their herds.'

'Kazakhs,' Piotyr said, nodding, 'are the descendants of the hordes of Genghis Khan. In Russian the word *kazakh* is an insult: it means free rider and outlaw.'

'When the Russians,' Harper continued, 'for want of a better word, colonized Kazakhstan, Stalin tried to force the Kazakhs onto collective farms. Do you know what their response was? Rather than accept collectivization, working for the state and being tied down to one place for the rest of their lives, they massacred their herds: the history books say that 24 million sheep and goats, 5 million cows and 3 million horses were slaughtered. And then hundreds of thousands of Kazakhs died in the resulting famine.'

'But that is history, Kit,' Evans said, shaking his head. 'You just said so yourself.'

'But,' Harper sighed, 'the mind-set of the Kazakh and the Russian is still totally different. Compare the two farms we have seen. On the control site there were oil lamps: here there are generators and electricity. There the buildings were in disrepair, here they are well maintained. When I went for a walk to Lake Zaysan, it was well into the morning before any Kazakhs were up and about and in the fields: here, they start at dawn – and they also work on Sundays. Like Françoise, it seems – but we can come on to that later. Had you, like me, forgotten that today was Sunday? So it isn't just the psychological make-up of the two peoples that is fundamentally different, it is the working practices, too.'

'So you're saying,' Charly said, her eyes narrowed in concentration and her fingers nervously running over her lips, 'that Mueller, who designed this trial, chose these two sites in Kazakhstan in order to fiddle the figures – to make it appear that the enzyme was performing better than the existing methods?'

'I wish that was all that I was saying,' Harper said. 'I think there was a much more sinister and devious reason. A much more evil motive. Something that explains what Piotyr calls the curse on this land.'

'You were beginning to win me over,' Evans said. 'Until you started talking of curses. Magic and science are incompatible.'

'To a scientific ignoramus like myself,' Harper said, 'all science can seem like magic. The impossible happens before your very eyes.'

Evans shook his head sadly. 'You sound like Crazy Man again.'

'I'm beginning to regret that incident,' he said.

'Then don't,' said Charly, smiling up at him.

'OK,' he said, smiling back. 'I repeat my question. Why Kazakhstan? That is the mystery. You don't need to travel all the way to central Asia to rig an experiment. If it were simply to fiddle the difference in yields of crops, it could have been done in other countries much nearer to home. There is something, I believe, that made Kazakhstan the only possible choice for Mueller. Think back to our journey from the airport to the control site.'

'I'd rather not,' said Charly, giving a shudder.

'What did you see through the windows of the jeep?'

'Nothing,' Evans said. 'It was pitch-black most of the time.'

'For which Kazam was very grateful.'

'And I was asleep most of the way,' Charly said. 'As you well know.'

'When we were stopped by the *militsia*,' Harper said, 'it wasn't simply a random check. I think they patrol that road – and probably others in that area, too – on a regular basis. For a very specific purpose – to make sure people carry on driving.'

Charly gave him a puzzled look.

'Immediately before we were stopped,' he explained, 'there was one strange thing I noticed. Mile after mile of electrified fence. I thought I knew what might be on the other side, but I got Saul to do some checking.'

'And?' Charly said.

'The fence encloses another sort of test site. Where the Russians tested their nuclear weapons.' Harper paused to let the import sink into Evans's mind. 'Between 1948 and 1992 an average of fifteen atom bombs *a year* were exploded at that site south of Semey. Their testing programme had two side effects on the people living nearby. The first was genetic mutations. At the control site, according to Ned, the girl who served us at dinner had six fingers on each hand.'

'The state that Ned is in most of the time,' Evans said, 'I wouldn't place too much emphasis on his ability to count. He could even have been hallucinating.'

'But I wasn't,' Harper said. 'When I was on the shores of Lake Zaysan, I saw a fish with an extra pectoral fin.'

'Jesus Christ, Kit,' Charly said. 'Are you saying that the Gaia enzyme causes genetic mutations?'

'Tell them,' he said to Piotyr.

'There have been three cases among the workers in the last two years,' the Russian said, frowning. 'A boy born with webbed feet; another with only one eye; a girl with no arms, her hands growing directly from the shoulders.'

Evans stared into the far corner of the room, unwilling to meet Piotyr's gaze.

'There's worse,' Harper said. 'I believe the product of the Gaia enzyme also shares the same property as the other side effect of the nuclear testing. Cancer. I think the fertilizer somehow causes cancer. And that explains what Piotyr regards as the curse on the land.'

'But it can't do,' Evans protested. 'Gaia was rigorously tested in our laboratories before this trial. I did the first small-scale tests myself. Then, in the larger-scale laboratory tests at the special facility in Den Haag, the fertilizer was used on a range of different crops and they were fed to a wide variety of animals from mice to monkeys. There were no cancerous side effects.'

'If the dead could talk, Andrew, there are some in Balqash graveyard who would dispute that point. And one of those would Piotyr's late wife.'

'So Piotyr's wife died of cancer?' Charly said.

It wasn't a question; it was a statement, and one that, to Harper, carried an unmistakable message.

'I know what you're thinking, Charly,' he said. 'That I've let my judgement be clouded because Piotyr and I share a common history – a common tragedy. But it isn't like that. This isn't some bitter grief-ridden conspiracy theory, it *is* a conspiracy. Kazam, with his talk of non-existent wolves' – Piotyr gave a mocking laugh and tossed his head – 'and his guided tours, has done his very best to keep us from seeing anything that would raise any suspicions, doubts or fears. You both have to come to terms with the fact that Mueller chose the control site at Lake Zaysan because he knew it would disguise the mutagenic and carcinogenic side effects of the Gaia enzyme. He must have found out what was occurring when animals were fed the fertilised crops during the laboratory trials and then he covered up the deaths of those animals.'

'Oh, God,' Evans said. 'That was the facility where GreenWay released all the animals.'

'Jeremiah was adamant that GreenWay had nothing to do with it,' Charly said. She paused for thought. 'So you think that Kazam is involved in this conspiracy?' Charly said. 'And that he has been protecting himself by restricting our movements?'

'Kazam,' Piotyr said, 'told us not to mention the deaths of the people or the farm animals – cows, sheep and pigs have died too: he ordered us to burn the carcasses and bury them in a pit. Then he paid us a special bonus, and promised us another when you had all been and gone. Kazam knows I speak English and he gave me strict instructions that I was not to talk to anyone on this visit, or permit you to wander around on your own.'

Harper nodded. 'Kazam, along with Mueller, was responsible for choosing and recruiting Piotyr and his family. Kazam, I presume, is also the person who feeds the results of the trial back to AUC headquarters, and edits out anything that would suggest that Gaia isn't the miracle product we have all assumed it to be. But there *has* to be someone else involved.'

'I hope you're not suggesting,' Evans said angrily, 'that I have followed in my predecessor's footsteps?'

'If I didn't believe in your honesty and integrity, Andrew, you wouldn't be sitting here now. The risks are much too great.'

'Then who else?' asked Charly. 'Oh, no,' she said. You're not suggesting—'

'Consider how many fortuitous coincidences there have been lately. Laurelle about to experience a drop in share price because of the link with Iraq. The attack on the jogger in the park – someone who just happens to be the EC commissioner who would probably have rejected the takeover of Laurelle by AUC, or at the very least delayed it for a few months, and has now been replaced by a deputy who I believe is being blackmailed into giving swift approval. And finally the email today claiming that the inhibitor has been discovered. There's only one person who could orchestrate – order – all those events. It's your grandfather, Charly. Sir Angus is pulling the strings on this conspiracy. *He* is behind it, and everything else that has happened.'

'You don't give up on your theories, do you? I remember you once saying that all business is corrupt, and the bigger the business the more corrupt it is. A company takes its lead from the top. If you're trying to prove that point, I can tell you one thing for sure. My grandfather would not kill anyone.'

'So you buy Mueller's death as simply the result of a serial killer at work? Even despite all the other coincidences? Well, I hope you're right, but I don't think so.'

'And I hope I'm right too, Kit. For one thing, despite all his faults, I love my grandfather and I cannot believe he would be involved in anything like this. For another, and more selfish reason, this could ruin me.'

'No one can place any blame on you, Charly.'

'I didn't mean ruin my reputation – although the mud will stick to everyone in AUC if this comes out – I meant ruin me financially. When I was twenty-one my grandfather gave me one hundred thousand shares in AUC. How much do you think those shares will be worth if the company faces a law suit from Piotyr here and it emerges that there has been a cover-up of Watergate proportions?'

'The share price will drop,' Harper said, 'but—'

'The share price won't just drop, Kit, it will plummet. And I happen to have borrowed against my shares to buy the apartment in Brussels.'

'Ring your broker tomorrow. Sell the shares while you can still get a decent price.'

'Won't that alert whoever is actually behind all this. Won't it signal that I know what is going on?'

'That may not matter.'

Charly stared at him.

'Unfortunately,' he began to explain, 'there are three things that worry me more than a past killing. The first is that we have all been eating the product of Piotyr's cursed land. We may well have been exposed to whatever muta-gen or carcinogen has got into the food chain here. There's little we can do about that now, but perhaps, Piotyr, we can stick to fish and food bought from Balqash from now on.'

'I will arrange it,' he said.

'My second anxiety,' Harper continued, 'is that I took comprehensive notes when Saul phoned to give me the facts and figures on Kazakhs and nuclear testing and its side effects. Someone has been snooping around my room. My fear is that Kazam read those notes and has told Sir Angus their contents. In which case, your grandfather can assume I have worked out what has been going on, or at least have suspicions and am on the right trail. And that makes me a marked man. But, to look on the bright side, that might put you in the clear – I could have advised you to sell your shares without giving you any reason.'

Evans looked at Harper and frowned. 'So far in this conversation,' he said, 'you have always started with the least of the evils and worked up from there. I, therefore, hesitate to ask, but what is your third worry?'

'Let me ask you a question. Do you accept my theory of why Kazakhstan was chosen, and everything that follows from it?'

'It's very hard for me, Kit. The Gaia enzyme was my discovery – my baby, if you like. I don't want to believe it is anything but the miracle chemical it appears. And, as I said before, I conducted the first small-scale tests myself.'

'Why do you do these extensive trials?'

'Because you can't replicate real life in a laboratory.'

'And because large-scale can be a different dimension from small-scale?'

'Yes, of course. I would have thought that was blindingly obvious.'

'When you and Françoise demonstrated the oil-eating enzyme—'

'You're not going to tell me there's something wrong with that as well,' Evans interrupted.

'Not that I know of. No. It was just that you were very precise in the demonstration about the temperature.'

'Because each enzyme operates best at one specific temperature. I explained that to you at the time.'

'When I was looking around this morning I saw the silo where the biode-grading process – the chemical reaction – takes place. I not only saw it, but I touched it too. The silo was hot. Very hot. And, more relevantly, Kazam has taken pains to try to cool it down: there are fans surrounding the silo and a roof panel has been removed to let some of the hot air escape. To me that suggests the heat is important.'

'There was no heat generated in the tests I conducted,' Evans said, screwing up his mouth, 'but I suppose it *is* possible that when the chemicals are in bulk, greater heat is generated and then not dissipated.'

'What might the effects be?'

'It's hard to say.'

'Speculate, please.'

'It might cause a somewhat different reaction.'

'Sufficiently different to cause the side effects I have postulated?'

'It is not unknown,' Evans said.

'Come on, Andrew, lives depend on this. Give me a straight answer.'

'There are some substances – polynuclear aromatic hydrocarbons, PAHs for short – that form when fossil fuels are burnt and have been found to contaminate soil if buried. PAHs are known to be both carcinogenic and mutagenic. The heat generated by the biodegrading process operating in bulk might have resulted in PAHs being produced.'

'Then let us say for the moment that my theory is right. One last question, Andrew. Do you think Françoise has *really* found the inhibitor?'

'Why should she lie?'

'For money. And for your job.'

Evans shook his head dismissively. 'But I'll discover the truth as soon as I get back and run tests on the inhibitor myself.'

'*If* you get back, Andrew,' Harper said. 'If any of us get back, for that matter.'

'Isn't that a bit melodramatic?' Evans said. 'Do you really think Sir Angus – or whoever is behind this – would have us all killed?'

'One bad deed inevitably follows another. And the deeds get worse. It would simply be a natural progression – an escalation of past crimes. He is left with no other option, not if the secret is to be kept concealed.'

'I'm not saying that I go along with your thinking,' said Charly, 'but, assuming you are right, is there nothing we can do?'

'Andrew is the one who is at the greatest and the most immediate risk: he must leave here as soon as possible. For the rest of us, I think we're safe until the shooting of the commercial is finished and the video tapes are sent off. However, Charly, I think you should go too.'

'No way,' she said. 'This commercial is as much my responsibility as yours.

And it's the physical demonstration that I'm fit for the top position in AUC.'

'Which may not be worth having,' Harper pointed out.

'Then let's just say that I don't like leaving a job half-finished. I stay until the end.'

'Very well,' Harper said. And, he might have added, blood is thicker than water – whatever else happened, surely Charly would be spared. 'I'd like to sneak Andrew out in the morning. Piotyr, can you take him to Balqash and put him on a train to Alma-Ata?'

'If we can find an excuse for both our absences.'

'Once we have filmed the biodegrading and recycling process, Andrew will feign sickness and return to the farmhouse while the rest of us troop off with Kazam to the other locations. And if Piotyr has to go to Balqash to pick up some medicine—' Harper screwed up his mouth and shrugged his shoulders. 'Well, hopefully, that should be sufficient to cover Andrew's escape. If we're lucky; it might even buy us time for the rest of the day – if Andrew *was* actually sick, he wouldn't want to be disturbed.'

'It's beginning to sound like there are a lot of *ifs* in this plan,' Charly said. 'But if it's the only one we've got, then I suppose we have to go with it.'

'When you get to Alma-Ata, Andrew,' Harper said, 'jump on the first plane travelling west – an indirect route home will give you the best chance of not being spotted if Kazam starts to suspect something and arranges for someone to watch the airport. Then, once back in Brussels, go to your office and search the files for any trace Mueller might have left of the enzyme having side effects. We need concrete evidence if we are to be taken seriously when we finally blow the whistle. Only when the incontrovertible truth is out will we all be safe.'

'OK,' Evans said. 'I'll do what you say. But I still think you're letting your imagination run wild.'

'Me, too,' said Charly.

'Indulge me, both of you,' Harper said. He stood up, signalling the end of the meeting. 'It's a big day tomorrow. You ought to go back to your rooms and get some sleep.'

'Sleep! Very funny,' said Charly. 'How the hell do you expect us to sleep after the bombshell you've just dropped?'

26

If Sunday afternoon and evening had been about killing time, then, comparatively, Monday was a chronological bloody massacre.

Harper rose an hour before dawn and went downstairs, where he was met by an enveloping darkness, a brooding silence and the smell of last night's fish. He entered the kitchen, opened the side door to clear the air, made a pot of strong coffee, poured himself a large mug and took it into the main room. Throwing some kindling and a log on the dormant fire, he poked at the ashes until a soft red glow appeared. As the twigs of apple wood caught alight, he sat down and stared at the flames. Maybe a different focus would help him resolve matters.

He had slept little, if at all – he couldn't even be sure of that simple fact. It had been one of those interminable and confusing nights when even if he had dropped off for a while he had dreamt that he was awake. His mind had been too active, too preoccupied with intense emotions: desire and loving for Charly; an equally deep loathing of her grandfather who seemed capable of anything and willing to stop at nothing; and a heavy burden of responsibility. Apart from Andrew and Charly, both of whom for different reasons should not be at risk, there were eight others in his group; if his worst fears were realized, how was he going to get everyone away safely? He couldn't warn them; couldn't sit them all down around the table and explain his theory: that would only further arouse Kazam's suspicions and might precipitate exactly the action he feared. And anyway, Ned, for one, would just shake his head incredulously, smile pitifully and then call him Crazy Man. Maybe he was crazy.

'Penny for them,' Drew said, interrupting Harper's tortuous and tortured thought processes.

'Sorry?'

'You seem a million miles away.'

'That's where I'd like to be, I suppose,' Harper said, unable to bite back a sigh. 'I'm homesick, Jeremiah. How about you? Would you like to leave early? Maybe get away from here as soon as filming is over for the day?'

'I think Patrick is planning on having a big party.'

Harper groaned.

'Ned's very keen too,' Drew said.

'You surprise me,' Harper grunted.

'It's not a bad idea, Kit. A celebration of our role in a little slice of the future history of our planet. And this *is* Patrick's first commercial, after all. That occasion merits marking. Not to mention that we will all have worked very hard to shoot the whole thing in just a couple of days. Why not let everyone unwind before the long journey home? Where's the harm? If they have fat heads in the morning, what does it matter? They can sleep in the jeeps and the plane.'

'I guess you're right,' Harper relented, appreciating the potential of the idea. 'If they want to stay awake all night, that's fine by me. I tell you what though, let's make it really special. Let's all get dressed up.'

'I'm not sure that anyone has brought anything suitable.'

'If we can't make it a black tie event, we'll settle for second best – everyone must wear black. We might be able to borrow some clothes from Piotyr, if necessary. Or get him to buy some for us.'

'I'll talk to Patrick,' Drew said. 'He can make the arrangements with Kazam. Organize a special meal, perhaps even see if they have any wine around here. It would make a pleasant change from vodka.'

'I'll chip in a few hundred dollars of the agency's money,' he said. 'Get Patrick to make a list and Piotyr can drive into Balqash and pick up whatever is needed.'

Harper made his own mental list: untainted food, strong liquor, jet-black clothing – oh, and a couple of machine guns might not go amiss.

By dawn everyone was knee deep in the land of cotton. Harper wondered if he was the only one trying hard not to whistle Dixie. In the middle of the field, Drew, the sun rising spectacularly behind him, was clutching handfuls of the fluffy white balls and showing them to camera; on the outer edges, a hay fever-suffering production assistant was sneezing and Evans was clutching his stomach and groaning loudly. The sound engineer, his headphones amplifying every noise, declared himself to be 'not a happy bunny'.

Harper took Evans aside and led him out of earshot. 'All packed and ready to go?' he asked.

'Yes,' Evans replied uncertainly. 'But I must admit, in the cold light of day, your theory now seems a little far-fetched. If there are these side effects you claim – and I am reserving my judgement on that – then perhaps it isn't the Gaia enzyme that is the problem. Maybe the enzyme was contaminated at some point in the production process.'

'Then take a sample and analyze it when you get back,' Harper snapped at him. 'If it makes you happy.'

Evans nodded, then frowned. 'Don't take this the wrong way, Kit, but I can't help feeling you are totally on the wrong track.'

'Andrew,' Harper said, poking his finger in Evans's chest, 'just make sure *you* are on the right track as soon as Piotyr drops you at the station.' He shook his head in exasperation. 'Look, if I am wrong then what have you lost? One extra day of vodka drinking, that's all. But if I am right, then we have gained the element of surprise. You can be digging into the AUC files before anyone even suspects you are missing. Contact me on my mobile as soon as you have any concrete evidence.'

Evans shrugged.

'Don't give me any shrugs, Andrew. It implies a lack of faith. And,' he said with a wink, 'it's impossible to shrug and clutch your stomach convincingly at the same time.'

Harper turned and trudged back into the field to check on progress. The last thing he wanted was for the schedule to slip and for them to have spend another day and night here.

The camera had moved. Now it was directly behind Drew.

Harper walked up to Charly; tried to ignore the tanned legs and arms emphasized by the yellow shorts and vest and the way her hair shone like fire in the morning light; failed miserably. 'What's Patrick up to now?' he asked.

'Trying another POV, apparently,' she said, rolling her big brown eyes and sending Harper weak at the knees. 'Whatever that is.'

'Point of view. And this one seems to be the point of view of the sun. Must be something deeply symbolic about it. The fruits of Gaia witnessed by the dawn of a new era? Or it might just be that Jeremiah's make-up has run already and the rear view is his only option left.'

'How's Andrew?' Charly said, looking over her shoulder at Evans.

'Having second thoughts.'

'Can't blame him, I suppose.'

'Not you too, Charly?' Harper groaned.

'Look at it from his POV, Kit. Gaia is Andrew's baby, after all. He's bound to defend his *wunderkind* against any attack.'

'Oh, well,' he shrugged. 'Just as long as *you* still believe in me.'

She looked away. Suddenly seemed very interested in camera angles, or the optical effect of the spectrum of the dawn sun's rays as it intensified the whiteness of the cotton. Or anything but him.

'Thanks a bunch,' Harper said.

'Let me ask you a question, Kit,' she said, still staring across the field at the sun. 'Do you believe in God?'

'The concept is appealing,' he said. 'Yet the execution does not seem to be without flaws.'

'Don't duck the question,' Charly snapped back.

'Sort of,' he said. 'That's the best answer I can offer you. Whether it's a bloke with a long white beard who created Heaven and Earth and was responsible for such diverse events as the flood and the Judgement of Solomon, I don't know.'

'How about the bit about omnipresent, omnipotent and omniscient then?'

'I'd like to believe that, but—'

'I feel the same,' she said, turning her face towards him. 'About God and you. Because I don't buy the whole package doesn't mean I don't like the product.'

'I'm sure there's a compliment in there somewhere,' Harper said. 'If only I could work my way past the treble negatives. Even then I have an uneasy feeling it might prove to be backhanded.'

'Then don't analyze so much.'

'Expect little, and be satisfied with less, eh?'

'It's time you stopped using that maxim,' she said. 'And that's not just my opinion, it's Saul's too. That Sunday we had lunch at his place, when you were setting the table and Saul and I were in the kitchen with Cassie, he said it was better to think in terms of there being no such things as problems, only opportunities.'

'I've always struggled with that one.'

'Always?' she said, tilting her head.

'Come on,' Harper said, setting off in the direction of Patrick. 'It's time to put some pressure on.'

'Yes,' Charly said. 'My sentiments entirely.'

An hour later the cotton was forgotten (but not the conversation), the flock of sheep munching grass had passed into celluloid (well, videotape) history, and Harper stood with the rest of the group in the barn housing the silo. There was no sign of the giant fans, the roof panels had been replaced (somewhat hastily it appeared, judging from the small gap that let in a single – symbolic? – slanting ray of light) and the temperature was a few degrees lower than on Harper's first visit. But there were beads of sweat running down Kazam's brow.

'What do you think?' Harper asked Evans.

'It's hot, I grant you.'

'Thank you. I rest my case.'

'But not as hot as I had expected from what you reported last night.'

'It's had another day to cool down, that's why. Give it another hour or so and Gaia gobbling away at a fresh meal of plastic and we'll soon be back to Swedish sauna temperatures.'

The conveyor belt began to roll and all eyes switched their focus to the top of the silo.

'Time to get your sample,' Harper said, 'while attention is directed elsewhere.'

Evans took out a penknife and made a small slit in one of the sacks containing the enzyme. Using the blade of the knife he scooped some of the grey powder into a tobacco tin that Leonid had discarded.

'That ought to do it,' he said, putting the lid on the tin and placing it in his trouser pocket. 'Enough here to degrade a lorry load of plastic, so more than ample for the tests I want to run.'

From the top of the conveyor the first items of plastic began to roll off the black rubber belt and drop to their doom inside the silo. Three video cameras were capturing the moment from all available points of view except that of the plastic itself. With luck, Patrick would not call for volunteers to climb the steel ladder and descend into the silo.

'Cut,' shouted Patrick in a bored voice after a couple of minutes of what was admittedly pretty unspectacular footage. 'OK, Jeremiah, foot of the silo, please.'

Drew took up position by the lever which released the biodegraded product and fed it into a waiting trailer. The make-up artist ran in, straightened Drew's tie, dabbed lightly at his brow and brushed a little powder over where the perspiration had broken out.

'On my cue,' Patrick called, 'pull the lever and fill the trailer. Then cup both hands to take a scoop. Make sure you grab lots. I'm going for a close-up here of the stuff spilling from your cupped hands.'

More symbolism, Harper sighed to himself. Unmistakably heavy-handed this time. Our cup(ped hands) runneth over!

'Action!' Patrick commanded.

Drew turned to pull the lever.

'No, no, no,' Patrick said, shaking his head. 'Keep facing the camera, Jeremiah, love.'

There was then a heated discussion between actor and director as Drew questioned how he was supposed to move the large lever with both hands while still pointing his body at the camera, and Patrick suggested that the obvious answer was to use one hand only, dear.

'Action,' Patrick finally said.

Drew placed his hand on the lever. And withdrew it swiftly with an accompanying wince.

'Cut,' Patrick groaned.

'Sorry,' Drew said. 'Couldn't help it. Natural reaction. The handle is damned hot.'

'Try to remember, Jeremiah, that you're a star,' Patrick said, 'not a baby. Bear the pain, eh? It's only for a second. Right. And action.'

Drew, after a shrug that would presumably be edited out, swung at the handle with his right hand and knocked the valve open. Light-brown sand-like grains poured into the trailer to form a picturesque cone. He bent forward, head unnaturally upright but to camera, cupped his hands and dipped them into the trailer.

Drew screamed. Held his hands in the air, then blew on them before finally tucking them under his armpits.

'What the hell now?' Patrick asked in a tone which betrayed a distinct lack of sympathy and forbearance.

'It's burning hot,' Jeremiah said, hopping from one foot to the other, his lips drawn back in pain.

'Told you so,' Harper whispered to Evans.

'No need to sound so smug.'

'Every need, Andrew. I think it's about time you started groaning again.'

Evans doubled up as if in pain, clutched his stomach with both hands and let out a loud moan.

'I do not believe this,' Patrick said, grasping his head in both hands. 'Take five, everyone. Take bloody five.'

Five turned out to be more like thirty. Drew left the barn to plunge his hands in cold water, a hunt took place for a suitable pair of gloves (white –a supposed contrast, if anyone ever asked, to the colour of the sandy grains), the trailer was emptied (for continuity purposes) and put back into position ready for what would seem like countless takes of the now be-gloved Drew, and Evans took to his sickbed (under a blanket in the back of Piotyr's jeep). Harper had wanted to shake his hand and wish him good luck, but you don't do that to a man who is suffering from a bad case of the Turkic trots.

When the shooting of the biodegrading process in the barn had been completed, they all left to film cows in pastures green. All, that is, apart from Piotyr and Kazam. Piotyr left for Balqash, bearing a list long enough to provide him with an excuse for leave of absence for a good few hours; Kazam stayed to supervise the switching off of the conveyor belt and the shutting up of the barn. And, presumably, to heave a big sigh of relief that although shooting the scene had not gone off totally without incident, at least there had been no embarrassing questions.

After a short break for lunch they had spent hours in a field of corn waiting for a changeable wind to blow from exactly the right direction and with exactly the right force to make the ears ripple in the precise patterns that Patrick had in mind. At last it was all over, the commercial was in the can and the tapes, having passed through Kazam's hot and sticky hands, were on their way, like Evans, to Alma-Ata airport. If Harper was right, this was the beginning of the period of maximum vulnerability.

He was stretched out on the bed in his room, hands behind his head, staring at the ceiling and trying to plan for eventualities he couldn't even begin to imagine. Beside him was his rucksack containing a change of clothes, his passport, wallet and mobile phone. At the foot of the bed his suitcase was packed, save for the clothes he was wearing and those for the party. On the chair was a pair of loose fitting trousers, baggy shirt and long jacket – all in jet-black – courtesy of Piotyr and his bulk-buying swoop on the local market. There was nothing more he could do.

'Hell!' he said, getting up from the bed and stripping off to change into his camouflage outfit. Prepared for everything and nothing, as usual, Harper, he thought. If all else fails, stick close to Charly, that's the best strategy. Charly was family; Charly was blood: she would be inviolate, and those near to her safe. So all you can do now is enjoy the party, and hope. Hope that no one suggests playing silly games – charades and consequences might be too near the mark.

As he went downstairs he could hear the sound of laughter. Entering the main room, it was as if he had gate-crashed a wake. The lights had been switched off and black-clothed individuals, drinks in hand, were silhouetted against the red glow of the fire or the flickering light of candles on the table. Ned, like a refugee from *Four Weddings and a Funeral*, was roaming around thrusting a video camera in people's faces, intent of capturing for posterity every moment of the celebration of the completion of Patrick's very first commercial.

'Kit,' said Patrick, clasping his arm and leading him to the table where bottles and glasses had been placed, 'I can offer you red or white wine, courtesy of Kazam.'

The Kazakh shrugged modestly, but beamed a wide smile, his gold tooth flashing in the light of the candle. 'It is only Chinese, I am afraid. But the best that Alma-Ata could provide. I had the driver pick some up on his way back from the airport this morning, together with another product of China that I thought might be appropriate for your celebrations. But that I will keep until later as a surprise.'

Harper was just about to tell Kazam how much he hated surprises when the room went quiet and Ned's camera swivelled in the direction of the stairs. He turned around in time to see Charly make her grand entrance.

No wonder everyone had fallen silent. She was wearing a black dress in a fabric – jersey, cashmere, spray paint? – that made what little there was of it cling tightly to her body. The dress was teamed with black stilettos that gave the illusion – or maybe it was reality – that her legs were endless. Her shoulders were bare, apart from the waterfall of long red hair and the two dental floss straps that came from the sides of the dress to criss-cross around her neck. Her brown eyes shone brightly, her heart-shaped lips smiled warmly. Harper returned the smile and let out the breath he realized he had been holding. He crossed the floor and held out a crooked elbow to escort her to the table.

'You must allow me the privilege of the first dance,' he said.

'There isn't any music, Kit,' she pointed out.

He started humming.

'Corny,' she said. 'Very corny. And stolen from some old film, if I'm not mistaken.'

'*The Dirty Dozen*,' Philip said. 'Stunning dress, Charly.'

'A girl should never travel without a little black dress,' – *little* being the operative word.

'Our table awaits, ma'am,' Harper said. 'You look good,' he said simply.

'Is that it?'

'Jesus, you look good.'

'Oh, well,' she shrugged. 'Such a relief to know that the two hours spent getting ready under adverse conditions was all worthwhile.'

Everyone took up their places. The crew clustered around Patrick on the side of the table facing the windows at the front of the farmhouse; Harper, Charly, Ned, Philip, Drew and Kazam were on the opposite side, their backs to the door and only a glimpse of the night coming from the one window at the back.

'Is Mr Evans not joining us?' asked Kazam.

'I think food is probably the last thing on his mind,' Harper said.

'Then we shall begin,' said Kazam, signalling to the two *babooshkas* waiting by the kitchen door.

'Speech!' Ned called, using one hand to point the camera at Patrick and the other to reach out for a bottle of red wine.

Patrick rose his chair. 'Charge your glasses,' he said, smiling, 'or, should I say, tumblers. And be upstanding, darlings.'

Chairs scraped on the floor as everyone stood up. Tumblers of wine – or, in Harper's case, boring old apple juice, were picked up in readiness. Piotyr, Leonid and the two old women paused at the kitchen door with platters in their hands.

'One could not have had a more difficult task for a first commercial,' said Patrick. 'Nor a more difficult location.' Kazam translated simultaneously for the benefit of the Russians who stood expressionless, reserving judgement. 'And yet we surmounted those difficulties; leapt each hurdle in our path until we held the gold medal in our grasp. This is our *Chariots of Fire*. For that I must thank the hospitality of our hosts,' – smiles at last from the Russians – 'the administrative skills of Kazam' – characteristic shrug – 'and the professionalism and hard work of my crew and every one of their helpers, especially Jeremiah.' – loud applause – 'Lastly, we must not forget the contributions of JKL, who showed great judgement in hiring me, AUC for their chequebook' – cheers – 'and the Gaia enzyme for providing the catalyst to an end product which will be hailed as an epic chapter in the history of advertising. Ladies and gentlemen, I give you Gaia.'

'Gaia,' they echoed.

'Gaia,' Harper joined in. 'But not her children,' he added under his breath.

For nigh on two hours they sat and feasted. Patrick was treated as if he were the central character in some sacrilegious re-enactment of the last supper: the crew could barely restrain themselves from washing his feet.

It was not the most balanced of meals – smoked fish with a creamy horse-radish sauce followed by poached fish with a creamy dill sauce – and neither was the Great Wall wine in the running for any vinticulture awards (the white being described as more like apple juice than the apple juice), but the atmosphere of conviviality made up for any shortfall in the creativity of the menu or the lacklustre nature of the accompanying alcohol. Tension was released; adrenaline levels, heavily depleted after the last few days, reached an all-time low; heads became light and mouths free-flowing as they were lubricated to the point where everyone seemed to be talking at once and giggling at everything in general and nothing in particular. Or, at least, that was

Harper's view, as the only sober one among them.

Ned's camera roamed around the table the whole time, although more shakily and with less apparent rationale behind the subject matter as the evening wore on. After a dessert of pancakes and berries, Kazam, a gleam in his eye, took his leave, claiming that there was much still be organized before their departure in the morning. The wine ran out: Piotyr and Leonid distributed bottles of chilled vodka and tiny glasses around the table. Harper caught Piotyr's eye and mouthed the single word *Go*. The drinking became more serious, the conversation even less so. And then, suddenly, a hush fell on the table.

Bang!

Outside, a loud explosion had split the air.

Harper, nerves as taut as piano wires, jumped six inches into the air. Then he saw the startled expressions of those facing the windows turn to wonder as a rain of gold and silver sparks fell down.

'Fireworks!' Ned shouted, leaping up from the table with camera at the ready. 'Kazam has organized fireworks. Wow, man. Brilliant!'

There was a rush to the door.

'No!' shouted Harper, pushing Charly back in her seat as instinct issued a red alert.

Heedless of his warning, the door was flung open and people followed Ned outside. Lambs to the slaughter. Harper ran after them, clutching at bodies and trying to pull them back inside.

Another rocket shot up into the air. The dark, moonless sky, and everything underneath it, was lit up. Forty or so yards away Harper saw three men standing upright, machine guns at the ready. Kazam's gold tooth flashed as he shouted an order. And then, along with the thunder of the rocket exploding, came the first elongated burst of gunfire.

Ned was the first to fall to the ground. Drew followed, then all the members of Patrick's crew.

Screams rent the air. The bright light of another rocket showed panic frozen on the faces of those pushing and shoving each other, trying to force their way back through the door. As they passed him, Harper flung himself down on to his stomach. He crawled outside, feeling the warmth of freshly spilt blood soak into his shirt. He stared at the bodies, unwilling to believe the evidence of his own eyes. Drew's face, pulverised by a hail of bullets, was barely recognizable. Only Ned was breathing.

'Bastards,' Harper shouted into the night. 'Bloody bastards.'

Coming to his senses, he jumped back into the main room, slamming the door shut behind him. He grabbed hold of a chair and wedged it under the handle of the door.

'Help me,' he called to Patrick and Philip. 'We have to move the table to block up the front door.'

They dragged the table across the room and manhandled it against the door. Then they clustered around Ned. As Harper knelt down, Charly, tears in her eyes, looked at him and shook her head.

Harper, knowing it was a lost cause, felt for a pulse.

Nothing. Not the faintest beat.

He bent down so that his ear was against Ned's gaping mouth.

Nothing. Not the faintest whisper of the breath of life.

Seeking the smallest sign of movement, his eyes scanned the body.

Nothing. Just blood. Lots of blood from a gaping hole in the centre of Ned's chest.

Ned was still holding the camera, his finger jammed on the trigger. Harper gently bent back the fingers and the machine stopped recording. He took the video tape from out of the camera, stood up and watched as Philip put his hands underneath Ned, lifted him upright and cradled him in his arms.

'What do we do now, Kit?' Charly asked.

Harper paused to take stock. Christ, just four of us left. Defenceless. Outnumbered. Both exits covered.

'We can't stay here,' he said.

'If we go outside,' Patrick said, his eyes white with fear, 'they'll just mow us down. It's madness to leave here.'

'It's madness to stay,' Harper said. 'Sooner or later they'll break down the doors and then we're cornered. Sitting bloody ducks. But if we make a run for it, we might just have a chance.'

'Might?' said Charly.

'It's the best I can offer.'

'Then tell us what to do,' she said.

He knelt down again and took hold of Philip, who was rocking backwards and forwards with Ned in his arms. He broke Philip's grasp and laid Ned back down on the floor. Gently, he lifted Philip to his feet.

'Come on,' he said softly. 'You can't do any more for Ned. We have to look after ourselves now. It's time to leave. Follow me upstairs, everybody.'

At the foot of the stairs he saw Patrick out of the corner of his eye reach out a hand. Harper grabbed it and forced it down.

'Don't turn on the light, for chrissake,' he said, letting out a sigh which was part relief and part frustration. 'Now, grab your passports and a coat and meet me in my room. And Charly, change your shoes.'

Harper felt his way along the corridor and into his room. He found his rucksack, slipped the video inside, slung a strap over his shoulder and crept to the window. Inch by inch he slid up the bottom section. Gingerly poking his head outside, he looked all around and then, for an instant only, down. He saw nothing, but then it was pitch black. Unless another rocket was set off, they – and especially he – would just have to trust to luck.

Patrick and Philip came up behind him, and then Charly, wrapped in a dark cardigan and with the ginger suede desert boots on her feet.

'Well?' she said. 'What now?'

'I want the three of you to lower yourself out of the window and drop to the ground. Then, as quietly and as quickly as possible, make for the barn where we were filming this morning. Wait for me there. The moment you see me coming, fling open the doors and go inside.'

'And what will you be doing?' Charly asked.

'Drawing their attention to the barn.'

'Don't go crazy on us again, Kit. Not now, when we need you so much.'

'Kazam and his trigger-happy buddies can't afford for any of us to survive. It's a case of dead men, and dead women, tell no tales. They have to – will – kill us all. Unless, that is, we can trick them. Buy some time to make our escape.'

'But it's suicide to go into the barn. We'll be cornered.'

'That's what I'm hoping Kazam will think. That there's no escape, and that they can just saunter in at their leisure and pick us off as easily as shooting apples in a barrel. Our only chance is to appear to walk into a self-made trap.'

'But there's a way out of the trap?' Charly asked uncertainly. 'Please tell me there's a way out.'

'Yes,' Harper said. 'But I don't want to think about that now. One step at a time. Just trust me, Charly.'

'Who else is there to trust?' she said.

Terrific, Harper thought. She trusts me. When I'm the last resort. The forlorn hope.

'Right,' he said. 'I'll leave you three to decide who goes out of the window first. But don't take too long about it. We may not have much time. I'll give you a minute's start. See you at the barn.'

He went downstairs, counting full-length seconds – one elephant, two elephants – and stood for a moment in front of the window that looked out onto the back of the farmhouse. It was a single pane of glass, not designed to be opened. Perfect.

Harper picked up one of the wooden dining chairs. And waited. Forty-seven elephants. Forty-eight elephants.

There was a pounding on the front door. Forty-nine elephants.

The door began to cave in; the table moved a few inches. Fifty elephants.

Hell! What is an elephant or ten between friends?

He smashed the glass with the legs of the chair.

Behind him the barricade finally gave way.

He was diving through the window as the first of his pursuers entered the room, took aim and fired. The bullet thudded into the rucksack. Harper felt a sharp pain in the middle of his back as he fell to the ground.

27

Harper lay there for a moment on the ground, expecting to feel warm blood soaking into the back of his shirt and to hear a choir of angels beckoning upwards. All he heard was the sound of running feet; all he felt was fear.

Leaping up, he ran round the side of the building and sprinted zigzag-fashion to the barn. Bullets – aimed at the sound of his shoes on the hard earth rather than the unseen black figure in the dark – bounced and ricocheted all about him.

Charly, alerted by the noise of firing, had the heavy barn door ajar and now, aided by Philip and Patrick, swung it outwards. They stepped quickly inside, Charly looking back anxiously. Harper covered the last few feet in a flying slide along the ground that took him yards into the barn and lay breathing heavily in the dust as the door was closed behind him.

'Move the trailer towards the door and upend it,' he called out as he pulled himself up on to his feet.

He heard Philip gasp. Saw him stagger back from the trailer, holding his mouth.

'You'd better come over here,' Patrick said.

Harper stepped over to the trailer and followed the direction of Patrick's gaze. Inside the trailer were four bullet-ridden bodies – Piotyr, Leonid and the two *babooshkas*. His stomach turned.

'I told him to leave,' he said. 'I didn't know this would happen.'

'Would it have been any different if they had stayed with us?' Charly said. 'The old women wouldn't have been up to jumping out of windows. You did what you thought was best. Come on, Kit, there's work to do.'

On autopilot, Harper took hold of the front of the trailer and, staring straight ahead, began to tug. Patrick and Charly went to the other end and pushed.

'Well,' Charly said, when the trailer had been wheeled into position – but not upended: that was something none of them could bear to do. 'You've successfully got us into the trap. Now how the hell do we get out?'

'The only way there is. The one way that would never even cross Kazam's mind – as far as he is concerned we're stuck here, no exit, and he can pick us off whenever he wants. The plan is to climb the ladder to the top of the silo, cross to the conveyor and crawl down the belt.'

'So there was a method in your madness, after all,' Charly said.

'Yeah,' he said, trying to sound confident. 'Philip, you first, then Patrick. Get climbing.'

Harper took the rucksack off his back. There was a neat, round bullet hole at the bottom.

'Take this,' he said, holding out the rucksack towards Charly. 'It contains everything you'll need. You'll find money inside, my mobile and the video that Ned took. Keep it safe. It's the only concrete evidence we have so far of AUC's involvement in this bloody massacre – Kazam's on it somewhere, grinning and flashing that unmistakable gold tooth. There's an orchard about half a mile down the track toward the lake. Wait for me there. Give me five minutes. If I'm not with you by then, go on to Balqash and hide up until the train to Alma-Ata arrives. Good luck, Charly.'

He put his hand on her shoulders and bent his head down to kiss her.

'Hang on,' she said, pushing him away. 'What do you mean, *wait for me*? Aren't you coming with us?'

'I thought I might take my chances here.'

'But you said there was no chance here. Shooting apples in a barrel, remember?'

'Then maybe I can slow them down for a while. Buy you some time to get clear of here.'

'Bullshit,' she said, spitting out the word. 'I don't understand. There's something you're not telling me.'

'Get going, Charly. Philip and Patrick are near the top of the ladder. I'm relying on you to get them to safety.'

He pushed her toward the ladder.

'Quit shoving, Harper. I'm not moving an inch until you tell me what the hell is going on.'

'Just do as I say for once,' he pleaded, his voice quivering. 'Without bloody question. Scram, Charly. Goodbye and good luck.'

'No, Harper. I'm not going without you.'

'Then you're a fool.'

'That makes two of us.'

'But you can't leave Philip and Patrick.'

'You seem prepared to.'

'Only because I can't help them,' he said, shaking uncontrollably. 'I'm terrified of heights, Charly. Scared witless. Understand? Even the thought of it turns my legs to jelly and causes my brain to cease functioning. Do you get the bloody picture? I can just about control it in a plane by concentrating on the inside and pretending it's on the ground. But I *cannot* climb that ladder, Charly. I just cannot do it, not for love or money.'

She put her arms around him. Hugged him tight, trying to stem the trembling of his body. Kissed him on the cheek. Tasted the salt of his tears.

'Think of Cassie,' she said. 'She's already lost a mother. She needs a father even more now.'

Harper closed his eyes and sucked in breath.

'Think of Piotyr, too,' Charly said. 'The grief you share and the promise you made to help him. And if that doesn't work, listen to this, buster. If you think I'm climbing *that* ladder in *this* skirt while *you* stand here on the ground, then you better think again.'

'I won't look,' he said.

'That's right, Kit,' she said. 'You won't look. You're going to close your eyes. I'll talk you up the ladder and down the conveyor belt. I'll be right behind you all the way. You can do it. Trust me.'

'But—'

The excuse he couldn't think of was cut short by someone or something hammering against the barn door. Shots were fired through the wood, more in frustration than in hope of hitting a target.

'If your plan is to work,' Charly said urgently, 'we have to be clear of the building and out of sight before they enter. Don't spoil everything for all of us. Come on, Kit. Close your eyes.'

She led him to the foot of the ladder. Placed his hands on the rails that ran up each side. They were hot. Harper tried to remove his hand, but Charly pushed them back down.

'Use the pain as a focus for your mind, Kit. You move your hands, I'll guide your feet. Ready? Left foot up. Now right. Good. Again, left foot.'

Slowly, step by step, they progressed up the ladder.

'We're going to have to move a little faster,' Charly said.

'Give me a break,' Harper said. 'I'm climbing by bloody Braille, for chrissake. I'm doing the best I can.'

'It might not be good enough, Kit. I kinda hate to mention this – no, don't stop, keep going – but seeing as you have your eyes closed, I feel I should point out that there are small packages fixed to the side of the silo. I hate to be a pessimist, but my guess is that they are plastic explosive. And I don't know whether they can be detonated from inside or outside the barn.'

'It was a better trap than I thought.'

'Not if we're not caught in it, Kit.'

She guided his feet more quickly now. Left, right, in a rapid procession.

'OK,' she finally said. 'We're at the top of the ladder. The next bit will be tricky. Sure you don't want a peek?'

'Hell, I don't know. I don't know anything right now.'

'Give it a try.'

Harper squinted through the slits of his eyes. All he saw was steel.

'Turn around,' Charly prompted. 'The conveyor is behind you and a little above. All you have to do is lift yourself on to it.'

'All I have to do? Wonderful!'

'And, Kit,' she said, 'don't look down, eh?'

It was an awkward manoeuvre, necessitating Harper twisting his body a hundred and eighty degrees, placing his hands a little way down the belt and then raising his knees on to the top of the conveyor.

'Charly,' he said, as he worked hard to coordinate hands and legs and not to look down, 'if I ever get another bright idea to extricate us from a mess, do me a favour, huh? Talk me out of it.'

He made it and crawled down the belt, ducking his head to clear the hole where it fed into the barn. Now he really felt exposed, the night air cold about him, the sky black above, the ground – well, he didn't bother checking that.

Charly pushed him along, using outstretched hands on his backside, and together they travelled down the thirty-degree incline. 'Help him off,' she whispered to Philip and Patrick as Harper neared the bottom.

'What kept you?' Patrick asked, raising Harper to his feet. 'We thought you were never coming.'

'So did we,' said Charly. 'OK, Kit. Lead on to Balqash.'

They crept along, keeping their bodies bent low. Harper tried to visualize the route he had taken on the morning he had explored the farm. He cut a little to the south and found the track that led past the orchard. From there it was easier going, the lights of Balqash acting like beacons.

They were still a mile away when the thunder, lightning and rain came.

The thunder was the boom of the explosion.

The lightning the flames that arced up into the sky.

The rain the sandy grains that fell from the mushroom cloud.

The silo had been destroyed. And with it the product of Gaia.

But the work of her infernal children would continue. Aided by the wind, the contamination was being blown across the land. Piotyr's 'curse' was spreading.

It had to be stopped.

Sir Angus had to be stopped, before he launched Gaia on an unsuspecting world.

Remember the dead, Harper told himself as he trudged on. And have no more faith in so-called *miracles*. Have faith only in Evans, that he will find something to prove the theory; in Charly, that she will be around whenever needed; and in yourself.

You may have won the battle, Sir Angus bloody Cameron; but you won't win the war.

STAGE FIVE

SIDE EFFECTS

28

The explosion woke the town of Balqash. The response was like a scene from the last ten minutes of a horror movie where the villagers are drawn magnetically to the castle to witness the final destruction of the vampire and the laying of the curse. Hastily clad Russians and Kazakhs rushed along the track towards the beckoning yellow flames, passing the strange-looking quartet, unwilling to stop and get involved. Perhaps they were deterred by the sandy dust that seemed to cling to every fibre of the black clothes and every strand of hair of the three men and the beautiful girl in mini dress and desert boots. Or maybe it was just that the action had moved on, the role of these actors deemed to be over.

There was to be no safe haven at the station. No waiting room to provide shelter nor a floor to collapse on for a brief respite. No one in the little ticket office of whom to enquire about the time of the next train. It was close to midnight, and Harper's guess was that nothing would be happening here until at least eight or nine o'clock in the morning. And that might well be too late: if Kazam or one of his hired guns were to overhear one of the townsfolk talking about the strange group heading towards Balqash, then the hunt would be on again. He looked at the shivering bodies and drawn faces of Charly, Philip and Patrick and knew that they needed somewhere warm to rest for a little while, some place to patch up their tattered nerves before the final dash for home. And Harper needed time to think, to consider the options available to them and their associated dangers.

He took them to the bar on the waterfront. He brushed himself down, now looking only mildly disreputable, led them inside and to a table in a corner where he could watch the door. Philip and Patrick slumped down in their chairs and gazed at some point in the middle distance with the fixed, unfocused expressions of zombies: the environment of relative safety had broken down an instinctive barrier and shock was setting in. Charly, probably undergoing the same process but displaying different symptoms, stared at Harper, her eyebrows slanting down as if her mind was locked on solving some inner puzzle.

You and me both, Charly, Harper thought. What he *should* do was go to someone in authority and lay out the whole story and ask for protection, but his dealings so far with representatives of officialdom in Kazakhstan – the man at the immigration desk at the airport skimming dollars off the inflated price of a visa, the customs officials who would loot your baggage or take a bribe not to, the militia who took your money and anything else they wanted; every damned one of them on the take – told him he could trust no one. For all he knew, Kazam, AUC's Mr Fix It, had already bought anyone who could have been of use to them. Or whoever he approached might be the godfather of the local branch of the mafia. No, they must keep their own counsel; survive without help until they got out of this bloody country.

The place, as far as he could tell through the lingering mist of tobacco smoke, was decorated in middle-period manic-depressive, gloomy and cheer-less, a combination of dark wood, nicotine-coated walls and a floor covering of ash and cigarette butts. Ideal it wasn't, but it would do for a short while. Apart from the grim-faced barman, there was just a handful of customers, most of them old men, all of them too drunk or feeble or both to follow the crowd to the farmhouse. He bought a bottle of vodka and took it back to the table along with three inadequately small glasses.

'Drink up,' he said, filling the glasses. 'It will do you good.'

They followed his instruction with all the emotion of well-programmed automatons. After draining their glasses, Patrick and Philip switched their inattention to the table, Charly shivered. Harper put his arm round her shoulder. There was no reaction, positive or otherwise.

'You may have been right about Gaia,' she said, 'but you're wrong about my grandfather. He's not behind all this. You only have to think about it for a moment to see that it doesn't make sense. Back at the farm they were firing indiscriminately at anyone and everyone. Kazam wouldn't act without orders. And my grandfather would never sanction my death. It has to be someone else. Someone who doesn't care whether I lived or died.'

Maybe, Harper thought. Or maybe, in the grand scheme of things, Charly was as expendable as the rest of them. He saw again in his mind's eye the bodies outside the farm and those in the barn. With his free hand he picked up the vodka bottle and took a long pull.

'What are you doing?' she said.

'Washing the taste of death from my mouth.'

'And has it worked?'

'Not yet.'

'Don't get drunk on us, Kit,' she said, turning her brown eyes pleadingly on him. 'We need you.'

'Don't worry, Charly. I'm not drinking to blot out the past. I exorcised one demon tonight by climbing up that silo and crawling down the conveyor belt. After that experience, I know that anything is possible. This drink is to the future – whatever that might turn out to hold.'

'What are we going to do?' she asked, voicing the question he had known was inevitable.

Harper took another pull at the bottle. 'We've got to get out of this place,' he said.

'Why is it that wherever we are at any given moment, you say we have to leave?'

'Because wherever we are at any given moment, someone always seems to want to kill us. We won't be safe until we're on a plane home.'

He dug inside his rucksack and took out his mobile phone and wallet. The phone had a neat hole in its centre, the wallet a bullet lodged in the thick wad of money. Saved by a miracle of modern technology and a fistful of dollars! He prised the bullet out and put it in his pocket, then tossed the useless phone onto the table.

'Would you like to use mine?' Charly said, digging into her shoulder bag.

She handed it to Harper. He called Saul first. His answerphone cut in after three rings. Where are you when I need you, Saul? Harper left a message, simply saying that he was safe, whatever Saul might hear on the news, and passed the phone to Charly for her to dictate her number into the machine.

Next he tried his home. Saul answered.

'Saul?' Harper said. 'What are you doing there?'

'I've been trying to phone you on your mobile,' Saul said.

'Out of commission,' Harper said. 'Why were you trying to contact me? Is anything wrong?'

'I can't talk now, Kit. Can you give me a number and I'll ring you back?'

'But—'

'Don't say any more, Kit. A number, please.'

For the second time, he passed the phone to Charly. She gave her number, listened for a moment, put the phone down on the table and turned to Harper.

'Saul rang off as soon as he had the number,' she said. 'What's wrong?'

'I don't know,' he replied, frowning. 'Something's wrong for sure. Why should Saul be at my house? And why won't he talk?'

He rubbed at the scar, until Charly took hold of his hand and held it between hers.

'All we can do is wait for him to ring back,' she said. 'Whatever's the problem, Saul will solve it.'

Harper nodded, more to abate his own anxiety than in agreement with Charly's words. He rose from the table, picked up his wallet and stepped across to the bar.

'Taxi,' he said to the barman, hoping that the Kazakh or Russian word was similar sounding to the English, but adding a mime of rotating a steering wheel for good measure. 'Taxi. Semey.'

The barman shrugged his shoulders.

Harper took five hundred-dollar bills from his wallet and spread them out on the counter of the bar. The barman gave a wide stained-tooth grin, poured two glasses of vodka and took two paces back to where a phone sat among a clutter of bottles in front of a mirror. As Harper sipped the vodka, the barman gabbled into the mouthpiece and watched him in the reflection of the mirror.

'Taxi,' the barman nodded when he had finished. He tapped the face of his watch, held five fingers in the air, hopefully indicating minutes and not hours, pocketed one of the bills, placed a glass over the rest of the money and then used both hands to shoo Harper in the direction of the table. Charly's mobile rang as he was walking back.

'Yes,' she said. Then her face turned white. 'It's my grandfather,' she said.

Harper swore under his breath. Saved by a miracle of modern technology and then plunged straight back into danger by it! Frying pan to fire in one bloody leap.

Charly covered the phone with her hand and turned to Harper for advice. 'Kazam has telephoned him. Told him that the local *mafiosniki* attacked the farm because they couldn't get protection money out of AUC.'

So that was the cover story, Harper thought, shaking his head. Blame it all on the *mafiosniki* and, at the same time, score an ethical point for not swelling the funds of a criminal organization in order to be allowed to go about your business. Well, let's see who believes the cock-and-bull story when they see the evidence of the video.

'Kazam,' Charly continued, 'told him everybody was dead.'

In Kazam's bloody dreams.

'Just tell your grandfather that *you're* safe,' Harper said. 'And that you need the plane at Semey airport by nine o'clock in the morning. Then clear the line in case Saul rings.'

There followed a brief conversation in which Charly seemed to repeat the words yes, *grandfather* an infuriating number of times and Harper ran his hand across his throat in the international sign for *cut.*

He lit a cigarette and concentrated on inhaling smoke rather than exhaling a morale-destroying groan: Sir Angus Cameron now knew that there were survivors, and, Harper was willing to bet, it wouldn't be long before Kazam heard the glad tidings. He checked his watch. The promised five minutes had elapsed and still no taxi. If it didn't arrive shortly, they might just as well stand outside with their backs to the wall, blindfolds over their eyes and targets painted in the middle of their chests.

A scruffily dressed man entered the bar, scratched at three days growth of beard while looking around, and walked up to the barman. After a swift glass of vodka, during which the remaining four hundred dollars disappeared into the pocket of his tattered and torn overcoat, the man waved his hand at their table and gestured that they should go outside.

Not exactly the white knight of the road that you were hoping for, Harper thought. But beggars can't be choosers.

He and Charly helped Patrick and Philip to their feet and led them outside. A battered Wartburg stood by the kerb. The taxi driver opened the passenger door and the nearside rear door. Harper watched as the others squeezed into the back of the car and then he climbed into the front.

'Why are we going to Semey?' Charly said. 'I thought the original plan was to head for Alma-Ata. It is nearer, after all.'

'We're not going to Semey,' he answered as the driver started the engine. 'I just wanted to throw any pursuers off the scent. Heading off in the wrong direction might gain us the time we need. God knows how long it's going to take in this crate. We need a head start on Kazam. Alma-Ata,' he said to the driver.

The driver shrugged. Travelling half the distance for the same money was fine by him.

The Wartburg had seen better days – the launch of the first Sputnik was Harper's guess. It was built like a tank – shared technology and production line, probably – and seemed almost as fast and manoeuvrable. Still, if the driver fell asleep and collided with a mountain, then it would be the mountain that came off worse. The heater didn't work, causing shivers even among the tightly packed occupants in the rear and the driver to wipe his hand continually over the windscreen to clear the condensation. The car chugged along at an estimated fifty miles per hour – the speedometer wasn't functioning either – its geriatric engine straining to cope with the unaccustomed weight of four passengers. At this speed it would take six hours to reach Alma-Ata. Assuming that Kazam would travel at seventy miles per hour at the most and that it would take him, say, an hour before he suspected he had been duped then. . . .

Charly's phone rang, interrupting Harper's complex calculations.

'Sorry it's taken me a long time to get back to you,' Saul said, 'but it was hard to find a public call-box that was working.'

'What's wrong the phone at my house?' Harper asked.

'Nothing, I suspect. I take it you didn't call in the engineers because of a noisy line: Nanny Trent didn't know anything about it.'

'Neither do I,' Harper said.

'Then I think we can safely assume that your phone is bugged. Now I take it from everything that has been happening here that there have been developments at your end. Give me a very brief résumé, Kit.'

Harper relayed the details of the destruction of the farm, including the deaths of Ned and Drew, and their current flight to Alma-Ata with the pursuers hopefully headed off in the opposite direction. 'I managed to get Evans away before we were attacked,' he added. 'By the time we get back I hope he has dug up something from the files at AUC. What with that, Charly's corroboration of my version of the attack and a video we have, we should be in a position to call in the police and hold a press conference.'

'I wouldn't advise that,' Saul said. 'Not for a while yet. There's something you need to know, Kit. At school today—'

'Cassie?' Harper screamed into the phone. 'What's happened? Is Cassie all right? Jesus Christ, Saul, is she OK?'

'Don't panic, Kit,' Saul said.

Saul had said some pretty incomprehensible things in the past, but *don't panic* topped the lot.

29

Andrew Evans sat at a terminal in the computer room at AUC systematically working his way back into the history of the Gaia enzyme. The digital clock on the wall told him it was five o'clock in the morning; his internal body clock, its movement out of kilter from a day of travelling and a five-hour time difference, desperately wanted to disagree but had no better chronological answer. Evans was unwashed, unshaven and dressed in the same clothes, now creased and stained with sweat and grime, that he had put on nearly twenty-eight hours ago; his hair, unbrushed for the same amount of time, had taken on a style that might have been copied from a caustic fashion review of what every badly dressed mop was wearing last season. From time to time the computer operator, upset at the disruption of the simple nocturnal routine of running back-ups and fine-tuning the system parameters, looked across at him as if to check that this intrusive vision of a mad professor was reality and not something out of a strange drug-induced dream.

After leaving the farm, Evans had caught the slow noon train south from Balqash towards Bishkek, changing at a terminus north of that city for the even slower eastbound train to Alma-Ata. From there he had caught the first remotely convenient plane headed westward, landing in Amsterdam just after eleven in the evening. The final leg of his journey had been a long drive in a hired car along the motorways to Brussels. He had entered the AUC building at four o'clock and gone straight to the computer room. It was there that he had first heard the news of the attack at the farm. Details were sparse, and all the more worrying for that: a *mafiosniki* raid; prolonged gunfire; a violent explosion; a number of bodies found, some unidentifiable; only Charly known definitely to have survived. Any last lingering doubts he may have harboured about Harper's theory evaporated into the sterile air of the room.

Evans had started by checking the current file on Gaia. It was exactly as he had last seen it – nothing incriminating, and nothing new. If Françoise had indeed found the inhibitor, then she had neglected to write up the results of the experiments. And that was completely out of character for such a thorough person, and one who would have liked nothing better than to have staked her claim on the discovery. He knew now that he had to work quickly, get out of the building and go into hiding. Yet he had a long task ahead of him. In the cool of the room, beads of nervous perspiration broke out on his forehead.

He had formulated a plan of action during his journey. At some stage in the testing of the Gaia enzyme, Mueller must have noticed an embarrassing pattern in the data: an abnormally high level of mutations, cancers and associated deaths. That was the point at which the file would have been changed, the data altered to remove the threat to the future of the enzyme. But Mueller was computer illiterate, unfamiliar with the system and ignorant of the mechanics of how it operated. The current file could be changed to leave no trace of incriminating evidence: the back-up system files could not. History could not be completely rewritten.

Each day the whole system was backed-up on to one of the massive disks; at the end of each week, the last disk was kept and the daily disks recycled; and so it went on, with only the monthly and annual disks being write-protected and stored for posterity. This methodical procedure had two advantages: firstly, in the event of a devastating crash or attack by virus, the whole system could be recreated with the loss of at most one day's work; secondly, the memory of the computer could be optimized by deleting non-current files in the safe knowledge that if ever there was cause to refer to the originals then the relevant back-up disk could be loaded.

Evans rose from his chair, stretched his aching limbs and walked over to the computer operator. 'Back one more year, please,' he said.

'If you told me exactly what you are looking for, maybe I could help and save us both time,' the operator said, not bothering to hide his annoyance.

Evans shook his head and stood looking down threateningly at the young operator. The man sighed, walked over to the steel rack that ran along one wall of the subterranean room, and slid out a disk. With more than a little petulant huffing and puffing, the disk was carried over to the cabinet housing the drive and installed in place of the one already consulted without success.

Sitting himself down again, Evans typed in the reference number of the Gaia file. Why, he wondered as he waited for the file to come up on his screen, had the original programmers chosen a numerical filing system rather than the more logical option based on names? Cost probably. Or something to do with simplicity of design taking priority over ease of use.

He scrolled through the file, concentrating on updates on the trial from the Den Haag research facility. All of a sudden, he blinked. He had seen a difference. Not an alteration as such, but instances of data which, to an informed and searching eye, suggested the emergence of a pattern. A shiver of excitement ran through his body. He had identified the year in question, now he had to find the precise month that Mueller had cleansed the file.

Over the course of the next half an hour, Evans moved forward in time, becoming more impatient with the delays when each monthly disk was loaded. The April disk bore conclusive evidence of Gaia's deadly side effects: the May disk portrayed the enzyme as squeaky clean. Not only had Harper's suspicions been proven, but the timing had thrown up another coincidence: May was when the laboratory had been attacked, the animals set free and the records conveniently destroyed. He picked up the telephone and punched out the number of Harper's mobile with trembling fingers.

Damn, no answer. Just a recorded announcement to leave a message. His heart sank. Was Harper one of those unidentifiable bodies? Had he died without knowing for sure that he had been right all the time? Had he been wrong to trust Charly? Betrayed by a blood relation of the man behind the slaughter of the innocent?

Evans slumped back in the chair, sad, dejected and depressed. He thumped the desk with his fist, bringing forth a librarian-style glare from the operator. Be positive, he told himself. Harper had saved his life – because he had *predicted* that something would happen. So Harper must have had a plan of escape. The only useful, and comforting, assumption was that Harper was alive and making his way back to safety. Or maybe he was hiding, in some situation where it was too dangerous to have the mobile switched on, alerting the searchers of his presence if it rang.

Evans sat there for a while wondering what to do. Then the scientist in him took over. He went into the word processing package and typed in his findings, his conclusions and the all-important reference to the disk that contained the evidence. Having finished, he realized that he could not leave the document sitting there in a folder with his name attached to it: too easy for someone to spot and delete. He had to hide it somewhere. Somewhere in the thousands of numerical files where it would take a lifetime to find. All he had to do was choose a number – one that he would not forget and, if the worse were to happen, which would be obvious to Harper.

Think of a number. Wasn't as easy as it sounded. The two of them didn't have much in common. He liked Gilbert and Sullivan, Harper like blues. He was a scientist, Harper – well, he wasn't really quite sure how to define Harper; didn't seem to fit in the neatly labelled boxes of skills or personality traits by which we all categorize people. Not a scientist, by his own admittance; but not an artist either. And then it struck him – the perfect number.

Evans entered the file of his chosen number, deleted the entire contents except for the first page (the one which would appear on the screen when the file was opened), returned to his word document, cut and pasted it to the file. It was then a simple process to delete the word document, and its automatic back-up, eradicating all trace. Congratulating himself that he had thought of everything – Harper would be proud of him – he was just about to log off when a very uneasy thought struck him. Perhaps he had not thought of absolutely everything, after all.

'Can you load another disk for me?' he asked the operator.

Fifteen minutes later, he wished he had left well alone.

'Damn you to hell,' he said to himself, as he added to the contents of the file.

Ronnie Stoker sat up with a jolt. He must have dozed off. He shook his head, part in self-admonition, part to clear his brain. He looked at his watch – six-fifteen – and swore loudly into the silence of his office. Two hours! He hadn't dozed off: he had bloody slept for two hours.

It had been a long, frustrating evening, followed by an even longer and more frustrating night. And all so unnecessary. If you wanted a job done properly, Stoker thought, then you just had to do it yourself. But he couldn't be in three places at once.

It should have been so easy. All his men had to do was go to the bloody school and snatch an unsuspecting little girl. Keep her safely tucked away somewhere so he could put pressure on Harper to keep his mouth shut. Of course, Harper would have had to be eliminated eventually – he knew every-thing, that was plain from Kazam's call – but the kidnap would have bought some time. Time for the image campaign and Gaia to be launched, for AUC's share price to soar and, the ultimate prize, for the acquisition of Laurelle to go through. If he could have bought that time, then he would have been spared the necessity of organizing the very public bloodbath in Kazakhstan. The silo could have been destroyed, and Evans with it, as had always been the plan. But they had bungled it. The kid wasn't safely tucked away. Not now. And never had been. Not the *right* kid, that is.

Harper was a lucky bugger. He gives his kid some damn stupid name – Cassandra, what the hell kind of name was that? – that will make her stand out a mile in the playground the very first time one of her friends or a teacher uses it, and what bloody happens? The hired help – *fired* help, as of now – swoop on some kid called Sandra instead!

Surrounded by incompetents – that's what he was.

With no hope of putting pressure on Harper, he'd had no option but to let Kazam have a free hand – kill the lot of them, if necessary. The bloody Kazakh is tooled up with machine guns and Semtex: how could anyone survive? And yet both Charly (to whom Sir Angus had spoken on her mobile) and Harper (who, according to the tap on his telephone, had spoken to some-one at his home) had somehow escaped – maybe others too, for all he knew. He had needed to take remedial action. Institute measures inside AUC as well as contacting the phone company for Charly's mobile line. He had explained the situation – not the real one, of course, but the scenario where Charly was fleeing from the *mafiosniki* – and asked them to put a trace on the phone: whenever it was used the local node was identified and its location relayed to him for onward transmission to Kazam. But so far only transmissions using the node in the vicinity of Balqash had been made. The day, the night, had just gone from bad to worse. He banged his fist on the desk in frustration.

The screensaver on his computer cleared with the action.

The message shone out at him.

SPECIFIED USER LOGGED ON TO TERMINAL 05 AT 04:07.

Evans!

Stoker let out a stream of expletives. Terminal 05? Where the hell was that?

He consulted his list. Computer room! What the hell was Evans doing there? Frightened to use his own office, probably. That meant Evans knew everything.

Stoker raced from the room and along the corridor as fast as his good leg would carry him, cursing everyone, including himself, all the while. If he hadn't fallen asleep he would have seen the message he had set up especially to alert him to Evans's use of the computer. But then the system warning had only been intended as a failsafe – he wasn't really expecting anything to happen. Hopefully not at all, if Kazam had done his job properly, but certainly not this quickly. It wasn't possible. Not only had Evans survived, but he was in the building. How could he have got back from Kazakhstan so quickly?

Stoker stormed into the computer room. Looked around. Marched up to the operator, grabbed him by the throat and raised him into the air.

'Where's Evans?' he screamed into the operator's frightened face.

'Gone,' gasped the operator. 'You've just missed him. He left five minutes ago.'

The operator was dropped back into his chair. He watched with relief as Stoker left the room, slamming the door behind him. What a night! First Evans and the constant interruptions, then physically assaulted by Stoker. What a temper! And what language! He didn't even know what some of the words meant. He could make an educated guess, but didn't need to. One thing was clear. Stoker was not a happy man. Not by any stretch of the imagination. And when Stoker wasn't happy there was only one answer – keep your head down and pray that some other poor soul would be the victim of his wrath.

30

'What's wrong?' Charly asked. 'You've hardly said a word since Saul phoned. I thought you would be relieved.'

Harper felt the nose of the plane jerk upwards as it took off from the runway. The city of Alma-Ata spread out below him, the lake and green fields of Gorky Park an oasis in a high-rise architectural desert, before the first layer of cloud blotted everything from view.

Relieved?

Maybe he should have been.

Cassie had not, as intended, been kidnapped and should now be on her way with Saul and Nanny Trent to safety in a secret hideaway. On top of that, he had the video to prove his case and bring the villains to justice.

But when you're a man who knows the blues, you accept that an attack can strike any time, any place, any where. And not even the adman's miracle of a taste of Martini can act as an effective antidote.

'I feel responsible,' he said through gritted teeth.

'What for?' she said, swivelling around in her seat and looking into his eyes.

'Everything,' he said. 'Six of our group killed. Then there's Piotyr and his family. And the trauma that Cassie's friend Sandra must have suffered after being kidnapped. A few weeks ago I was perfectly happy—'

'Perfectly happy?' she interrupted.

'Maybe not,' he admitted. 'But I can't help feeling that if I hadn't got involved with AUC, then maybe none of this would have happened.'

'You had no alternative *but* to get involved. Klein and my grandfather made sure of that. How could you refuse? Not with Cassie to bring up and the threat of becoming unemployed and unemployable hanging in the air.'

'Hanging in the air is not a good phrase to use just at this moment.'

'Sorry,' she said, taking hold of his arm. 'What I meant was that you were thrust into the AUC account because of me – as bait for me, remember? If anyone is responsible, then it's me.'

'No,' he said. 'You wouldn't have had the alarm bells of intuition ringing in your ears. You wouldn't have dug around until the evidence was incontrovertible and the consequential chain reaction had been set in place and become irreversible.'

'Maybe that says more about me than it does about you. You can't blame yourself, Kit. How is it that you like to see planners? Catalysts? Well, you didn't cause the reaction; you just speeded it up, that's all. Sooner or later someone else would have had the same suspicions and gone through the same investigative process. And the farmhouse was never going to be allowed to sit there with its red-hot silo, or Piotyr to live to tell his tale of the curse of the land.'

Harper shrugged.

'And,' she continued, 'those who have given their lives have done so in a good cause. If you hadn't got involved – if you don't stay involved – AUC launches the Gaia enzyme. How many mutated babies and cancer deaths around the world will that cause? Hundreds of thousands? Millions?'

Harper nodded. 'Maybe you're right, Charly,' he said. 'And at least you've convinced me of one thing – this is too big for us. As soon as we land at Heathrow, we go straight to the police; tell them the whole story and hand over the video.'

'I'd rather we didn't do that, Kit,' she said.

He looked at her with narrowed eyes. 'But why not? We have to shed the burden of responsibility.'

'By placing it on my grandfather? I keep telling you, he's not behind this. Let me speak to him. Grandfather will know what to do – how to track down who is responsible inside AUC. If we go to the police, then he'll be arrested. And that will only serve to alert the real culprit, and give him a chance to escape. Give me a little time, Kit. That's all I ask.'

'No, Charly. That's not all you ask. You're asking me to risk my life and yours. Because, until we tell the authorities, we're still a threat. Both our lives will be at stake.'

'Do it for me, Kit,' she said, biting her lower lip. 'Please.'

Hell! He never could bear to see a woman cry.

At Heathrow, Harper changed his remaining dollars into pounds and despatched Philip and Patrick in a cab to hole up in a hotel, giving them enough money to pay in cash and strict instructions not to come out until they heard from him that it was safe to do so. Harper and Charly bought a few clothes and toiletries in the concourse mall, cleaned themselves up and changed, and then caught a cab to Oxford Street. Now all they could do was wait – with his mobile out of action, the only contact number which Evans would know was that of the agency. If Sir Angus were to be confronted, then Harper wanted the evidence to be incontrovertible.

It was gone midday when they arrived at the agency. Harper tried to walk quickly past Reception – no questions, please, about Ned, not now – and head off in the direction of his office, but a crowd gathered before he had moved more than a couple of paces. He was rescued by Klein and the same summons of 'My office' that had started the whole bloody business.

'Leave the talking to me,' Harper whispered to Charly as they followed Klein along the corridor.

'I think you had better tell me exactly what happened,' Klein said before they had even sat down.

Welcome home, Harper! Good to see you, Harper! He hadn't wanted to be hailed a hero and be given a Roman-style triumph, but the odd smile and word of commiseration would not have gone amiss. But what could he expect? He *wasn't* welcome. It *wasn't* good to see him. It would have been a whole lot simpler for Klein if Harper, like so many others who had set off on the shoot, had never returned.

'I don't know any more than you,' Harper said, intending to stay calm and give nothing away. 'Probably less, I imagine. We were attacked by gun-toting hoodlums. When they got bored with shooting people, they set off a bomb.'

'What about Philip and Ned? Where are they?'

'Philip's in a state of shock, but safe. Ned didn't make it.'

'Didn't make it? Is that all you can say?'

'He's dead. And so are Drew and four members of the film crew.' Harper felt his raw nerve of responsibility painfully reawakened. 'Do you want the gory details? The bullets thumping into bodies? The blood? The faces shot to pulp? The terror and the blind panic of those who could see nothing but their own inevitable death? What do you want to do, Klein? Recreate the whole scene in some future advertisement?'

'Not a very good advertisement, is it?' Klein said. 'Not for our agency, that is.'

'Jesus Christ!' exclaimed Harper. 'I do not believe this. Innocent people killed and you're worried about our image?'

'What are our clients going to think, Harper? Who the hell is going to want to come on a shoot with us ever again?'

'At least something positive has come out of this episode then,' Harper grunted.

'I'm serious,' Klein said, frowning. 'This is bad for business. It could do us a lot of harm.'

'Oh, that's it, is it? Stray bullet ricocheted and hit you in the wallet, has it? Worried about internal bleeding from your bank account, are you? Just count yourself lucky that I went to Kazakhstan in your place.'

'And look what a mess you made of it.'

Harper clenched his fists and breathed deeply. Charly placed a restraining hand on his arm.

'That's hardly fair,' she said to Klein. 'None of this is Kit's fault.'

'Harper was in charge of this shoot. I hold him entirely responsible for everything that happened. As of now, he is off the AUC account.'

'We'll see what my grandfather has to say about that,' she said.

'I wouldn't bother,' Harper said. 'Klein's only following your grandfather's orders, although I suspect he is doing it with relish as well as obedience. Klein and Sir Angus have their campaign and their commercial, and now I'm expendable.'

'From now on, Harper,' Klein said with that twisted-lip smile of his, 'you will have nothing more to do with the AUC or any of its employees – and that includes Miss Mendoza here. Is that clear?'

'I can't agree to that.'

'You have no choice, Harper. That is a direct order from me, in accordance with the client's understandable wishes. If you disobey that order, you will be knowingly putting the future of the account in jeopardy. I could only consider that to be a flagrant dereliction of your duty to the agency and would have no alternative but to terminate your employment.'

'I've had just about enough of you telling me I have no choice,' Harper said. 'But for once in your life, you are right. You do leave me with no choice.' – Klein looked surprised, Charly looked anxious – 'I am sick of this job, this agency and, above all else, sick of you, Klein. You sit here in this office, well out of the firing line, with no thought for the people who produce the goods and the profits – except, that is, when they pose any threat to you, and then you sack them, like you did to Saul, and like you were going to do with Grayson. You don't give a damn about anybody: not even Ned – art directors are two-a-penny in your book. You care about nothing but yourself. And if I never see you again in the whole of my lifetime, then that will be much too soon. So my choice, Klein – the only choice – is to resign.'

Harper stood up. Saw Klein reach for a folder which was lying handily on his desk. Read his name on its front and knew it was his personal file, containing every detail of his life, both private and working, from original job application form onwards.

'If that is your decision,' Klein said, taking the topmost sheet of paper from the file, 'I would like it in writing.' He slid the piece of paper across the desk. 'This is your letter of resignation. Sign at the bottom, please.'

Klein picked up a pen and held it out to Harper.

'Don't bother,' Harper said, drawing his hand back. 'I won't need your pen.'

His fists were still clenched with rage.

Which was just how he wanted them.

Leaning across the desk, he swung a right hook and punched Klein hard on the nose. There was a sickening crunch and an instant flow of blood. Harper reached out, dipped his index finger in the blood and used it to make a cross on the dotted line of the resignation letter.

'You always wanted blood, Klein,' he said. 'Now you've got it.'

Klein sat there, head tilted back, handkerchief clutched to nose, for a little while after they had gone. When the flow of blood had eased sufficiently, he picked up the phone and pressed the one-touch button which dialled a number at AUC.

'They're on their way,' he said nasally.

'You shouldn't have done that,' Charly said.

They were standing side by side just inside the door of Harper's office. He was rubbing his sore knuckles – hell, it was worth a little pain – and survey-ing the room for the last time.

'Shouldn't have done what?' he said. 'Hit Klein?'

'No,' she said, smiling proudly at him. 'Stopped at just one punch.'

'It was tempting, I admit,' he said. 'But my berserkometer needs a better reason before the needle jumps into the red zone.'

'I hate to sound like a recording,' Charly said, 'but what are we going to do now?'

'The same as we always do,' he said. 'once we've heard from Evans, we get out of this place.'

He walked over to his desk, sat down and looked at the two framed photographs, the recent one of Cassie in her school uniform and the much older one of Heather.

'I had intended to clear the office,' he said, 'but there's nothing here I need.'

'I'm glad to hear that,' she said.

'Charly,' he said tentatively, 'did you sell your shares?'

She blushed. 'I didn't get round to it,' she admitted.

'I'd hate for us both to finish up destitute.' He picked up the phone and passed it to her. 'Better call your broker now.'

While she was on the phone Harper picked up the pile of telephone messages that had accumulated during his absence. Only one demanded any action.

'All sold,' Charly said, putting down the phone.

'I hope you didn't lose too much.'

'On the contrary,' she said. 'The price has gone up this morning.'

Harper stared at her.

'According to my broker, who has his ear firmly to the ground,' she said, 'there's a rumour going round that the destruction of the test site wasn't simply about the *mafiosniki* dealing out a lesson to those who won't pay their protection money. The word is that it may have been sabotage. By a competitor – and Laurelle's name is on everybody's lips – who would benefit from the project being put back.'

Harper couldn't believe it. Somehow AUC had emerged from the ordure smelling of roses. Christ, how did Sir Angus do it?

'Brussels,' he said, keeping his thoughts to himself and reading the one important message a second time. 'We go to Brussels. But first I want to introduce you to Mab.'

'Mab? Who is Mab?'

'Someone who can provide us with a smile, a drink and, hopefully, an answer.'

'An answer to what? All our problems?'

'No. Even Mab's not that good. But I'll settle for a stiff vodka and an answer to this riddle. Come on,' he said, handing her the message from Evans. 'You can read as we walk.'

'Kit,' Mab shouted, jumping up excitedly from her chair and running over to Harper. 'I heard the story on the news. I was so worried. It's so good to see you.'

She threw her arms around him, tears running down her cheeks and held him tight. Then she must have noticed Charly. Harper felt Mab's grip slacken and she stepped away from him.

'The return of the prodigal calls for a celebratory drink,' Mab said.

'I was hoping you would say that. Vodka all round, please.'

'All round?' she said. 'Kazakhstan was that bad, was it? Or' – examining Charly intently – 'was it that good?'

'This is Charly Mendoza,' Harper said. 'Charly, this is Mab – an old friend.'

'Not so much of the *old*, Kit, if you don't mind,' Mab said, nodding perfunctorily at Charly while busying herself with fetching the vodka bottle and glasses from the fridge. '*Friend* is bad enough. Sit down, the pair of you.

You look as if you have the weight of the world on your shoulders.'

'How right you are, as always,' Harper said.

He sat down in his usual chair facing Mab, Charly pulled up a seat beside him. Mab slugged back her vodka and immediately poured a refill.

'Uncanny,' she said, looking at Charly. 'And even more beautiful than the glowing reports suggested.' She sighed wistfully. 'Well, Kit, you had better tell me everything that has happened over the last few days. On second thoughts, perhaps not everything.'

'It would take too long to tell you even the half of it. And we have very little time, I'm afraid. Anyway, I suspect Klein is penning an all-staff memorandum right at this minute.' He lowered his voice. 'I'm sorry to be the bearer of bad news, Mab. Ned is dead.'

'Mary, mother of Jesus!' Mab said, closing her eyes. 'I'll miss him. He was a one-off.' She began to cry. 'Oh, Kit,' she sobbed.

Harper walked round the desk, knelt down and put his arms round her. She buried her head into his chest. He felt the wetness of her tears soak into his shirt; placed a hand on her hair and pulled her even closer.

'That's not the only bad news,' Charly said. 'Kit has resigned.'

Mab looked up and stared at her. 'Don't you think that could have waited a moment or two?' she said.

'As Kit said, we don't have much time.'

'If you say so,' Mab said, straightening up and reaching again for the vodka bottle. 'You better sit back down, Kit.'

Harper let her go and walked towards his chair, glaring at Charly as he did so. She just shrugged.

'So,' said Mab, 'tell your *old friend*, was it resigned or iced?'

Iced! Management speak – comfortable euphemism. No one got sacked any more, they merely suffered an Involuntary Career Event. Still meant you didn't get any salary, though.

'Thought I would jump before I was pushed,' Harper said.

'I suppose it was inevitable,' Mab said. 'Been building up for a long while, hasn't it? Well, are you happy now?'

'Not yet. There's still something I have to do.'

'A man's gotta do what a man's gotta do? Don't let me hold you up any longer. Thanks for dropping by. Both of you.' Her hand shaking, she picked up the glass. 'You better go,' she said, turning her head away.

'Don't be like this, Mab,' Harper said. 'I don't understand.'

'You never did, Kit.'

'We need your help,' Charly interrupted. 'We need to look at a map of Brussels.'

'And to pick that brilliant brain of yours,' Harper added.

'Oh, so that's why you came. Is that all I'm good for? I suppose I should be grateful. And pleased.' She squinted enquiringly at Harper and saw the hurt look in his eyes. 'Very well,' she sighed. 'Tell me what you want to know.'

She got up and stepped over to the shelf where the maps were stored. 'Brussels? Ah, here we are.'

Harper spread the map over the desk and peered down at it.

'What do you make of this?' he said to Mab, handing her the message.

'*Meet me at six o'clock,*' she read from the slip of paper, '*Or eight. Or ten. My choice of venue. Evans.* Who is he anyway?'

'Head chemist at AUC,' Harper explained.

'Well, he certainly wasn't giving much away.'

'Recent events have taught him to be careful,' Harper replied. 'And to trust no one.'

'Except you, it would appear. Where would *you* expect to meet him? His office, maybe.'

'Too obvious. And too dangerous.'

'*Six, or eight, or ten,*' Charly said, 'suggests he will keep coming back at two-hourly intervals if you can't make the first time. But where?'

'*His* choice of venue,' Mab said, walking round the desk to consult the map. 'That's the only possible clue in the message. Where would he choose to go? What does he like? Open spaces? Art? Music?'

'He's a keen Gilbert and Sullivan fan,' Harper said.

'There's the Theatre Royal,' Charly suggested. 'That's where the *Opera National* performs. Although I don't think Gilbert and Sullivan merits being included in their repertoire.'

'Mikado,' Harper said, thinking back. He had admitted to the chemist that he knew Evans's passwords. So, maybe Mikado was the clue. 'Is there anything particularly Japanese in Brussels?'

'Half a dozen restaurants,' Charly said. 'So which to choose? And in any case, Andrew never struck me as someone who would find sushi satisfying. More a steak and chips man.'

'Not the opera, not a restaurant,' Mab said, thinking aloud. 'Museum? Art gallery?'

'A whole host of them,' Charly said. 'Costume and lace, music, ancient art, modern art—'

'Too much choice again,' said Harper. 'And Andrew was no art lover. Art and science rarely make good bedfellows.'

'That's it,' said Mab. 'That's the clue.'

'Bedfellows?' Harper said, raising his eyebrows in puzzlement.

'Science,' said Mab.

Harper's mind flashed back to the view from the window of the AUC boardroom. The structure that dominated the distant skyline. He stabbed his finger at a point on the map. 'The Atomium,' he said. 'The bloody Atomium. Mab, you're a genius.'

'I owe it all to clean living,' she said. 'Unfortunately.'

'We have to go,' Harper said, standing up. He kissed Mab on the cheek. 'Thanks, Mab. For everything.'

'Keep in touch, Kit.'

'I will. I promise.'

Harper gave her one last smile and headed for the door, Charly following hard on his heels.

Mab grabbed Charly by the arm. 'She'll see you outside, Kit,' she said.

'Let go of me,' Charly protested.

'Just one thing before you go,' Mab said, her face close to Charly's. 'You make sure you look after him. Or you'll have me to reckon with. And we Irish have wicked tempers. Understand?'

'Message received,' Charly said, jerking her arm from out of Mab's grip. 'Loud and clear. Over and out.'

31

It would soon be over. That was crystal clear to Harper as he and Charly trudged wearily along the walkways from the arrivals gate to passport control. It wasn't just receiving the cryptic message from Evans – an obvious signal that the vital evidence had been found. Harper's every instinct told him that he was being carried along on the upward wave of the crescendo towards the inevitable climax.

It was a quarter past eight when they emerged from the airport terminal and saw the long queue for taxis.

'How long do you think Andrew will wait?' Charly asked.

'Not this long,' Harper said. 'He will have heard by now about the deaths and destruction at the test site – Andrew won't be taking any chances.'

'Taxi?' said a tall man wrapped in a dark-blue padded anorak. He had sidled up to them from the direction of the terminal while they had been talking.

Harper nodded and the man signalled for them to follow him across the road to the short-term car park. As they set off, the man was growled at and jeered by the first few taxi drivers in line. Harper looked questioningly at Charly.

'Like most airports,' she said, 'there is an official system here for pick-ups. Taxis are supposed to join the end of the queue and take their turn. This man is a queue-jumper. He won't win any friends, and risks a rebuke and a fine from the authorities, but he'll save half an hour of sitting around empty and wasting fuel while he moves forward a few metres at a time.'

They climbed into the back of the black Mercedes and Charly told the driver their destination. He set the meter running, pulled out of the car park and dutifully radioed his base.

Dusk was falling as they travelled the familiar route towards the city centre. It was twenty minutes before the driver veered off in an arc that ran along the side of the wide Canal de Charleroi to the north of the city. By then, the sky was black and the illuminated globes of the Atomium seemed to hang impossibly in the air without any visible means of support. Although Harper had not been to the top of the structure – Heather had gone alone and taken panoramic photographs of the city while he had cowardly smoked a cigarette in the reassuring safety of ground level – he knew the history. The nine aluminium-covered steel spheres with their interconnecting lattice of struts was a representation of an iron crystal, magnified 200,000 times. The structure had been built in 1958 in the Parc des Expositions for the World Fair: its slogan had been '*Bâtir le monde por l'homme.*' – building the world for mankind. Harper wondered whether this had either directly or subconsciously influenced Evans's choice of venue.

They walked through the park, circled the Atomium and, having seen no sign of Evans, retreated to a café on the Quai du Commerce to while away an hour.

'We pitched for a cigarette account once,' Harper said, while drinking his third double espresso and smoking his fourth cigarette. 'Didn't get it – Ned's creative "solution" was to play up the dangers of smoking to make the brand more attractive to those who aspired to be seen as reckless rebels, and the client, quite naturally, had cold feet – but I learnt a lot. Did you know that cigarettes are the only drug where the therapeutic effects depend on the smoker's mental state? If you want to feel enervated, then they will act as a stimulant: if you want to relax, they will act as a tranquillizer.'

'I didn't know,' Charly said, savouring the froth of her cappuccino, 'but it doesn't really surprise me. We're still learning about precisely how drugs function.'

'So Andrew was telling me. We had a long discussion about thalidomide and the recent discovery of time-windows.' Harper checked his watch: ten minutes before the next appointed time. 'Let's go,' he said. 'But I warn you, my system is so awash with adrenaline, nicotine and caffeine that you'll have to hold my hand tightly to stop me floating up into the stratosphere.'

'Only if I must,' she said. 'Or if it makes us less conspicuous.'

They walked hand in hand back to the park, looking to all the world like lovers on a casual stroll before returning home to bed. Huddling together under a clump of trees, they watched the approach to the Atomium. As the bells of St Catherine's tolled ten o'clock, the unmistakable round figure of Evans came waddling comically into view.

Harper and Charly emerged from the shadows and set out to meet him. Evans saw them, acknowledging their presence not with a wave or a smile, but merely by increasing his pace. The chemist stepped into the light radiating from the lowest sphere.

And the sound of a shot rang out.

Harper pushed Charly in the small of the back, sending her flying forwards onto the grass and then dived down beside her. He peered at the shape of Evans spread-eagled and motionless twenty yards away.

'Keep down,' Harper ordered Charly. 'Make your way back to the trees. Phone for an ambulance and the police. Tell them it's urgent. Very urgent.'

He crawled on his elbows and stomach until he was alongside Evans. Felt his heart sink as he saw the gaping hole in his friend's chest where the nose of the bullet had opened out on impact to produce a deep red crater. There was a dark circle of blood – God, hadn't there been enough blood spilled? – spreading out rapidly over the front of Evans's check shirt.

'Hang on,' he said, gripping Evans's hand. 'An ambulance is on its way. You'll be all right.'

Evans summoned his rapidly fading resources of strength to shake his head. He moved his lips inaudibly.

Harper bent close.

'Files. AUC,' Evans gurgled, blood in his mouth, tears in his eyes. 'Sorry.'

'It's my fault, Andrew,' Harper said. 'We must have led them to you. Forgive me.'

Evans stared into Harper's eyes. Opened his mouth one last time. Framed the words *No . . . forgive. . . .*

But no sound came out, except the death rattle.

On the first occasion Harper had heard that sound it had turned his blood to ice. Neither time nor recent harsh familiarity had diminished its effect. With a shudder that came from both the past and present, he searched the body. Wiping his bloody hands on his jeans, he slipped the only item of any use into his pocket.

There was no point any more in waiting for the ambulance, even less for the police. That would only slow them down. There was work to do. Another death to be avenged.

When the wailing of the sirens was close enough to frighten off even the most foolhardy killer, Harper ran back to Charly. She was standing a little apart from a small group of people who had arrived on the scene. Some were looking suspiciously at Harper, others tentatively at the body on the grass; all were wondering what to do.

'Come on, Charly,' Harper said, putting his arms around her. 'We have to go before the police arrive and want to ask questions – that's something you said you didn't want. Let's go. We can't help Andrew any more.'

He led her around the back of the Atomium and across to the far side of the park. Once on the wide boulevard running east, he pushed her along – keep her moving, stop her thinking – glancing frequently back over his shoulder to scan the traffic. After a couple of hundred yards he saw the yellow sign of an empty taxi and stuck his arm out into the road.

'Where are we going?' Charly asked as they climbed inside.

'The AUC building,' Harper said to both Charly and the driver. 'Evans mentioned the files. I have to retrace his steps, rediscover the evidence he found.'

'What's with the *I?*' she said. 'I thought we were in this together.'

'Someone always seems to be one jump ahead of us. There's no sense in both of us walking into what might well be a trap.'

'There's every sense,' she said. 'I want to speak to my grandfather.'

'Now isn't the time.'

'OK then, tell me this, how are you going to get through security without me?'

'I have Andrew's pass card.'

'If it still works,' she said scornfully. 'And even if it hasn't been cancelled, you have to get past the guard. Don't you think he might notice the odd subtle difference between you and Andrew? Like height, weight and facial features for instance. Your only chance of getting into the building is with me.'

'But—'

'We do it together, Kit,' she said. 'Unless you'd rather I did it on my own? It's entirely your decision.'

'And, as usual,' he sighed, 'I don't have any choice.'

The taxi drew up outside the building. Lights shone brightly on the top floor and dimly on their night setting in the reception area. Harper paid off the driver and followed Charly to the door. She pressed the buzzer. The guard turned away from the bank of security monitors flashing different scenes of rooms throughout the building, recognized Charly, gave a little nod to himself and rose from his desk. He unlocked the door with his master pass card and stood there for a moment analyzing Charly's cheap jeans and T-shirt and hiding his disappointment that she wasn't wearing something more revealing – not that from the look in his X-ray eyes it would have made much difference to the vision in his mind.

'Ms Mendoza,' he said, running the back of his hand across his mouth, 'I didn't know you were back.'

'A lot to catch up on,' she said, brushing past him and heading for the lift. Charly turned back towards Harper, shook her head and sighed. 'Come along there. We don't want to be here all night.'

Harper gave a shrug, rolled his eyes at the guard and hurried after her.

'Let's walk up,' he said loudly.

Charly swiped her card through the slot at the door to the stairwell and they stepped out of sight. Harper, unwilling to break the eerie silence, pointed down the stairs and they descended one floor. It needed another swipe of Charly's pass card to exit the stairwell and one more to gain entry through the heavy security doors to the main laboratory.

The vast room was in total darkness. Harper took out his lighter, spun the wheel and in the flickering light walked on tiptoe to Evans's office.

'Isn't this all a little unnecessary?' Charly said. 'Lighters and tiptoes! We're below ground level, so no one would see if we turned on the lights. And, unless the guard has the hearing of a mole, no one can hear us either.'

'What about the security cameras?' Harper said, feeling a little foolish. 'Won't they pick up the lights?'

'It's just I would have thought it was better to act normally, rather than like a couple of cartoon burglars. If anyone did pass by and spot us, then we couldn't look more suspicious if we were wearing striped jerseys and masks and carrying a bag marked *swag.*'

'A little less criticism and a little more solidarity wouldn't go amiss,' he grunted, entering the office and sitting down at Evans's desk. He flicked on the anglepoise lamp. 'Satisfied?'

'Now what?' she shrugged.

'There was nothing in Andrew's pockets, so whatever he found is still somewhere inside the computer system. Let's see if he left us a note.'

Harper switched on the computer and tapped his fingers while the machine whirred into life.

'You'll need my password,' Charly said.

Harper shook his head. 'My guess is that eventually we're going to have to delve into the scientific files. I'd be surprised if even you had that level of clearance.'

At the computer's prompt Harper keyed in MIKADO.

'How did you get to know Andrew's password?' Charly asked.

'Photographic memory,' he shrugged. 'Simply watched as he typed it in and then replayed the scene in my mind.'

'Thanks for warning me,' she said.

Harper, having been given entry to the first security level, gave a sigh of relief and double-clicked the email icon on the screen.

'Hell!' he said, seeing the long list of mail.

'Andrew's an important man in AUC and the scientific community in general,' Charly said. 'His mail will have built up while he was away.'

'He checked his mail on Sunday evening,' Harper said. 'Remember the email from Françoise claiming to have discovered the inhibitor? There must be nearly fifty items of mail here, and none of them seems to have been read, unless he didn't delete them afterwards.' He scanned down the list, examining the screen names of the senders – none leapt out at him as a possible clue. Next he checked the companion file of mail sent. 'Out of luck, Charly,' he said. 'I was hoping he would have sent mail to either himself or to one of us.'

'You said yourself that he wouldn't be taking any chances,' she said. 'If there's a clue somewhere it will be a subtle one.'

Harper exited the mail program, went into the word processing package and saw an equally lengthy and unpromising list of document names. No clues, subtle or otherwise. He sat staring at the screen, hoping for inspiration. Pulling out the top drawer of the desk, he started a systematic search – for what he didn't know.

There was all manner of junk stored away in the desk. Harper's mind flashed back to his schooldays as he examined the collection of pens, pencils, boiled sweets (fruit flavoured), two packets of mints and candy bar wrappers: all that was missing was a prize marble, a comic, a piece of knotted string and a ticket to Hampstead Fair – only the brave deserve the fair! His eyes settled on the stainless steel box that contained the sample of the Gaia enzyme. A perfect hiding place for a message. His spirits rose as he took it out and opened the lid. Then fell again: no note, just dull-grey powder. He put the box in his pocket as potential evidence and turned back to the screen.

'Let's try the Gaia file,' he said as he typed in the second level password.

He closed his eyes to picture the reference number, and keyed it in. Next he reduced the size of the layout until it was a whole page, so that the type-script would match that of the hard copy he had read. It took only a couple of minutes to scan through the document, comparing the picture on each screen to his mental image of the physical page. The file appeared to be exactly the same as the one he had worked his way through less than a fort-night ago. Was it really so little time since he had sat in this office last? So much had happened, so many lives lost, since Evans had wittered away enthusiastically while munching sandwiches.

'There's nothing here,' he said, sitting back in the chair and rubbing away at the scar with his finger.

'Surely it would have been too obvious,' Charly pointed out. 'Too easy for the bad guys to spot. Wouldn't he take the same precautions he did when leaving the message about the venue? Use a cryptic clue or code? Something that you might break, but wouldn't mean anything to anyone else?'

'Any ideas?'

She shrugged.

Harper backtracked out of the Gaia file and into the index. It ran to more than a hundred pages – thousands of numbers.

'It would take a lifetime to go through this lot,' he said. 'We're missing something, Charly.'

'What exactly did Andrew say?'

'Just three words – all he could manage. *Files. AUC. Sorry.* Then some-thing about forgive. The *sorry* I take as an apology for getting shot, for letting us down by dying before the job was finished. *Files* and *AUC* seemed obvi-ous. I didn't expect to be faced with the prospect of trawling through thou-sands of numbered files.'

'Maybe he had a lucky number,' Charly said.

'Well, it sure didn't work for him tonight.'

'What about the date then?'

'Which date? Today's? Yesterday's? His birth date? The battle of Waterloo?'

'Don't snap at me, Harper. I'm only trying to help.'

'Sorry, Charly,' he said, reaching into his pocket for his cigarettes.

'Not here,' she said, pointing at the smoke detector on the ceiling and adding to his misery and frustration.

He yanked at the desk drawer and took out a packet of mints. Popped one surreptitiously in his mouth as if concealing a punishable offence from a schoolteacher. Then every synapse in his brain clicked open.

Harper leapt up from the desk, threw his arms around and kissed her.

'You're wonderful,' he said, dancing around her with delight. 'Bloody wonderful.'

'True,' she said. 'But why tell me now?'

'Because you were right. It *is* the date. It must be. I'd stake my life on it.'

'So which date? Waterloo, is that it?'

'No,' he said, shaking his head vigorously. 'Waterloo is in Belgium, I grant you, but not Andrew's period of history.'

'Then what, for chrissake, Kit?'

'Andrew and I are two opposites,' he said. 'We have absolutely nothing in common. Except a shared passion.'

Charly looked at him as if he had finally flipped.

'Andrew told me,' he began to explain, 'that while he was at school he studied Latin. Couldn't get on with the language, but loved the history. Roman history. Tales of courage and bravery, heroes like Horatius defending the bridge over the Tiber against a whole army.'

'What the hell has all this to do with the date?'

'What's the precise date today?' he asked.

Charly sighed and told him in a bored voice.

'Wrong,' he said. 'You got the day and month right, but you're out by a mile on the year. If you calculate it according to Roman history, that is. The Romans had a different base for their dating system. *Ab urbe condita* – since the founding of the city, it means. Shortened to AUC. That must be what Andrew meant.'

'So where is the evidence? What is the magic number?'

'Rome was founded, in their terms, in the year Zero AUC – 753 BC according to our system. Whatever Andrew found is hidden in file number 753.'

Harper punched out the number and waited with pounding heart for the file to load.

'Shit,' he said as the first page came up on the screen. 'Shit bloody shit.'

'What is it?' Charly asked.

'How the hell do I know?' Harper answered, pointing at the screen. 'A whole lot of scientific gobbledegook. I don't understand a word of it. Doesn't seem to relate to Gaia either. It looks like it's back to the drawing board, Charly.'

He moved the mouse to close the file.

'Wait,' said Charly. 'You had a flash of inspiration, and followed it up with sound reasoning. Don't give up so easily. Maybe this was Andrew's final safeguard. Scroll down a page.'

Harper did as she said. The top of the next page bore his name.

'We've done it, Charly,' he said, reading quickly through the first paragraph. 'We have bloody done it. Looks like it's all here.' He read on a little. 'The vital evidence is contained on two back-up disks in the computer room. Can you use your feminine charms and royal blood to get them?'

Harper took a piece of paper from the holder on the desk, wrote down the dates of the two disks and handed the paper to Charly.

'Be as quick as you can,' he said. 'Once we have the disks we're out of here. Then you can call your grandfather and tell him everything. And then we go to the police.'

'Give me five minutes,' she said, bending down and kissing him on the cheek.

While she was gone, Harper continued to read Evans's note. When he had reached the end, he went back and re-read the last few paragraphs. Then he sat back in the chair and stared up at the ceiling, lost in thought, tears streaming from his eyes.

Evans – brave friend, nothing would ever change that – had done a thorough job. Left no stone unturned. And uncovered the maggots wriggling beneath. More maggots, feeding off more dead bodies, than Harper had expected.

Everything was now clear to Harper.

AUC was finished. It would never survive the scandal, the recriminations, the claims for damages. It was as dead as Andrew, Ned, Drew . . . the list seemed endless.

Vengeance is mine, thought Harper. Vengeance will be mine.

He got up from the desk and made his way out of the office and towards the door.

It opened as he approached.

In the light from the corridor he could see Charly clutching the two disks.

She took a pace forward.

There was an arm around her neck. And a gun pressed against her head.

'We meet again, Harper,' the man with the gun said, limping into the room.

32

'Sorry,' Charly said. 'I've blown it, haven't I? I was just on my way back from the computer room when Stoker here bushwhacked me.'

'Stoker?' Harper said. 'Good to have a name at last. You were the thug who smashed the jogger's legs at the park. And shot Andrew, too, I presume?'

'I'm a man of many talents,' Stoker said.

'None of them endearing,' Harper replied.

'You should be nice to me, Harper. I haven't decided yet quite what to do with you. A bullet seems too quick for all the trouble you've caused us. Maybe I'll strangle you like Mueller. I find killing with bare hands is so much more satisfying.'

Harper paused to assess the situation.

Psychopathic killer. Gun pointed at Charly's brains. His own imminent death. No means of escape. No handy weapons to make a fight of it. Didn't look very promising.

The first priority, he decided, was to get Charly out of danger, preferably with the disks. How exactly to do that was another matter.

'Since I'm going to die anyway,' he said, playing for time, 'why not humour me by answering a few questions.'

'As long as you return the favour,' Stoker said. 'And don't mind me at the same time doing a bit of lateral thinking on the manner of your death.'

'Whatever turns you on, Stoker.'

'So nice to be given carte blanche by your victim.'

'First question,' Harper said. 'Who the hell are you?'

'Stoker, Ronald, but you can call me Ronnie – for the next few minutes at least. Head of Security.'

'Insecurity, more like. But then there's a lot to feel insecure about.'

'How much do you know, Harper?'

'Pretty much everything. And what I don't know I can guess. I take it Mueller was blackmailing AUC? That's why you killed him.'

'Don't shed any tears for Mueller,' – not a snowball's chance in hell, thought Harper – 'he was a pathetic, selfish, greedy little man. Do you know how much he wanted to keep quiet about the enzyme? Five million pounds. Fucking stroll on!'

Chance would be a fine thing, thought Harper.

'And the murders of the other businessmen – the Nazi serial killer strikes again! – were just a cover?' he asked rhetorically. 'Slot Mueller somewhere among a series of apparently racially motivated deaths and switch the focus of attention away from AUC?'

'Good plan, beautifully executed,' said Stoker.

'Not in the eye of this beholder,' said Harper, taking a step forward.

'Stay where you are, Harper. Don't make the target too easy for me. I'm good with a gun, don't spoil the fun.'

'Catchy slogan,' Harper said. 'But if you're so good, why smash the legs of Charbonnier? I know he was against the acquisition of Laurelle, but shooting him would have been a more effective way to stop him vetoing the takeover. Quicker, too.'

'You've just answered your own question. My motto, Harper, is a man should get the maximum enjoyment from his work. Sir Angus didn't want Charbonnier killed' – he looked sideways at Charly – 'sorry if I disillusion you about your grandfather, Ms Mendoza, but he thought it might create too much of a stir within the European Commission, or, much more inconveniently, that Charbonnier might be replaced by someone apart from his perverted deputy – but he left the choice of how to take him out of the action up to me.'

'What a fertile mind you have.'

Harper shook his head, using the gesture to glance round the room. There would be chemicals in the cabinets, but they were under lock and key, and he wouldn't know which to use as a weapon in any case; probably finish up flinging some liquid in Stoker's face only to find out it was AUC's new improved skin cleanser. There were four different fire extinguishers by the door, but the path to them was blocked. He returned his gaze to Stoker and noticed that he was looking around too. Trying to predict Harper's moves, or something more sinister?

'Did Kazam report to you,' Harper continued, 'or direct to Sir Angus?'

'To me. Pretty much everything goes through me, except a few personal sources of Sir Angus. You were very careless, Harper. Taking notes and leaving them lying around.'

'Lying around *inside* a suitcase *inside* my room.'

Stoker shrugged, brushing aside the naïve criticism of industrial espionage. 'Once we knew you were on the trail, we hoped to frighten you off by kidnapping your daughter. What the hell kind of a name is Cassandra, anyway?'

'Greek mythology. Daughter of Priam, king of Troy. As a punishment for rejecting the love of Apollo, Cassandra was given the gift of prophecy, but with the rider that she was never to be believed.'

'Ain't that fitting,' Stoker grinned. 'Anyway, when we snatched the wrong girl there wasn't any option but to kill you. Evans, too, before he found out there was no inhibitor. And, to make it look good, everybody else.'

'Did that include Charly?' Harper said. 'Did your orders from Sir Angus include Charly?'

'Ah, Charly,' Stoker said. 'What are we going to do with you, eh?'

'You could let her go.'

'Good suggestion, Harper,' he sneered. ''Tell me, should I let her take these disks too? "And they all lived happily ever after!" You've got me confused with someone else. I don't do fairy stories.'

'You surprise me.'

'I hope so,' Stoker said. 'Charly's coming with me to see Sir Angus. He can decide her fate. Meanwhile, Harper, you can cool your heels down here. See that gas chamber over there? Get in it.'

Stoker took the gun away from Charly's head for a moment, used it to wave Harper in the direction of the airtight chamber and then returned it to its position of maximum threat.

'What if I refuse?' Harper asked.

'Then I lighten Sir Angus's decision-making burden by taking one for him. I'll shoot Charly. And then you. Now stop fucking around and get in the chamber.'

'Only because you ask so nicely,' Harper said.

He walked across the room and placed his hands on the drop-down front of the chamber.

'I might need some help with this,' he said.

Stoker cocked the gun.

'On second thoughts,' he said, 'I think I can manage.'

He squeezed himself inside and got his legs into a position where he could kick up at the front when Stoker attempted to move the handles into the lock position.

Stoker manoeuvred Charly to the chamber. 'Lock it,' he said.

'Sorry, Kit,' she said, turning the handles. 'I don't know what else to do.'

'Don't worry, Charly,' he replied with a smile. 'I'll be all right. I have a secret weapon.'

Stoker frowned.

'Right will always conquer might,' Harper said.

'You had me worried for a moment,' Stoker admitted. 'But you got it the wrong way round. Might tramples over right every time. Now, try and be a good boy while I'm gone. And don't use up all the air before I get back. I've thought of something really slow and horrible for you.'

'I can hardly wait.'

'But please do.'

Whoever had designed and built the airtight chamber had done a good job – unfortunately. The controls for the fans and to flush the inside with clean air were, quite logically, out of reach on the outside. The Plexiglas walls were thick and impenetrable. Harper had spent the first few minutes kicking furiously at the drop-down front: the thing didn't even wobble, let alone budge. Next he had tugged at one of the rubber gloves dangling inside; had managed to wrench it off, only to find that the flap covering the armhole was locked and as solid as everything else about the cabinet. All he succeeded in doing was wasting precious time and air and making himself hot, more angry and breathless. The walls of the chamber were now beginning to steam up.

Estimating the dimensions of the chamber, he tried to calculate how many cubic litres of air was inside, and, by remembering the days of scuba-diving holidays, convert that into minutes of survival time. Maybe he'd got the answer wrong – fifteen minutes didn't sound good. But then maybe it didn't matter that much. It all depended on how long it would be before Stoker returned. If it was a short while, then Harper would still be trapped and a sitting duck for whatever gruesome fate was in store: and if it was a long time, then not only would he have suffocated but probably the delay would have been caused by Stoker taking time out to kill Charly.

It can't end this way, Harper thought. Not if there is any justice in this world. *Dum spiro spero* – while I breathe, I hope.

He concentrated on controlling his racing pulse and slowing his breathing, but the beads of perspiration running into his eyes made that difficult. Contorting his body, he stripped off his jacket and tossed it behind him. The jacket made a dull clang when it landed.

The box! The stainless steel box!

He reached behind and took the box from his pocket. Opened the lid and stared at the dull-grey powder. There seemed so little of it. And the Plexiglas was so thick.

'Gaia,' he said aloud, sprinkling the enzyme over the plastic around the locks of the drop-down front of the chamber, 'we started out with such high hopes for you. A miracle product! Well, right now, that's what I need. A miracle.'

Harper stared at the locks, willing the surrounding plastic to dissolve before his eyes. Nothing happened. His mind flashed back to the conversation with Evans. *Each enzyme works at a specific temperature.* Was it too hot in here? Surely not, think of the temperature in the silo. Was it too cold then? Can't be – what's the use of a product that will only work for part of the year in the hottest parts of the world? Gaia needed time. And that was the only thing he didn't have.

He felt his eyes closing – fifteen minutes had been an overestimate, the oxygen in the air was already running low. Breathe deep and slow.

Through flickering eyelids he saw the bottom of the Plexiglas flap begin to glaze over. Felt the heat of reaction radiating out towards him.

Sleepy. So sleepy.

'Wake up, Daddy,' he heard Cassie say.

'Wake up, darling,' Heather said. 'For me, Kit. You know what you must do.'

A chemical aroma – burning oil? melting wax? – hit his nose and acted like smelling salts. He shook his head, trying to clear his brain.

It was now or never. Wait any longer, Harper, and you won't have sufficient strength left in your body for the task in hand.

He kicked out at the plastic around the first lock. It separated from the chamber, leaving the lock still in position.

One last breath. One last kick.

He kicked out at the other lock with both feet, then immediately rolled his body toward the front of the chamber. The whole Plexiglas front gave way. Harper fell to the floor, gasping for breath.

He lay there for a moment recovering, and realized that time was still ticking away. Getting up, Harper reached into the chamber for his jacket, took out Evans's pass card and walked to the door. He swiped the card through the slot and pushed at the door.

It didn't open.

Charly had been right. The card was no use any more. Evans was dead and Stoker, not only a psychopath but also possessing the tidy mind of an anal retentive, had taken away his privileges along with his life.

Harper heard the click of the door lock retracting.

There was nowhere to hide, or, at least, nowhere he would not be eventually found. If he was going to make a stand, some kind of weapon wouldn't go amiss. He looked at the line of fire extinguishers, knew there was no time to consider the relative merits of foam, carbon dioxide, powder and water and simply chose the heaviest. As Stoker stepped through the door, Harper swung the extinguisher and hit him hard on the back of the neck.

Stoker stumbled forward a pace, regained his balance like an ice skater who has misjudged a triple salko by placing the tips of the fingers of his free hand momentarily on the floor, sprang upright and spun around, gun in hand.

Harper swung the extinguisher a second time, aiming at the gun hand and connecting with Stoker's fingers. There was a howl of pain. The gun dropped from Stoker's broken grasp and clattered to the floor.

Stoker, eyes narrowed in pain, bent down, his good hand reaching for the gun.

Harper brought the extinguisher in an upward arc, thumping Stoker under the chin and sending him flying backwards. Stoker used his forearms to break the fall, rolled over and jumped back to his feet.

Harper kicked out at the gun.

Stoker kicked out at Harper's leg.

They both connected.

The gun skittered across the floor, coming to rest against the base of one of the workbenches.

Harper was sent spinning, first around and then down.

Stoker made a dash for the gun. As he passed, Harper swung the extinguisher into his shinbones. There was a sickening crack.

'That's for Charbonnier,' Harper said, scrabbling to his feet.

Stoker's forward momentum propelled him across the floor. He slid, face down, across the polished surface. Towards the gun.

Harper ran forward. Stoker's left hand was already on the butt of the gun.

Too far away to use the extinguisher as a club, Harper was running out of options. Stoker, still lying prostrate on the floor, pivoted on one elbow and began to take aim.

So did Harper. He pointed the black cone-shaped nozzle of the extinguisher at Stoker and squeezed the trigger. A stream of white vapour gushed towards Stoker's face. Carbon dioxide, super-cooled by the pressure inside the extinguisher, penetrated Stoker's staring eyes and formed ice crystals on his lashes and brows. Blindly, Stoker swivelled the gun in the air, searching for a telltale sound which would pinpoint a target.

Harper stepped quickly to the side, avoiding the first wildly aimed bullet. He moved behind Stoker. Swung the extinguisher one more time. Brought it down on the back of Stoker's head.

'And that's for Evans,' he said.

Harper bent down, registered with mixed emotions that Stoker was breathing, and searched the unconscious man's pockets. He took the pass card in one hand, the gun in the other, and, determination etched on his face as visibly as the scar, strode purposefully towards the door.

33

There was a long rectangle of light coming out from underneath the double doors of the boardroom. The light at the end of the tunnel? Harper pushed opened the door and entered.

They were sitting on opposite sides of the long conference table, Sir Angus Cameron, in shirt sleeves and braces, with his back to the wall and Charly, the disks in front of her, with her chair turned to face the window rather than her grandfather. Every light in the room was on, even that in the display case containing Cameron's dress uniform, medals and ceremonial sword – maybe he needed to remind himself that he had, presumably, once been a man of honour.

'Harper?' said Cameron, his expression of surprise quickly turning to a frown when he saw the gun.

'Kit,' said Charly, swivelling round and smiling with relief.

She jumped up, ran across to Harper and threw her arms around him.

'I told you I had a secret weapon,' he said. 'How are you, Charly? Stoker didn't hurt you, did he?'

'I'm all right, Kit,' she said, hugging him. 'Couldn't be better now, in fact.'

Cameron placed his hands on the table and made to push himself up on to his feet.

'Stay where you are,' Harper said. 'I may not be much of a crack shot, but I doubt very much that even I could miss a target the size of your bloated body at this short range.'

'Put the gun down, Harper. You don't want to shoot me.'

'Don't be so sure of that.'

'I know you inside out,' Cameron said, the Scottish burr tinged with derision. 'Every little detail of your sad life. You're not the type to kill.'

'Even an expert in the subject like you can be wrong sometimes.'

Cameron shrugged, his huge body wobbling with the movement.

'Sit down, Harper,' he said. 'We need to talk.'

'You talk. I'll pace around. I've been a bit cramped up lately; it feels good to stretch my legs.'

'I've been discussing you with Charlotte. I'm prepared to make you an offer.'

'If it's to buy some time until Stoker rides in like the US cavalry, guns blazing, then don't bother – he's sleeping off a headache at the moment and won't be going anywhere when he wakes up. And if it's to buy my silence, save your breath.'

'Every man has his price,' Cameron said.

'I agree,' said Harper, 'but you won't be willing to pay mine.'

'You're trying my patience,' Cameron said, sighing blatantly.

'Patience is a virtue. Everything comes to him who waits.'

'Spare me the self-righteous crap, Harper, and listen. I am willing to offer you the sum of five million pounds, *if* you forget all about the enzyme and everything connected with it.'

'This five million pounds?' said Harper, 'it wouldn't happen to be the same one you paid to Mueller – the one that yo-yoed it's way back to you on a length of rope that was once wrapped around his neck?'

'Money is money, Harper. It doesn't matter where it comes from, only that it gives you power. You can spend it too, of course. Couldn't you do with some spending money? Expensive business bringing up a wee bairn, employing a nanny, finding school fees, paying a mortgage. Especially when you don't have a job and an income. Five million pounds would solve all your problems. Think about it. Five million pounds. Accept my offer, Harper. Why make life difficult for yourself?'

'Maybe because I have a credibility problem where you are concerned. Tell me, why should I trust you?'

'Because of Charlotte. My Charlotte. Your Charly. I've always done my best for her, Harper. That you must believe. It was for Charlotte's own good that I wanted her out of AUC. Sooner or later – five years, ten years after the launch of Gaia, who knows? – someone would have been bound to notice the increased rate of genetic mutations and cancer-related deaths and worked out the truth about the enzyme. Then the shit would hit the fan. That didn't matter to me – by that time I would have retired and spent a few peaceful years as the highly respected, and very rich, Lord Cameron. But I had to think of Charlotte – I didn't want her to have to take any of the blame, be burdened with any of the guilt.'

'I believe you,' Harper said, Cameron confirming his own suspicions. 'What I can't credit is that you were willing to sacrifice her in Kazakhstan.'

'I doubt whether it would have come to that,' Cameron said, waving a podgy hand dismissively in the air and smiling benevolently at Charly. 'Kazam would have found a way to save her.'

'Firing indiscriminately with machine guns and using plastic explosive is not the best way of singling out someone for salvation. Don't bullshit me, Cameron,' Harper said, his voice raised, the gun waving about. 'I work – I worked – in advertising: I've lived with bullshit for so long I can smell it a mile away. When it came to the crunch, Charly was expendable. Protecting her only mattered to you as long as she posed no threat. You care for no one, Cameron. No one but yourself.'

'Five million pounds, Harper.'

'I wonder,' said Harper. 'How much is that per head? Not for Charly and I, you understand. But how much for each innocent person across the world who will die because Gaia causes cancer? How much for each child whose life is ruined by being born with some deformity because Gaia causes genetic mutations? You don't value life very dearly, do you?'

'Six million. That's my final offer.'

'Not for fifty million,' Harper said.

'I told you so,' Charly said to her grandfather, a wide self-satisfied smile on her lips. 'Kit can't be bought.'

'My conscience wouldn't allow it,' Harper said. 'But then that's something you would never comprehend, Cameron. You have no conscience.' Harper walked over to the display cabinet and glanced at its contents while still keeping one eye on Cameron. 'I've had the misfortune to meet some pretty immoral people in my time,' he continued, 'but you are totally amoral. You have no moral code at all.'

'You can't afford morals in business,' Cameron said. 'That's my philosophy.'

'And a philosophy that was absolutely apparent to your staff, for many of them followed it – Mueller and Françoise, to name but two. A company takes its direction from the top – isn't that what we once said, Charly? Protect oneself – priority number one: protect the company – priority number two. That leaves no room for other priorities. You, Cameron, have bred an organization which cares nothing for its fellow man, and which shares your contempt for the whole of humanity.'

Harper looked away from Cameron as if it were the only way to prevent himself being physically sick. He raised the gun and smashed the barrel into the glass of the display cabinet. Cameron jolted in his seat.

Sticking the gun into the waistband of his jeans, Harper reached into the cabinet. He took out the sword, drew the blade from the scabbard, threw the ornate sheath contemptuously on to the floor and walked across the room until he was standing directly over Cameron.

'A sword of honour?' Harper said. 'Isn't that what this is called?'

'Don't break it,' Cameron said. 'The sword is precious to me.'

'Snap it in two across my knee? There's a thought. But no, I have a much better use for this sword than merely to make a symbolic gesture.'

Harper placed the point of the sword on Cameron's white shirt. Pressed down until he saw fear in Cameron's eyes. Then drew it swiftly from side to side across Cameron's chest.

A porcine squeal came from between Cameron's lips.

Charly looked at Harper as a line of blood, running directly under both swollen quasi-feminine breasts, appeared on her grandfather's shirt.

'What are you doing?' Cameron said.

'Do you know how many times my wife was cut open?' Harper said to Cameron.

He shook his head, unable to speak for once.

'And I thought you knew so much about me,' Harper mocked. 'Still, I don't blame you for not being able to answer. Even I lost count in the end. That means I'll just have to guess.'

Harper flashed the blade down Cameron's right side. Another line of blood, wider and more deeply furrowed this time, spurted out on the shirt.

'I had nothing to do with your wife's death,' Cameron said, his voice an octave higher, the words tumbling out of his mouth in panic. 'She died of cancer, Harper. It's there in black and white in your file. Her death is one you *can't* pin on me.'

'He's right,' Charly shouted. 'Stop it, Kit. Please.'

'You're mad, Harper,' Cameron said. 'Charlotte, do something.'

'Why do you think there are two disks on the table?' Harper asked, slashing the sword down the left side of Cameron's body.

They both stared at him. Cameron clutched at the new wound with both hands.

'Andrew was a thorough man,' Harper said. 'You should have had more like him, Cameron. And fewer like Mueller.'

'Why are you doing this, Kit?' Charly said. 'I don't understand.'

'Andrew didn't just check on the Gaia enzyme,' Harper explained. 'He must have been concerned that if Mueller had fiddled the figures once to conceal evidence, he might well have done so on other occasions, on other products. Andrew delved into another file. Then he wished he hadn't. That's why Andrew said sorry with his dying breath. It wasn't because he felt he had failed us. It was a personal apology to me. He wanted me to forgive him.'

Harper moved the sword until the point was pressed against Cameron's windpipe.

'It wasn't Andrew's fault, though,' Harper said, his free hand feeling the scar. 'Granted, he had invented the product. But Mueller was the one to claim the discovery as his own and to take charge of the trials. And the one who kept quiet when the results showed a worrying singularity. The product, Cameron, is Excelsior – your wonder drug. The singularity was the existence of a time-window, just like for thalidomide.'

Cameron's mouth dropped open. Charly closed her eyes. The penny had finally dropped. But Harper continued, more for his own benefit – for catharsis? – than theirs.

'The time-window,' he said, 'was not, in this case, during a specific period of pregnancy. It was for another short period of time when the female body undergoes drastic physical and hormonal changes – after giving birth. If a woman, Mueller found out when the results of the full-scale trails started to come through, took Excelsior a few weeks after giving birth, the side effects could be disastrous. If there was a single cancer cell in her body, Excelsior acted as a catalyst to start a chain reaction of nuclear proportions. The cell multiplied a million-fold; the cancers spread so rapidly throughout the body that no amount of surgery could keep pace. Excelsior was the drug that my wife took. Now do you understand, Cameron? Now do you bloody understand?'

Harper's eyes filled with tears. He drew back the sword and raised it above his head.

'Go ahead, Harper,' Cameron said. 'Destroy me, and yourself at the same time.

Harper took careful aim.

'No, Kit,' Charly cried out, running around the table to try to stop him. 'Think of Cassie. Think of me.'

He brought the sword down with all his might.

And buried the blade into the thick wood at the edge of the table.

Harper turned away from Cameron and stepped forward to meet Charly.

'Phone the police,' he said, putting an arm around her. 'It's over. It's all over.'

He let go of her, picked up the two disks and prepared to leave.

'Give me your pass card, Cameron,' he said.

Cameron dipped into his trouser pocket, withdrew the pass card and tossed it on to the table.

'The police are on their way,' Charly said. 'What do we do now?'

'What do we always do? Get out of this place. I can't stand the sight of your grandfather for one moment longer. Without his pass card, he's not going anywhere.'

They walked to the door.

'Wait,' Cameron shouted.

Harper paused, seeing the pleading look in the man's face.

'Go get the lift,' he said to Charly. 'What do you want, Cameron?'

'Think of the consequences of your action, Harper.'

'You heard what Charly said – the police are on their way. It's too late to change anything now.'

'When this becomes public I lose everything – my reputation, my fortune, my hopes, my dreams, my knighthood, too – they'll strip me of that, for sure. And you've even taken Charlotte from me. Don't you think you owe me something, Harper? If only for Charly.'

'What do you want?'

'Leave me the gun.'

Harper went out of the room, not looking back at the pitiful figure.

But, just before he closed the door, he tossed the gun inside the room.

The shot rang out as he joined Charly in the lift.

Justice had finally been done.

STAGE SIX

CONCLUSIONS

34

Harper walked along Oxford Street, the collar of his raincoat turned up against the persistent drizzle. He paused on the threshold of the agency, looking at the dark-red logo of JKL and shivering. Red wasn't one of his favourite colours any more – struggled to get into his top twenty, in fact. Maybe, given time, the associations would fade: the flashbacks, however, – damn that photographic memory – would always be in the permanent album of his brain. As if to prove his point, a vision projected onto the screen somewhere inside his head: Evans – loyal, thorough, truth-questing and dream-shattered Evans – spread-eagled on the grass, uttering his misconstrued apology. Harper bit his lip and pulled open the door. Get it over with, he told himself. You have something to say, and, if ears are prepared to hear and minds to open, a reward to claim.

It was the first week in November and Harper was finding it hard to adjust to the noisy crowds and murky damp of London after the tranquillity and warm, soothing sun of the final week of their holiday.

The first few days after that long night in Brussels had been taken up by a series of repetitive interviews with the police: when Charly and he had finished telling their story to the Belgian authorities, it was the turn of the Metropolitan Police – the force working on the supposed serial killings – next, a multilingual old campaigner from Interpol who was coordinating information and working with the law enforcement agencies of Kazakhstan. And when the police had sucked them dry, it was the turn of the media. No wonder they felt they had to get away.

The reunion between Cassie and Harper had been tearful (on both their parts), and he had decided that they needed to spend a lot of time together. Charly had asked to come along – separate rooms if he wished, she'd leave father and daughter alone whenever they asked, no commitment necessary, no promises but. . . . How could he refuse? Even if Cassie hadn't been quite so insistent. In his mind the holiday would be a hothouse; it would be the quickest and surest way to find out how they both felt.

The choice of destination had been difficult – neither Harper nor Charly wanted to go anywhere they had visited before – and so, with unsubtle prompting from Cassie, they had settled on Florida – theme parks the first week, the Keys the second. It was four days into the holiday when Charly stared across the dinner table into his eyes and said, 'My grandfather and Klein were right, you know. When they set their trap and baited it. I did fall for you in the end, Kit.'

'I have an appointment,' Harper said to the receptionist at JKL..

'You're to go straight in,' she said, smiling at him. 'I suppose I should give you a visitor's badge but—'

'I shouldn't worry about that,' he said. 'Instead, can you give me a couple of minutes before you phone and announce my arrival?'

She nodded at him and he made his way to The Planning Zone. Took a look at his office, empty but with all possessions in cardboard boxes. Poked his head round another door; was pleasantly surprised to see both Grayson and a tidy office.

He thought briefly of calling in on Philip, but couldn't face the prospect of seeing the room without Ned. Making his way back along the corridor, he stood for a moment outside the door of the boardroom, then knocked and immediately entered.

The cynically termed Three Wise Men of JKL – Jackson, more soberly dressed than usual; Klein, soberly dressed as always; and Lottersby, the collar of his shirt hanging loose about his neck – looked up at him.

'Harper has got something to say to you,' Lottersby said to Klein.

'If it's to apologize,' Klein said, after recovering from the shock of the bad penny turning up, 'then don't bother.'

Harper looked at him, registered the kink in the aquiline nose, fought back a smile and sat down at the table. 'I think there are some vacancies here,' he said.

'Like one art director,' said Klein, causing Jackson, the late Ned's boss, to wince. 'You don't have the qualifications, Harper. Nor the temperament.'

'I agree entirely, Klein. But I wasn't referring to Ned's job. I was thinking more of the dual roles of managing director and head of planning.'

'Didn't I tell you he was mad?' Klein said to Jackson and Lottersby. 'Those are *my* jobs, Harper. Haven't you done enough damage to me and to this agency? With AUC in receivership, not only is the takeover dead and buried but we're also saddled with a bad debt that is going to hit cash flow and profits hard. We are now in a period of retrenchment – it isn't the time to take on more staff. And even if it was, *you* would be last in the queue for the post of office cleaner, let alone my job. Now, stop wasting my time. Get out of here.'

'Hear him out,' said Lottersby, his face pale and grim.

Klein sat back in the chair, shook his head in disbelief, and stared petulantly at the yellow blinds.

'I had a lot of time to think while I was on holiday,' Harper said.

'Lucky you,' said Klein. 'Some of us have been too busy on damage limitation to swan around on holiday.'

'Shut up and listen,' Jackson snapped at him.

Klein grunted, unused to any attack from that direction.

'When Charly and I left this building and went to Brussels,' Harper continued, 'we were followed from the airport. Unwittingly, and very unfortunately, we led the hounds to the Atomium, and to Evans. Someone tipped off Sir Angus Cameron that we were on our way. That someone effectively signed Evans's death warrant. I think that someone was you, Klein.'

'I'll see you in court, Harper. That's a slanderous accusation, and one you can't substantiate. In front of witnesses, too.'

Klein looked at Jackson and Lottersby for support.

'Sorry,' said Lottersby. 'Must have dozed off for a while there.'

'Me, too,' said Jackson. 'Now, what were you talking about, Kit?'

'Traitors in the ranks,' Harper said. 'That was the subject.'

'I'm not prepared to listen to any more of this,' Klein said, standing up.

'Sit down,' said Lottersby. 'Kit isn't finished yet.'

'You see,' said Harper, 'there is something else that has been bothering me. But, wait, where is your normal politeness, Klein? I forgive you for not enquiring about my health, but surely you should ask after my daughter.'

'Cassandra? What's she got to do with anything?'

'Everything,' said Harper. 'You see, I got to thinking just how much the late and unlamented Cameron knew about me. Where I lived, the parlous state of my finances, my job, or should I say, jobless, situation. Not to mention where my daughter went to school, and her first name. Someone was feeding him information. Now, who could that have been? Who is the only person who refers to my daughter as Cassandra? You, Klein. You set up my daughter to be kidnapped. If the attempt had been successful, then Cameron would surely have bought my silence – every man has his price, as he rightly said. But, because they were listening out for the name *Cassandra* instead of *Cassie*, the kidnapping failed. And because it failed, everyone in Kazakhstan had to be eliminated. I lay the deaths of Ned, Drew, all the others, at your door, Klein. I hope you rot in hell.'

'Why?' Lottersby asked Klein. 'Why did you do it? Why betray everyone? No account can be worth what you have done. Get out, Klein. Get off these premises now. Our lawyers will be communicating with you.'

'You can't do this to me,' Klein said, banging his fist on the table.

'Shall I call security?' Lottersby asked. 'Or the police, perhaps? Do you want your exit to be as undignified as the rest of your behaviour? Get out of my sight.'

Klein stood up. Walked across the room. Pressed his face closed to Harper's – closer than had ever been possible before, now that there was the sideways kink in the long nose. Quickly stepped back a pace when he saw Harper clench his fist.

'Are you happy now, Harper?' he said, spitting the words out. 'Now you have my job.'

'You've got it wrong again, Klein. You've never understood me, have you? But then that went for all of your staff. I don't want your job. This agency needs someone to rebuild it. To re-establish some loyalty and bind everyone together into a team. Someone to nurture and grow new talent. And some-one who is totally committed to advertising. That's not me, Klein. I've lost my faith. Did so a long time ago. The job's not for me. It's for Saul.'

Klein staggered from the room.

Insult had been added to injury.

'So what are you going to do?' Lottersby asked. 'I hate to mention this, but your only experience is advertising. And your academic qualifications don't seem suited to much that goes on in this modern world.'

'Looking back over the last few weeks,' Harper said, 'I realized I was perfectly qualified for what I want to do – what I feel I have to do.'

'And that is?' Lottersby said, his brow furrowed as he tried to work out what he had missed in Harper's *curriculum vitae*.

'Poking my nose into other people's business,' Harper said. 'And exposing the corruption within. Charly and I are going to work for GreenWay. She feels she should make amends for the sins of the grandfather.'

'And you?' Lottersby asked. 'What exactly are you making amends for? No, don't answer that. I think I can guess. I wish you good luck for the future.

For the future of the future, we might say. And, Kit, one last thing. Forgive us advertising men our trespassers.'

35

Three months later.

What a day!

Charly was the most beautiful bride there had ever been; Cassie, her hair an exact duplicate of her new stepmother's, the prettiest bridesmaid; Harper, simply the luckiest man alive.

Saul's speech was witty – well, at least the parts the audience understood. (*Sed aliquando bonus dormitat Homerus*: you can't win 'em all.)

And Mab, using the shoulders of Nanny Trent as a fulcrum to leap high in the air, caught the bouquet.

Ronnie 'I don't do fairy stories' Stoker would have hated the wedding.

And that thought made it just perfect.